Based on a True Story

Based on a True Story

A Novel

Elizabeth Renzetti

ANANSI

This edition published in 2014 by
House of Anansi Press Inc.
110 Spadina Avenue, Suite 801
Toronto, ON, M5V 2K4
Tel. 416-363-4343
Fax 416-363-1017
www.houseofanansi.com

Distributed in Canada by
HarperCollins Canada Ltd.
1995 Markham Road
Scarborough, ON, M1B 5M8
Toll free tel. 1-800-387-0117

House of Anansi Press is committed to protecting our natural environment.
As part of our efforts, the interior of this book is printed on paper that contains
100% post-consumer recycled fibres, is acid-free, and is processed chlorine-free.

18 17 16 15 14 1 2 3 4 5

Library and Archives Canada Cataloguing in Publication

Renzetti, Elizabeth, author
Based on a true story / Elizabeth Renzetti.

Issued in print and electronic formats.
ISBN 978-1-77089-313-9 (pbk.). — ISBN 978-1-77089-314-6 (epub).

I. Title.

PS8635.E59B37 2014   C813'.6   C2013-906990-9
                        C2013-906991-7

Jacket design: Kathryn Macnaughton
Text design and typesetting: Alysia Shewchuk

Canada Council   Conseil des Arts   ONTARIO ARTS COUNCIL
for the Arts   du Canada   CONSEIL DES ARTS DE L'ONTARIO

We acknowledge for their financial support of our publishing program
the Canada Council for the Arts, the Ontario Arts Council, and the
Government of Canada through the Canada Book Fund.

Printed and bound in Canada

For Doug, who gave me the title and much more.

"Her heart was broken perhaps but it was a small inexpensive organ of local manufacture."

—Evelyn Waugh, *The Loved One*

one

It was not the first time she'd been asked to leave a clinic. Augusta huddled into her coat as the wind cut across the porch. The nurse who'd come to say goodbye remained inside, as if afraid to leave the safety of the foyer. One hand held out in farewell, the other on the handle of the door. The paint was peeling down the side, Augusta noticed. The other clinics had been much smarter than this.

She took the outstretched hand, their cold fingers meeting. This nurse, Jennifer, had been her sole friend and ally over one long week, which should have been two.

"We'll not see you here again," Jennifer said.

"No," said Augusta. "You'll not see me here again."

"Well," said the nurse, "you know you can always ring me, any time, if you do feel yourself slipping. My mobile's on there." She fished a card from the pocket of her blue tunic. Augusta looked at it, and realized with some surprise that the nurse she'd been calling Jennifer was in fact named Claudia.

The door inched shut, and Claudia turned back inside

to tend the drunks and wastrels who knew how to obey rules. Augusta watched her go. She really should have made more of an effort to hide the pills, but who knew that her roommate would be such a quisling? She walked to the curb, where a minicab sat idling. Someone had drawn a penis in the dirt on its side, elephantine testicles dangling below.

"My chariot," she said. A copy of the local newspaper tumbled along the pavement and wrapped itself around her ankle. "Walthamstow Shopping Centre to Celebrate 25 Years," read the headline on the front page. Walthamstow, boil on the neck of London. Where she'd begun and, against all best efforts, where she had washed up.

She kicked the newspaper aside and reached for the door of the minicab. Alma Partridge sat in the back, wrapped in an ancient fur as stiff as a sarcophagus. Augusta slid in beside her, inhaling the mingled smells of her old friend's musty coat and the driver's luncheon kebab.

Alma gave him an address in Camden, and he pulled out into traffic. After a moment, Alma placed a dry and papery hand over Augusta's. "You look well, my dear. How was the sanatorium?"

Augusta closed her eyes against the pain of the last afternoon light. "It was fine. Fewer meetings than usual, thank Christ. But, if you really want to know, a bit on the cheap side. Thin gruel."

She felt Alma's hand withdraw. "Perhaps if you had stayed the course it would have proved more useful."

Despite herself, Augusta laughed. "You have a positively maternal gift for the barb, Alma. How I missed that when I was inside. All they spoke about was vulnerability and forgiveness and reaching out and recovering one's footing."

"Not such bad things."

"And journey, as a verb."

Alma shuddered. "That is disgraceful."

With an effort, Augusta wrenched one eye open. "I am grateful that you came to collect me, darling. Really. You are my dearest friend."

"I am your only—"

Augusta brought her hand up. The broken tip of one fingernail dangled like an unlatched gate. "I am well aware. It does not bear repeating."

Each retreated to her own corner in rankled silence. "No photographers outside when I left," Augusta muttered. "I thought the rags loved this kind of filth. Fallen celebrities."

Alma raised one pencilled brow at the word "celebrities." She said, "I believe what they're searching for is the *unexpected* fall." She ran a hand through her nimbus of white hair, coaxing the sparse strands higher.

As the car sped south, the lights of shops and restaurants glowed in the gathering dusk. It seemed that every second window advertised a pub quiz, pitchers of draft on sale, discounted trays of shooters.

"So," Augusta said brightly. "Drink?" She felt Alma stiffen next to her, and reached to clasp her friend's hand. "A joke, darling. Merely a joke."

two

The answering machine shuddered to life when Augusta pressed one gummy button. Amazing that it still worked. She had a ridiculously sentimental attachment to the thing. Once, after she'd spilled a drink on it, it had expired with a sigh. She'd found a man in Kentish Town to fix it, and when she placed it on the shop's counter he'd looked at it as if she'd presented him with an ear trumpet.

"Has this been out in the rain?" the fix-it man asked, as he poked its innards. "It's completely sodden."

Aren't we all, Augusta'd thought, but had merely smiled.

"Augusta? Are you back from holiday?" The answering machine made everyone sound like Orson Welles. Even the high-pitched voice of her agent, David, came out as a bass rumble. "Looking forward to breakfast next week. Bright and early, don't forget. There's a journalist from the *London Advance* who wants to do an interview about the book, now that it's coming out in paperback. Lovely timing, it was starting to fade a bit. Another little push, my love." His voice took on a wheedling quality and she clicked the message to a halt.

Across the room, her book stood out on the shelf, its title, *Based on a True Story: A Memoir of Sorts*, set in neon-green type. The publisher had favoured this vulgar display over her protests, arguing that a more tasteful colour would have been, in essence, false advertising. Neither she nor her agent had expected the book to do as well as it had, but they had stumbled by accident into a fad for the unearned memoir. A newspaper excerpt featuring Augusta's ecstatic encounter with a shaman had given the book a certain momentum leading into the holiday season. Augusta did not delude herself that its minor success equalled literary merit: the first week it landed on the bestseller list, *Based on a True Story* was sandwiched between the confessions of a disgraced DJ and the autobiography of a badgers' rights activist.

She wished her father could have lived to see the book published. Giovanni was certain of very few things: one, that the only books worth reading had been written by men who'd worked by candlelight, and two, that his daughter's trajectory, from a young age, was toward hell in a handbasket. But Giovanni had been in his grave for more than twenty years. She imagined her father marvelling from above, or more likely below, at the improbable mid-life success of his only child.

Although the book was soon to appear in a new edition, her sojourn in rehabilitation had prevented her from doing any publicity. God bless David for drumming up an interview now. The *Advance* was a rag, but it was read by half the commuters on the Tube every evening.

Rehab. What a loathsome word. It suggested new fabric

on a knackered sofa. She went and stood by the window. Below, the Regent's Canal shimmered dark and oily in the towpath's lights. A couple sat on the bench at the water's edge, kissing, and she watched them for a moment. Two weeks ago, she'd hurled a tin of tomatoes at a couple rutting in the shadows, but that was a different time. It was the drink that had powered her throwing arm. There was no drink in the flat now; Alma had seen to that. She'd even found the shampoo bottle filled with Amaretto.

Odd that David had mentioned her book, but not the role that would return her to her rightful place in the public eye. Augusta cast a quick eye around the room: Surely she'd left the *Circle of Lies* script here when she'd left for the clinic? That morning had been ever so slightly shrouded in fog.

No matter. She'd find it and make the lines her own before they met for the first table reading. It was a good role, a small one but with meat on it. There was Channel 4 money behind it, which meant there might even be a car and driver. David had sworn to her reliability, practically in his own blood. Back in front of the camera. Useful. It would make all the difference.

One message in seven days. It was not a pleasing number. Should she even bother checking her email? Augusta sat at her desk, where Alma had piled a week's worth of post. There was a hysterical taxation notice from Revenue and Customs, which she dropped in the bin, and a flyer for a new Thai takeaway, which she placed in the top drawer.

A fine film of dust covered the two photographs that sat on her desk. The first showed Augusta and Alma in the week they'd met, thirty-two years before. Augusta had been little more than a child, and Alma already well into middle age, with a lifetime of roles and men behind her, equally chewed to gristle. They'd starred in a dreadful pantomime in Cromer, the December sea wind lifting Alma's enormous wig every time someone opened the stage door. The actor playing Widow Twankey was a crème de menthe drunk, gassing the matinee crowds with great minty bellows.

The other photo... with the corner of her sleeve Augusta wiped away the thin layer of grit. Such a handsome boy, her son, with serious dark eyes that reminded her of an unplaceable someone. Could she still call him "son" when they hadn't spoken in seven years? Perhaps there was a statute of limitations on these things.

She placed the photo back on her desk and walked back to the tiny nook that served as a kitchen. The silence in the flat was unnerving, and she reached for the answering machine. Perhaps there was a reward at the end of David's message. Augusta hit the play button again.

His voice broke the stillness, a welcome presence. He gave the time and place of their meeting, and offered a few tantalizing details about mutual acquaintances. In the time she'd been away, one surgery had gone badly awry, and two marriages had crumbled.

Augusta stood half-listening, wondering if a glass of water would do anything for her thirst, when a name pierced her reverie. Her stomach lurched. She spun toward the answering machine, breath caught. She couldn't possibly have heard what she thought she'd heard. Sobriety was playing evil tricks.

With a shaking finger she jabbed the rewind button and David's voice rose again. She sank into a chair, unseeing, as he spoke the awful words again: "Speaking of publishing, I heard some news from California. Did you know your old mucker Ken Deller's writing a book? I think it might be about you."

three

Steam hissed from the silver machine on the café's counter. Augusta turned to glare at it. In her day, coffee makers had been discreet things, properly overshadowed by massed rows of liquor bottles. While she'd been preoccupied they had grown vast, bristling with levers and wheels and dials, tended by white-aproned acolytes.

It was not the Soho she remembered. Where were the tarts and the toilet traders? All gone. Once, many years before, in the dregs of a May night, Augusta had seen someone who looked very much like Francis Bacon having a pee against a tobacconist's on the corner. Now it was a shop selling reusable luncheon containers.

She was lost in a memory of the bottles that used to stand behind the bar in a magical skyline when a voice pierced her thoughts: "So, there were just a few other things I wanted to ask..."

Augusta focused on the girl who'd been sent to interrogate her. Was she from a newspaper? A magazine? No, the women from magazines displayed military precision in their grooming, every hair terrified into place, shoes and nails gleaming. This one was smudged around the edges.

"I wanted to ask you about the time you worked at the greyhound track in Walthamstow," the girl said. "When you were young."

"That long ago?" Augusta said, and the girl ducked her head. Her eye caught the empty bottle of Montrachet on the next table over. Two gin-blossomed City boys had made short work of it. How awful would it be to order a brandy at lunch? Brandy was what they drank at Oxford. It barely qualified as a spirit.

She tore her eyes away from the empty wine bottle. She'd been five days without a drink, each of them hard-won. As she slipped into her cold bed every night, she told herself that she had just climbed Kilimanjaro in a wheelchair, and congratulated herself on a lack of self-pity. The girl sitting across from her, nervously tugging a strand of dark hair straight, knew nothing of her struggles. She was a pretty, fine-featured thing, but did herself no favours with a Marks & Spencer cardigan sized for a rugby prop.

Augusta smiled. "A stunning place, the dog track. Such glamour, very East End. Wide boys and their ladies, the women all had mountains of hair and smelled of Youth Dew. I was just a pot girl, collecting glasses at the end of the night, but if you caught the eye of one of the smooth types he'd peel off a tenner and stick it down your top. Depending on how well he'd done on the dogs." She tipped her water glass up, drained the last drops. "Of course, it's all gone now. Possibly it's a Poundland today."

The girl leaned closer. Her fingernails, newly varnished

and even more recently bitten, tapped the cover of the book that lay on the table between them. On the cover of her memoir Augusta looked as if her eyes doubted what her lips were saying. She knew she seemed younger in the photo than she did in person.

"Princess Margaret really came to the dog track one night?"

Augusta traced the ring her water glass had left on the table. "I think she liked a little slumming. A bit of rough and then back to Kensington. She ordered a double gin with ice, and then sent it back because the ice wasn't cold enough. A memory I shall take with me to the grave."

"That was incredible, that part. I mean, the Queen's sister at a dog track in Walthamstow."

A smile spread slowly across Augusta's face. "You're wondering if any of it's true," she said. "I suppose I opened myself up to that, given the book's title. Not that it matters. It's entertainment, darling."

The girl's pen scratched on her notepad.

"Oh, for God's sake, child, don't write it down! Leave some things to your readers' imagination. The resonant space between the lines."

"But I don't get paid for the spaces."

For the first time that afternoon, Augusta laughed. "Then you need to negotiate a better deal, Stella."

"Probably I should," the girl said. "I'm not very good at that end of it." She paused for a moment and said, in a rush, "It's Frances, actually."

"Ah. And I've been calling you Stella all afternoon."

"No, you called me Jacqueline once. But it's kind of you to look for a more interesting name."

Augusta shrugged. "Why paint the walls cream when they could be orange?"

Her eyes were drawn to the door, where an elderly lady wearing a fur coat that looked suspiciously like orangutan struggled with a shopping trolley. Outside the café, pedestrians scurried along the narrow Soho pavement, intent on phones rather than feet. Taped to the window of the sex shop opposite was a cardboard sign, its message written in blue felt-tip: ARTISTS MODEL UPSTAIRS. NO APPT NECESARY. DOOR IS OPEN. A sign on the townhouse next door, neater and more official, said: THIS IS NOT A BROTHEL. The last surviving bit of old Soho, flashing its grimy wares at the tourists.

The waitress arrived at their table. "Ladies," she said, picking a hair off her apron. "Anything else?"

"A cappuccino for me, please," said the girl. "Augusta, would you like something?"

Augusta knew that she should join the sorority of coffee drinkers to signal that her afternoon, too, was packed with purpose. The thought of a coffee made her stomach heave. A single brandy would smooth the wrinkles from the day.

She hesitated a moment. Alma's voice in one ear. The distinctive throb behind her left eye urging her in the other direction. No one knew her here. Certainly not this girl. Alma's voice won; Augusta made a note to ring her and tell her of this victory.

"I'll have a coffee," she said. "One of the disgusting ones filled with milk."

* * *

The book lay between them; its pages bristled with yellow sticky notes. Frances tugged it closer, panicking, for a moment, at the thought that Augusta might open it to see the notes she'd scrawled inside: *Page 24: She gets Tylenol 4s from her doctor? Is there even such a thing as Tylenol 4s?!? Maybe only for celebrities! Page 62: Steals pills from her father. No way!! Page 117: Can you really put a tab of acid on your eyeball? Ask.*

But she hadn't asked, not yet.

The woman across from Frances bore little resemblance to the fiend in the book's pages. A grain of rice was stuck to her bosom, framed in the reckless V of a not-nearly buttoned blouse. Faintly glittering eyeliner drifted from the corner of one brown eye. There was a slight trembling in her hands.

Ask the question, Frances whispered fiercely to herself. *Just ask the question.*

"I hope I'm not keeping you too long," the girl said. "I've just got a few more questions."

"And I hope I'll have the answers." The dull pain behind Augusta's eyes began pulsing along to the sound of the Thompson Twins on the café's stereo. Every song that played brought her back to the 1980s.

Their coffees arrived, and Augusta began shovelling sugar into hers.

At this, Frances plucked up her nerve. "Now that you mention it, there are some pretty glaring—I guess you'd say omissions—" Her courage fled as a cloud crossed Augusta's face. "That is, there are things that are brought up... and are never returned to...which might be considered important, or at least relevant, and painful I suppose..."

Frances reached for her coffee, in order to drink instead of babble. Augusta gazed at her in silence, as she might have watched a thief slowly twist at the end of a rope.

"Your son, you only mention him once, I think, and I was wondering why —"

Augusta pushed her chair back. "The story I told is the one I wanted to tell. There wasn't the need to drag the whole world into it. You'll excuse me, won't you, Frances?" She balanced carefully on her orange-velvet platforms and pushed off from the table. With a wriggle, she inched her skirt a fraction lower and tottered away.

Was she gone to the toilet or just gone? Was that a strop? What the hell was a strop, anyway? No interview subject had ever left Frances's table in dudgeon, high or low, although once she had accidentally made a famous children's author cry by mentioning her husband's resemblance to Marty Feldman.

Twisting in her seat, Frances looked for the waitress. Time to collect the bill and skulk back to the office to admit she had botched an interview and had failed to get an answer to the one question that might have given her a nice scoop. Time to face Stanley's scowl and, worse, his disappointment.

Stanley Pfeffer, features editor of the *London Advance*, was the man responsible for Frances's increasingly outré daily assignments. When a pop star was found on a farmer's stolen tractor with six times the legal limit of alcohol in his blood, Frances had been dispatched to the pub to see if it was possible to get that drunk without falling into a coma. She swam in the Serpentine in December to test new data about hypothermia from the University of Edinburgh.

"You're a godsend, Frances," Stan would say as she filed her latest story. "I can't get that lot to do anything except scratch their arses, and even then they ask for overtime."

He'd shown a faith in her that no one else ever had, encouraging her at work in the morning and in the pub in the evening, where they sat and moistly reminisced about the good old days of newspapers, which Stanley remembered vaguely and Frances not at all.

A scraping noise caused her to look up, and there was her subject—crimson lipstick fresh and rust-red hair minimally neatened—taking her seat again at the table. An unspoken accord hung in the air: Let's try this again, shall we? Frances flipped open her notepad, searching for something anodyne to settle the mood.

"So you grew up in Walthamstow? I read somewhere that you said, 'I was born to leave.' Was it really so bad?"

"I take it that you've never been, Frances. Really, for your own sanity, it should remain that way."

"But it's the suburbs, isn't it? Nice houses and parks?"

Augusta's laugh turned into a small burp, which she caught with the back of her hand. "It's not America, darling. There were no cheerleaders bouncing around. The houses were tiny. Wet. They were so tiny and wet that the men would build themselves sheds at the bottom of the garden and spend all their time hiding from their women, doing God knows what. It was misery in a glass."

Her voice drifted off, and she turned a strained smile on Frances. "Where did you grow up? Your adorable accent tells me it wasn't London or environs."

This was the moment Frances always dreaded. The English asked where you were from, professing an interest, when really their minds had already calcified around a set of assumptions: Look at her, with her shiny teeth, even though she grew up on pop tarts and marshmallow sandwiches. Got her first passport at thirty. Wears panties that say "Property of Jesus."

"I'm American," Frances said, and regretted how defensive she sounded. "From California."

At the word *California* Augusta sat up straight. For a moment she said nothing, merely stared with an unnerving intensity. All at once Frances knew what a gazelle at a watering hole must feel like knowing there's a leopard hidden nearby.

Finally Augusta said: "Do you happen to know a fellow called Kenneth Deller?"

Startled, the girl shook her head.

"He used to be a journalist. Before your time, I imagine. He was old school, as you young creatures like to say. Proper Fleet Street. Christ, listen to me, I sound like I flew here on a biplane."

"I'd like to hear about him. I love stories from those days." Frances brought her spoon up to her lips, licked it clean. "I'll bet he smoked."

For a moment Augusta couldn't formulate a response. "Yes, darling, he smoked. He smoked in every possible way."

Even speaking his name filled her with bitterness. But sitting here in Soho brought back warmer memories, a sliver of light against the blackness of her current mood. She'd first met Kenneth in a Chinese restaurant on the next street over, when Soho was still filthy and worthy of love. That interview had started out much like this one, over lunch, and ended four days later in Salford, not one word ever appearing in print. It had been her first interview, conducted shortly after a punk production of *Hamlet* had lofted her from obscurity. Her reading of Ophelia trailed outrage in its wake.

When Deller showed up thirty minutes late at the Golden Fortune on Greek Street, Augusta had been on the verge of leaving. He sailed in on a cloud of Bell's and Benson & Hedges, his towering yellow quiff nearly bringing down the sign over the door that offered thousand-year-old duck egg.

"How lovely to meet you, finally," Augusta said as he arrived at her table and stuck out a giant pink paw in greeting. She ignored it. "No, you can keep your hand. I've got two of my own, and I'm thinking of using one of them to give you a good slap."

"Ooh," he said, unperturbed. "Get her."

He sat down anyway, unfolding long legs into the aisle so she couldn't escape. Augusta had never understood this male drive for territoriality, the way they spread their arms and legs as if they were ferns battling for every inch of sunlight.

Kenneth Deller lit a cigarette and watched her with an entirely unembarrassed grin. Augusta wondered that his hair didn't catch fire. It spread majestically upwards in defiance of gravity, a great blond cloud billowing above the horizon of his cheeky grin. From top to bottom he was a one-man fireworks display: the golden flare atop, the tight lavender shirt, the deeper mauve of his corduroy trousers. He was ridiculous. Augusta had never seen a peacock outside of a zoo, and couldn't take her eyes away.

"So, my girl," he said, leaning in close. "Tell me your story, Miss…Augusta…Price."

He tapped the back of her hand three times with his finger. Under the scotch there was another, vaguely sweet, chemical smell. It reminded her of her mother, the rare occasions her parents treated themselves to a night out at the Lord Palmerston. Hairspray, that was it. She pictured his bathroom, the spare canisters of Elnett in the cupboard, the ashtray balanced on the edge of the tub. Until that moment she'd been terrified, her first proper London interview and who knew if she'd muck it up? Then the fear fled. He was just like the boys she'd grown up with, only slightly more orange. And lavender.

Not for the last time, she made a decision in a second that could have benefited from a few minutes' scrutiny.

"Do you know what, Kenneth? I'm not sure I'm in the mood for Chinese."

He flashed a smile that had clearly served him well before, and stubbed out his cigarette. Stuffing his notebook into a shoulder bag more vibrantly patterned than anything Augusta owned, Deller reached for her hand. Stay where she was and salve her wounded pride, or follow the man with the orange flowered handbag? It seemed an oddly momentous decision.

"And so I followed him, darling," Augusta told Frances, watching a waitress squeeze past with a carafe of wine. "We ended up down the street at the Pillars of Hercules. Do you know it? Gruesome place. It always smells like they're pulling cat piss from the taps. Anyway, we got chucked out because Kenneth decided that the barman was ogling my bosom—I had misplaced a button or two over the evening, truth be told. My hero decided the only way to save my honour was to challenge the poor barman to a duel, armed with a wretched old cactus he'd found withering in a corner."

The girl turned up her hands expectantly. "And? Don't leave it there. Then what?"

"Well, the cactus was ancient, but somehow it had obtained quite a keen cutting edge, and how was Kenneth to know the barman was a hemophiliac?" The girl made a sound of horror or delight, and scratched a note on her pad.

They had fled through the night, hand in hand, Deller's ridiculous orange bag banging against his hip. At one point, skittering down the wet pavement of Brewer Street, they'd tried to help a dustman upend a rubbish bin into the back of his truck.

"Oi, mate," the dustman said, gently removing the overflowing can from Deller, who reeled under its weight. "Them's a job for professionals."

"It was sage advice," Augusta said. "Some things are meant for professionals. I wish I'd actually listened to that even once in my life." Her gaze was lost in the distance. "That particular interview went on for four days, and we ended up in Kenneth's brother's bedsit outside Salford. Not even Salford proper, you understand."

"Whoa," the girl breathed.

Enthusiasm always made Augusta nervous; she could never tell when it was authentic. But the girl seemed genuinely thrilled with the story.

"So," Frances began and halted. "Did you…and Kenneth…"

"Did we sleep together? My God, of course we did. We were in Salford, did I mention? For four days. In November. There was no heating, darling. Once we'd stolen all of his brother's ten-pence coins there was nothing to do but get under the covers."

Ten-pence coins? Frances wondered if this was some strange method of British foreplay. If so, where did the coins go?

"Of course, he turned out to be a bastard of epic proportions. And a fraud. He's reinvented himself as some sort of love guru in your home state." Her lip curled. "Mr. Romance, my arse." Abruptly she stopped, as if she'd suddenly realized who she was sharing a table with. She placed her handbag on her lap and snapped it shut.

"That story's not in your book." Frances reached over to check that the Record button was still lit on her tiny silver machine.

Augusta shrugged. "I felt like a tailor when I was writing it. The art is all in the cutting. And I hardly wanted to give Kenneth Deller the satisfaction of one more go-round between my covers."

four

The newsroom smelled, as always, of cold coffee and yesterday's air. Even when a rare breeze blew in off the streets of Farringdon, the office of the *London Advance* maintained the freshness of a Victorian coffin. Look closely and you'd see claw marks on the ceiling. Frances never looked.

In the corners of the newsroom, derelict printers occasionally spat out sheets of paper that no one collected. The grey vinyl floor was scabbed with cigarette burns, even though smoking had been banned for a decade—at least officially. A burnt tinge to the early-morning air spoke of a different reality for the late-shift reporters, whose lawlessness was overlooked as compensation for their punishing, and increasingly irrelevant, hours.

Frances slumped into her chair, temples pounding. The profile of Augusta sat open on her computer, a creature half-wrestled to the ground. Every time she felt she'd pinned part of her subject, Augusta slithered from her grasp. Frances wasn't used to this kind of frustration: normally, she wrote blithely, quickly, as confident with words as she was cautious in life.

She suspected that Augusta had sold her a counterfeit bill of goods, yet she was having trouble mustering a suitably indignant response. An actress had a tentative relationship with reality. So what? It was entertainment, darling. The heresy of that thought startled Frances, and she sneaked a look around the newsroom to see if anyone had noticed the traitor in their midst. Facts were her path; truth was the way. In the ten years she'd been writing down other people's words, she had never questioned this basic assumption.

Frances ground her palms into her eyes. It was almost four o'clock. Stanley would be escaping the afternoon meeting any time now, cheery or despondent depending on how his writers' stories had fared. His armpit stains frequently spoke of woe.

Lately his crankiness had been unleavened by any lighter mood. Each day brought dire rumours about the paper's fate—a new owner with deep pockets, said the optimists, while the half-empty brigade insisted they'd heard rumours that the whole operation would soon be moved online and staffed from a call centre in Tobago.

Pushing her chair away, Frances crouched above her desk to scan the newsroom. There was the usual spurt of near-deadline activity, not a buzz exactly, but more of a stuttering, as if the very cold engine of an ancient car had been coaxed to life.

Her email provided no relief from the day's anxieties. A message from Human Resources invited her to a stress-busting workshop on the first floor: **Please be reminded that lunch is not provided during the Lunch and Learn sessions.**

A note had arrived from her mother during the night. Mid-afternoon in California. Frances pictured her sitting by the kitchen window overlooking the ocean, the half-sized appliances neatly wiped down, a cup of fair-trade coffee by her elbow. A moment of peace while Frances's father napped. Frances skimmed the email, wincing at its muted admonition: **I wish you could find time to come and visit. I know how busy you are, but Daddy would love to see you while his good moments are still frequent.**

She jerked around as the chair next to her gave a wheeze. "You missed the cake," said her desk mate, Sue.

"There was cake?"

"The last of the purge. Arthur's leaving today."

Frances peered across the newsroom at Arthur, a cardiganned hobbit who'd been the *Advance*'s literary editor for as long as anyone could remember. ("Arthur buggered the Bard," read the graffiti in the men's toilet, or so she had heard.) The newspaper was culling the herd in a desperate attempt to fend off insolvency. Long-serving journalists had been invited in for a quiet chat with management and told that their contributions, while invaluable and magnificent, were not what the *Advance* needed in an era of linked digital strategies. Arthur and his fellow veterans were each given a large envelope marked Voluntary Severance Protocol. And a cake.

"Arthur's older than evil," said Sue.

"No," said Frances, "he's exactly the same age as despair."

They watched as the literary editor hoisted his Penguin bag over his shoulder. Stacks of books covered the surface of his desk, and more were piled on the floor around it. *Surely he can't mean to leave them all behind,* Frances thought. But he was already halfway out the door, radiating the bliss of the freed hostage.

He raised a hand: "The wallpaper is killing me," he said, and disappeared.

There was silence as the *Advance* journalists considered this latest loss, the perilous state of their careers, the attrition of the industry they loved. Then, as one, they rose and began to trot toward Arthur's desk.

"Come on," said Sue, who was already out of her seat. "Free books!"

Frances followed, because she would follow Sue anywhere. The *Advance*'s television columnist was her dearest friend in London — her only friend, it sometimes seemed. A single mother to three fractious children, Sue allowed all the mischief she denied herself at home free rein in the newsroom. At sixteen she'd escaped from a tiny town in Wales whose name had been bled dry of vowels.

The hordes had already descended on Arthur's desk by the time Frances and Sue arrived. Like ants, they took whatever they could carry. Frances noticed the crime editor walking away with a slab of a coffee-table book called *People of Antwerp*. Most of the mystery novels were already gone. Poetry and politics remained.

"I feel terrible for Arthur," Frances whispered to Sue. "It's like we're taking the pennies right off his eyes."

"Mmmm," said Sue. "Do you need a stapler?" She pulled out a hardcover from a teetering stack and held it out to Frances. "Augusta Price's memoir. Didn't you have to interview her?"

Frances did not need another reminder of the story that

sat, limply half-written, on her computer. She was busy extricating a biography of Lord Beaverbrook from a pile. *Stan will love this*, she thought, her heart thudding at the idea of handing it to him.

Sue began leafing through *Based on a True Story*. "I forgot she was still alive, until I read that excerpt in the *Mirror*. Was it true, that business about the shaman? Christ. The things that woman's survived. Is she still a drunk, or did one of those stints in rehab actually stick?"

Frances tucked the Beaverbrook biography under her arm; maybe she would see Stan at the pub later. He usually joined them for a drink.

"Did you know Augusta Price isn't her real name?" Frances asked. "She was born Anna Maria Ferragosto." She took the book from Sue. "But she doesn't write about that. Or lots of other things that happened to her. The book's hogwash, if you ask me."

"Hogwash," said Sue. "You really have to stop fouling the air with your profanity or Stan'll wash your mouth out with soap. Although," she said, feigning interest in a guide to gluten intolerance, "you might enjoy that."

"What is that supposed to mean?"

"Oh, I forgot. I'm not supposed to notice that you fancy Herr Big Arse."

"He does not have a big ass," Frances said indignantly. "He's just a bit pyramid-shaped."

It was humiliating enough to have a crush on her boss; that it was obvious to her colleagues was a mortification beyond words. Frances began to leaf through the Beaverbrook biography, although her thoughts lay in the past, when she'd arrived at Stanley Pfeffer's office door two years earlier, clutching a message of introduction from a mutual friend and a sheaf of clips she'd written for the *Bakersfield Californian*.

Pfeffer was barking at someone on the phone when she entered his office, and she stood nervously by his desk until he muttered, "Bye then, Mum," and hung up. He turned to face her, and waved toward a chair. He needed a haircut, and it looked as if he shaved with a chainsaw, but he had friendly, tired eyes and she liked him immediately.

He asked after their mutual friend, and flipped through the stories she'd carefully culled to showcase her strengths, stories about drought, foreclosures, homelessness. She noticed, with alarm, his eyes begin to glaze. He neatened the stack and pushed it back toward her. "Why'd you want to work here anyway?"

Frances flipped through her stock responses—change the world, make a difference—but she feared he would just sneer at her. Earnest American. The answers she'd rehearsed in the hotel mirror had evaporated. Her mouth was dry.

Pfeffer's phone rang, but he ignored it. "I mean, leave California for this—" he flapped a hand at the ash-grey sky outside his window. "You'd have to be mad."

Frances sensed a door closing before it had even opened. She blurted, "Journalism may kill me, but it'll keep me alive while I'm doing it."

He leaned forward sharply, cocking his head. "What was that?"

"It's just something Horace Greeley said. He was an American newspaper editor."

"I know who he was." Pfeffer gave her a small, sideways

smile, and she realized he was younger than she'd first thought. "Greeley was high minded," he said. "They called his newspaper the 'Great Moral Organ.'" He studied her, as if trying to solve a puzzle with no clues. "Are you high minded, Frances?"

She couldn't look away. Tentatively, she said, "Only if I'm required to be?"

He burst out laughing and rocked back in his chair. "Good. Because those sods out there all want to write about the plight of the downtrodden. I need somebody to find stories people might actually want to read."

Frances thought about the four-part series on corruption in the sewage-treatment industry that she'd written in Bakersfield.

"That's me," she said. "Only the stories that people want to read. Sex and death and animals."

Stanley rubbed his jaw. "It's your choice. The hours are crap and the pay's worse. The pub downstairs is all right, though."

He turned back to his computer and Frances realized, with a giddiness that filled her from head to toe, that he was offering her a job. It turned out to be a short-term contract with no benefits and no security, repeatedly renewed, but it didn't matter. Suddenly every morning was a doorway; every day sped by.

"There's your love now," whispered Sue, and Frances elbowed her, keeping her eyes on the senior editors leaving the meeting room. Stanley hurried past them, head between his shoulders, brows creased as he scanned a printout. His prematurely grey hair looked as if it housed a family of badgers.

For once, Stanley didn't turn to her and ask about her story, or share a sarcastic remark about the newsroom's collective laziness. Frances felt an odd shiver run down her back, but shrugged it off. She was being ridiculous. The purge was over.

A tobacco-rich voice spoke in her ear, making her jump. "We're sold to the Russians. It's the dole queue for us."

"The fuck we are, Gareth," said Sue. "I've heard nothing about it."

The office messenger had sidled up to them, and now he picked up a book from Arthur's desk. "This intel's pretty good," he said. "Some KGB fucker looking for an investment in London. He's bought the paper and he's going to give it to his kids to run. Run into the ground, innit."

Normally Gareth could not be induced to stir from his post at the back of the newsroom, where he sucked in an unending stream of Twitter feeds, aggrieved rants to radio call-in shows, and texts from dodgy friends in Peckham, then spat them back out as undisputed truth. It was troubling that he considered this gossip sterling enough to deliver in person.

"First thing," he said, "they gonna fire half the editors and reporters. Then they find someone to do it cheaper overseas. Next thing you know, *bam*"—he slammed his fist on Arthur's desk, making them both jump—"all your stories about *EastEnders* are being written in Bombay."

"Mumbai," said Frances, not really listening. A terrible feeling had come over her.

"Bollocks," said Sue, but she sounded uneasy. More than half her time was spent writing about *EastEnders*.

Thick as he was, Gareth somehow sensed their distress.

"Never mind," he said, and plucked a copy of *Heat* magazine off Arthur's desk ("Porky Princess's Shame-Stain Saturday!"). "Taking the piss out of celebrities. That's where the money is."

They walked back to their desks in silence. Frances slid into her seat. She tried not to imagine her future as an arctic slide through failure toward death. There were two months left on her contract, and it had never occurred to her that it wouldn't be renewed. It wouldn't make any sense for Stanley to let her go, would it? She was the equivalent of slave labour—cheap as chips. The newspaper didn't even pay her benefits.

An atavistic sense of preservation told her she should probably get out of the office as quickly as possible. She was just rising from her chair when she saw the door to Stanley's office swing open. Even from where she was standing, she could see that a Niagara of worry had spread under his arms and down his sides. Without stopping to talk to anyone, he made his way to her desk, eyes on the floor.

Not good, whispered a voice in the back of her head. *Not good at all. Miss Bleeker? Do you think you could come into the office to discuss the test results?*

Stan stopped at her desk, and clawed one hand through his hair so that it stood like a cockatiel's crest. He managed a smile, and that was when Frances's chest tightened. *Nurse? Could you leave us alone for a moment?*

"Hello, Frances," he said. "Do you think I could see you alone for a moment?"

five

Washed-Up Tales from a Soap Flake

BY FRANCES BLEEKER
London Advance

Augusta Price once haunted Soho, and now Soho haunts her. This is where the actress used to drink and score pills, when she was still drinking and scoring pills. Those days, she says, are history.

Price is perhaps most familiar to television viewers as Kit Gallagher, the hapless barmaid on the popular night-time soap *Canals* and as the vampire surgeon Helen Mount in the short-lived cult classic *The Blood Bank*. Those successes are behind her, but the actress, like a dowager leopard that refuses to give up the hunt, is preparing to pounce once again.

We meet for coffee on a street that is full of ghosts from her antic past. Thirty years ago, in a café like this one, Price met a journalist and immediately ran away with him. Their affair lasted until they had no more coins to feed the electricity metre in a Salford flat. Yes, that's right: They ran all the way from Soho to Salford.

You won't find that tale in her recent autobiography, *Based on a True Story: A Memoir of Sorts*. In fact, some of the most intriguing stories from an intriguing life are not present at all in the book, which was a surprise bestseller last Christmas. Other colourful tales are present, but gently tweaked. Price could have been a sculptor, rather than an actress, considering how adept she is at shaping the clay of her experience. More on this later.

Those experiences, dark though some of them were, have left only a few marks on the woman sitting across from me — and she's used all of her tools to try to erase them. Her dark eyes, ringed with eyeliner that Cleopatra would envy, are bright and shrewd. Her hair, the colour of an Irish setter's, catches the sunlight streaming in through the window. Her small feet are crammed into orange platform shoes, in defiance of her age and gravity. She seems to have forgotten to button the top of her blouse, much to the delight of the café's male patrons.

Although she won't reveal her age — published sources suggest she's 53 — Price seems not much older than when she left *Canals*, in which she played the dim-witted but kind-hearted barmaid. (Rumour has it that Ms. Price was sacked by the show's producers after a series of public contretemps, including a punch-up with a rival soap star in the loo at the Dorchester Hotel.)

"Stories are just that, darling — stories," says Price. "They are what we tell ourselves to make sense of our lives."

She sets down her latte with a grimace of distaste. (She's asked for "one of the disgusting ones filled with milk.") What she is trying to say, I think, is that the truth about her sacking lies somewhere between the producers' version and her own. In her memoir, she says only that "Kit had become threadbare, and it was time to find a new set of clothes."

Considering how entertaining her memoir is — and that its very title contains a warning to the literal-minded—only the most churlish reader would point out the various gaps between Price's account and the historical record. She claims, for example, to have resigned from her starring role in *The Blood Bank* over "script differences" with the show's producers. At the time, though, it was reported that she'd been asked to leave when she compared her character's vampirical desire for blood with "a priest's lust for tiny white bottoms."w

When the stories are this much fun, who really cares if she was in drugs and alcohol rehab once or twice (or more often), or whether she was arrested for pushing a shopping trolley off Southend Pier, or if she actually did serve Princess Margaret a drink when she worked at the dog track in Walthamstow?

"You're wondering if any of it's true," she says with a cat-like smile, the tiny lines at the corners of her eyes creasing. "I suppose I opened myself up to that, given the book's title. Not that it matters. It's entertainment, darling." Her voice is beautiful, low and whisky-tinted, pitched to draw the ear close.

Augusta Price has been an entertaining fixture on the minor-celebrity landscape since she left the North London School of Speech and Drama a little more than three decades ago. To her Italian-immigrant father, drama school was a betrayal of everything he'd worked and sacrificed for: "Why don't you just take your money and throw it off Blackfriars Bridge?" he screamed at her when she left the house for good at 17. At that point, she changed her name from Anna Maria Ferragosto to the more marquee-friendly Augusta Price.

"For him, being an actress was little better than being a whore," says Price. "And then in my first role at the Edinburgh Fringe I actually played a whore. Topless. He never really forgave me."

They were never entirely reconciled. The tangled skeins are hinted at in her book: she seems to blame him, at least in part, for her later problems with alcohol and drugs. Her father had injured his back while working as a stonemason, and lived afterward in a haze of painkillers. At 14, a curious Anna Maria stole one of his painkillers, washed it down with a glass of homemade wine, and never looked back. Or, as she writes, "I looked forward, with pinned pupils, for the next drink, the next high."

Yet, for a long while, Price's dalliance with substances did not affect her career — perhaps because she was hardly alone at the bar. After drama school, and a couple of years in tights playing regional pantos, she made a name for herself in the ITV miniseries *Highland Mist*, in which she played a London ad executive who is called home to Scotland to run her family's distillery. "Whisky flowed on that set, darling," she says, sounding somewhat wistful.

Price never married, though her memoir is dotted with men who vary from bad to worse. Somewhere along the way, she had a child, Charles, who is curiously absent from the book. When I ask her about the young man, who would be 24 today, she bridles. "The story I told is the one I wanted to tell," she says stiffly, before excusing herself to go to the ladies'. "There wasn't the need to drag the whole world into it."

Yikes! I wonder for a moment if I've blundered beyond repair (indeed, an acquaintance of Price's will tell me later that she and her son are estranged, and that the young man lives in California).

When she returns, though, all seems to be forgiven. Lipstick freshly applied, charm fully in place, Price is ready to answer all questions. So what does the future hold? Apparently she is now trying to decide between two high-profile television projects, both of which have meaty roles for her.

"Darling," she says, with such a pleasing smile that you really do want to believe her. "I'm not sure how I earned this much good fortune. I feel I should be knocking wood, or I'll jinx myself."

Six

The pestilent scourge of breakfast meetings had laid waste to early-morning London. Roustabouts no longer lolled in bed, nursing their hangovers. Instead, they arrived scoured like copper pots at restaurants like this, a vast, echoing space in Piccadilly that had once been a car showroom. It was the only place to properly advertise one's continued role in the running of things.

Politicians and their special advisers, dames and knights, censured comedians—all gathered on the leather banquettes, looking over their companions' shoulders every time the door opened. Menus the size of briefcases were placed in their hands by silently gliding waiters, but no one ever looked at them. They ordered what they always ordered, and lived for the day when the waiter would say, with a small smile, "The same again, sir?"

Augusta was no longer a regular here, or at any establishment with tablecloths. For the first few moments she'd gloried at being back in the thick of things, but the thrill soon died. The din was murder on her hearing. "What was that again?" she bellowed to the bearded man beside her. His voice was moist in her ear: "I was just saying that I remember it as if it were yesterday. I came like a V2."

She edged away from him on the banquette. "If we'd had relations in a makeup chair, Andrew, I would certainly have remembered."

He laughed and pulled a crumb from his luxuriant grey beard. The gesture rang a tiny, muted bell somewhere in the back of Augusta's mind. Of course she remembered, but the vain old goat hardly deserved the succour of her reminiscence. It hadn't been a makeup chair, it had been a frantic five minutes in the costume trailer, Augusta trying to remember her lines over Andrew's heaving back. A filthy Cardiff spring, twenty years before. Andrew had played a car thief turned football coach, and she had been…a paramedic? A social worker?

"Detective," Andrew supplied, sighing deeply.

He was now a television star, famous for playing a deaf veterinarian who solved crime in the Shetlands. Augusta had arrived at the restaurant uncharacteristically early, eager to meet her agent and draw the map of her comeback trail. As she sat by herself, assessing her crow's feet in the dull reflection of a butter knife, Andrew had spotted her and strolled over.

"I thought I might have made your book. Your *memoir*." He gave the word an exaggerated French pronunciation.

"You read it, did you?"

"Flipped through it anyway, at the newsagent's. Surprised to see there was no index."

That, Augusta thought, *is so vain twats like you would buy it.*

"Andrew," she said sweetly, "your presence is much too intense to be contained in a mere few pages. The paper would combust, and think of the lawsuits I would have on my hands."

He was edging one meaty thigh closer to hers when she was saved by the arrival of a tall, reedy man at the table.

"So sorry," said David, her agent, dropping into a chair in a cascade of scarves and bags. "Bloody awful on the Tube this morning. Passenger under train, again! Liverpool this time. Dear God, the sorrow in this city." He noticed Andrew and brightened. "Oh, hello! You're the vet off *Donkey Island*, aren't you?"

Augusta introduced the two men, and they briefly exchanged gossip about mutual acquaintances. *The London equivalent of dogs sniffing each other's arses*, she thought. Andrew finally left, after securing a promise that Augusta would call him one day soon.

David snapped his napkin across his lap. "You look well," he said. "Rested. The holiday worked marvels."

She searched his face for sarcasm, but there was none. Only familiar shrewd brown eyes, gazing at her over the top of Prada glasses that her fifteen percent had helped buy. A waiter poured mimosas at the next table, champagne meeting orange juice in a bright citrus explosion. It reminded her of a garden of orange poppies.

She tore her eyes away and took a sip of bitter black coffee. The urge to ask about Deller's book was overwhelming, but she fought it down. It would be better to get the good news first, and delay the sting in the tail.

"Now that I'm back," she forced a smile, "do we have the finished script for *Circle of Lies*?"

Six months ago, she had secured a job that would lead her back to the cameras. It was a small part, but gritty and eye-catching: she would play the wife of a Q.C. who was secretly running a European sex-trafficking ring. The wife, coddled in luxury, initially turned a blind eye to her husband's crimes but in the end, twisted by her conscience, reported him to the authorities. Augusta had auditioned, and pleaded, and lunched for weeks until the role was hers. Now, looking at David's darting eyes, she felt a stab of panic.

Her agent clung to his menu as if it offered the secret to life itself. She'd known him so long; this was not a positive sign.

"David?"

He appeared to be gathering himself. Finally he looked up. All the coming disappointments were forecast on his lovely, open face.

"There will be other work, Augusta."

She felt herself deflate in the chair, the air forced from her lungs. Surely everyone in the restaurant would turn and stare, smelling failure in their midst. In her head she was screaming, but only one word came out: "Why?"

David motioned to the waiter, who arrived with pen poised. Augusta was on the verge of asking for champagne in her orange juice. She bit the words back. Instead she ordered another coffee, and kept her hands in her lap to hide the trembling.

"Why?" she asked again once the waiter had gone.

David rubbed his spotless knife with his napkin. "They couldn't wait any longer. You were…away."

He'd left something unsaid. "And?"

Finally, he looked up at her. "And there was a problem with insurance. With insuring you."

It was out, hanging between them, impossible to retract now.

The waiter arrived with David's breakfast and her coffee. She reached blindly for his cuff. "I'll have a mimosa."

She took a deep breath. Suddenly she wanted to murder everyone in the place, to choke them with their words, their chattering, planning, scheduling.

"Well," she said finally. "Is there anything else on the horizon?"

"Absolutely," David said, with professional cheer. "I got a call about a reality program—don't give me that look—and you'd be perfect as the presenter. Just listen a moment. You'd be sent to live in a puffin colony in Northumberland, and you'd commune with them, you know, urbanite and bird, for six months…" His voice faltered at the look in her eyes.

"The title of this masterpiece?"

He coughed. "*Lonely Birds*."

"*Lonely Birds*." She drew herself up in her seat. "Just me, and a mountain of dung, and some penguins."

"Puffins."

"Darling, you know I was once nominated for a Bafta?"

"Things have changed, Augusta."

She remembered, suddenly, that it had been David who held her hair back when she was sick in the toilets at the Dorchester during the Bafta party. Alma Partridge had stood at the door, alternately berating her and anyone who attempted to enter the stall. Her army of two.

It felt as if someone were sawing at her throat. "Anything else?"

"Oh, Augusta," David said. He reached over to lay a hand on hers. "It's not so bad. The book's doing quite well, as you know. The publisher's interested in another."

"Another book," she said dully. "The first one took forever. You would not believe how much energy invention requires."

"Not another memoir," he said, jolly now that she had not actually impaled herself on her fork. "They're thinking maybe we could capitalize on…on…"

"My infamy?"

"Your unique perspective," David said. "Perhaps a kind of self-help book. A manual for overcoming disaster. I know it sounds horrendous, but in the right hands—in your hands—it could be good fun. Augusta, look at me. It's where the money is."

She shook her head slowly, watched the quartet at the next table clink their glasses together in celebration.

She said, "'There are millions to be made, and your only competition is idiots.'"

David looked up, fork halfway to his mouth. "Sorry?"

"Just something a wise man in Hollywood once said." She scanned the room for their waiter, but couldn't tell him from his fellows. In their white aprons they were like solicitous penguins, indistinguishable.

He seemed relieved that she hadn't screamed, or thrown anything. "And we'll find a ghost, a good one. That'll speed things along."

"Well, at least it shall keep me in nuts through the winter."

David shifted in his seat. "I've had a word with the publisher, and they would like to see a finished outline before they pull out the chequebook." He started to chuckle, then thought better of it. "You know, after the last time. A bit of carrot, much handier than the stick. A good ghost will be invaluable."

Augusta thought of her ghosts, drifting through the empty rooms of her memory. It was doubtful that any of them would want to help. She'd need someone biddable, and cheap, which ruled out most of London. A picture rose in her mind of the young American reporter in the dreadful cardigan. She'd been annoyingly tentative in person, but she left claw marks on paper.

The waiter arrived with her drink, setting it down with a chime. Her fingers closed around the cool stem, and she forced herself to count to thirty before taking a sip. She'd noticed on the cocktail menu that a single mimosa cost fifteen pounds. At least David was paying.

At the bar, Andrew was signing an autograph. She watched him replace the cap on his pen and slide it inside his jacket pocket. Such a small thing, a pen. So innocuous. A concealed weapon. She took a sip of her drink, already anticipating the next.

"So," she said, "tell me about Deller's book."

David appeared relieved that she'd circled back to the safer ground of gossip. "I don't really know much about it. I saw it in one of the U.S. catalogues. Some barking New Age publisher in California. It sounds like rubbish, but you never know with these things."

Augusta kept her voice as mild as possible. "But you think it might be about me?"

"Well, it seems to be about overcoming a broken heart. And you were the one who wielded the hammer, in his case." He pushed away from the table, worried perhaps that he might be in fork range. "Did you know he's reinvented himself in California? Apparently he's some sort of relation-ship counsellor." He shook his head, chuckling. "Which is a bit rich, when you think about it."

seven

"I have a question for you, Mr. Romance. Do you think it's possible for a mattress to be cursed?"

The question was a needle to his drifting thoughts. Deflated, Kenneth Deller came back to the radio studio with a bump and noted that the coffee in his mug was cool. It was only two minutes since he'd last looked at the clock on the wall. During some shows, like this one, its hands actually seemed to click backward, like a toddler slipping down the stairs. His mind would wander as he responded with stock answers—*You have to learn to value yourself, or how will* he *ever learn your true value?*

He cleared his throat. "Well, I guess that depends. Are we talking about a curse in the classical sense—that is, a hex placed by a supernatural force, in order to bring about painful retribution? Or are you just having bad luck in the bedroom?"

The woman on the other end hesitated, but only for a moment. They didn't call in to radio talk shows because they needed to be drawn out. "Bad luck, I guess is what I'm saying. You see, Mr. Romance, I bought it a year or so ago, and I've only managed to, you know, get lucky on it once. And that was with my ex-husband. So it's only, um, been christened once, and that was because we went out and got drunk after our divorce papers were signed. And no, um, party for two since then."

Where did they come up with these euphemisms? Boinking, schtupping, doing the baby dance, getting laid, scoring. Their shame radiated down the phone line. Where he came from, people were just as prudish: shagging, getting a leg over, on the pull. One word for love, a thousand for sex.

"And you blame the mattress for this?"

"You should see how fellas look at it. Like they know nothing good has happened there in a long, long time."

His producer, sitting outside the soundproof box of the studio, shook her head in disbelief.

"I think," he said, "that you're giving men a little too much credit for imagination. Usually when a bloke's in the bedroom he's not trying to channel supernatural messages from the furniture. He's thanking whatever kind fate brought him there in the first place."

"Actually, it's been longer than a year…the drought."

"It has?"

"More like five."

He pinched the bridge of his nose. "Have you thought about getting rid of the mattress?"

"Well, my sister's moving house. I'd thought she might want it, but I can't very well pass the curse on to her. She's already got fibromyalgia."

That was the highlight of his afternoon. The rest of the calls passed in an undifferentiated rush — boyfriends with porn addictions, boyfriends who wouldn't commit, boyfriends who were losers, wasters, slackers. Men rarely called; they were terrified someone they knew might hear them on the radio, asking for advice about love.

It was more than that, though: men seldom realized when their relationships were in trouble, usually not until an exasperated wife rose like a viper to disturb their lethargy. "I had no idea anything was wrong," they'd say, when they'd finally worked up the nerve to call. "Seventeen years, and we were happy. She never said."

"Are you sure?" he'd ask. No clues? No taut silences that stretched over days, no floods of inexplicable tears, no suggestions that you find a couples counsellor? "It wasn't that there were no clues," he would say gently, "it's that you chose not to notice."

When the hour was up, he slipped off the black padded headphones and stretched. The bottom button of his shirt popped open under the strain, and he reached down to do it up. His stomach may have grown, but at least it was still hard. His dad and uncles were big men with hands like Christmas hams and bellies like cement. "Soft bastard" was the worst insult in his father's vocabulary. Unfortunately, soft bastard seemed to be his job description these days. You couldn't go around calling yourself Mr. Romance and expect to be a hard man at the same time. The next time he was in London he'd have some new shirts made. If he could stand the humiliation of the measuring tape.

He spun his chair around to face the window and the mole-coloured suburbs spread out below. Before he'd arrived he'd thought California would be green and lush, nectar cascading from hibiscus on every corner. How cruel it had been to find the same palette as his mother's sitting room in Manchester, circa 1974: brown, orange, a thrilling splash of green.

He'd never grown used to the absence of clouds. That morning, as he was driving into the valley, he'd burst out laughing at the forecast on the radio. "Nice today," the weatherman had said. "Nice again tomorrow." A weatherman in Los Angeles. What a ridiculous job. Almost as ridiculous as a love adviser.

A city of wealth and warmth and privilege, yet it had to be the least romantic place in the world. People were afraid of food and abstained from drink, and as far as he was concerned those were the two major routes that led to sexual bliss. A city that contained the world's most rigorously rounded buttocks, its most exquisitely hillocked biceps, and all anyone could concentrate on was the millimetre of sag. They only got their kit off to compare how much further they had to go.

He liked to think that the city would wither and die without him, its wedding chapels and nurseries empty and forlorn. Sometimes he imagined trying to explain to his father his place in the world. His jerry-rigged career. "You see, Dad, I'm a love adviser, an expert on romance, an explorer of the heart's darkest corners." And then his father's fond, puzzled smile: "But lad, you were never much good with ladies, were you?"

The queer airlessness of the studio pressed on his ears; the sooner he was out of here the better. He fished his phone out of his pocket and turned the power back on. Seventeen new emails. He held it at arm's length and squinted at its tiny screen. Surely the print on his last phone had been much larger.

He sighed when he spotted the latest email from his publisher, Middle Way Books, asking if he could please deliver the manuscript by the end of the month. Closing the message hastily, he opened the next one. It was a brief note from Charles that made him smile, as always, with its formality: "Is tomorrow still fine for supper? Shall I make reservations?" There was a message from an engaged couple he was counselling confirming their next meeting.

His chair creaked as he sat forward suddenly, squinting at the next message. It had arrived from an address he didn't recognize, with no subject line. It seemed to have been typed by a child, or someone with hooks for hands. His breath caught as he read, **Write t hat book and you will rUE the day.**

eight

Across the turd-strewn courtyard of the George Cadbury Estate, a dog hung by its jaws from the seat of a children's swing. Even at this distance Frances could hear its rolling growls. Apart from the quivering and foam-flecked muzzle, it was completely still, suspended like a ham in a butcher's shop.

Its teenaged owner, hands deep in parka pockets, raised one foot and gave the dog a prod in the flank, which set its head whipping back and forth, meaty haunches dancing. *Looks like it's being electrocuted,* Frances thought. She recognized the ritual. In the park near her flat in London, half-chewed swings dangled above muscled, joyless dogs in spiked collars. They were being trained for fighting.

Once, when she still had a job she'd been sent on a quest to find out why these weapons dogs—as the *Advance* insisted on calling them—were so popular with shiftless youth.

"Find the hoodie with the ugliest dog," Stan had instructed, and so she had, approaching a spliff-smoking group with several panting beasts lying at their feet. It had ended, not quite according to plan, with Frances fleeing down a street in Bermondsey, the sound of her own screams and the boys' laughter in her ears, while a monster called Tiny galloped behind her trailing a spiked lead and a rope of saliva.

"'E just wants a kiss, darling!" was the last thing she heard before she dived into a Tesco for safety.

Frances had done everything Stanley asked, hunted down every story he assigned, and this was where her loyalty had led: to a shit-pocked, cigarette-stubbled patch of lawn on the outskirts of Birmingham. Once they had been friends, teetering perhaps on the edge of something more, but that was BS. Before Sacking.

Best not to think of that now, Frances thought. It wasn't a sacking, anyway, it was a "strategic distillation of resources," or that's how Stan had put it when he'd ushered her into his office. At least he'd had the grace to look ashamed.

"I feel like a prat," he'd said, refusing to meet her eyes. "But I'm not allowed to say 'sacked,' Frances, it's some legal thing. Bloody stupid, I always thought we were in the business of speaking plainly. Although I'm not sure we're going to be in any business in fairly short order."

He'd finally looked up at her, and immediately glanced away again. Frances couldn't swallow.

"Anyway, it's not so much…letting you go, as not renewing your contract. It's not just you. There are thirteen other people I have to tell by the end of the day." He was looking out the window at the fascinating view of the betting shop below. "I wanted to tell you first because I knew it would be hardest." His smile seemed controlled by electrodes at either side of his mouth, jerking at random intervals: "You'll be fine. You're better than this place. And we'll see each other. I'll buy you a drink and make sure you're okay."

Bastarding bastardy bastard, Frances thought. That one little phrase—*we'll see each other*—had given her a sick amount of hope. She checked her texts so often that her thumb hurt. Not one message from him. Not one.

Her fingers closed around the tiny voice recorder in her pocket. Taking the train two hours out of London to investigate some poor woman's misery for *Under the Skin* magazine was not the path she'd envisioned when she moved to this country. She sat on the freezing bench at the edge of the council estate, marvelling at how easy it was to slip down the ladder's rungs once your grip started to loosen.

Sue had arranged for her job interview at *Under the Skin*, calling in a favour from an old friend. At first, Frances had balked: *Under the Skin* was a magazine she scorned whenever she saw it at the newsagent's, with its headlines dredged from life's direst melodramas: "Who Would Steal Our Baby's Legs?" "Tumour Terror at 10,000 Feet." Once, just before Easter, she'd succumbed and bought a copy of the magazine, lured by the promise of its main story: "Cannibal Ate My Nan with Broccoli and Cheese Sauce."

These were desperate times, as the cash machine liked to remind her, and she had accepted an assignment from the magazine. Strictly on spec, said the features editor, whose name was Emma, or possibly Gemma. Frances would have to come up with the goods first.

"I've got a feeling about this story," Emma said over

the phone. "This woman's a fighter. And this man, this Les, this *monster*, is trying to bring her down. Crush her spirit. I can see the headline, Frances: 'Caged Sex Beast Kept Me on a Chain.'"

"Literally?" Frances had asked.

There was a long silence. "Not literally, Frances, no. But this woman—" Emma clicked through her emails—"this Sheena, she's trying to live a good life, works all night and goes to school. She's trying to be a good mum. She's lonely. Vulnerable. She becomes a pen pal with Les, the convict. And before you know it, he's preying on her from prison. Calling her every chance he gets. Telling her what to wear and who to see. Terrifying her. There's something here—yes, listen to this part: 'I want to tell my story so the young girls reading *Under the Skin* won't make the same mistake I did.'"

A day later, Frances was on her way to Birmingham to meet Sheena Henry, victim of a notorious sex beast, and wring every ounce of pathos from her story.

There are jobs and then there are jobs, thought Frances, shivering on the bench. Some people have to pluck a hundred chickens an hour. Some people repossess family homes. Some people shove giant hoses down public conveniences and watch a river of excrement get sucked into a waiting truck. And some people write for *Under the Skin*. Beggars, choosers. In the past few weeks, she had inched nearer to one pole than the other.

"It's not so nice as London, is it?" The woman had approached quietly and drew back in apology as Frances jumped. "I'm sorry, love. Didn't mean to startle you. You must be Frances."

The woman held out a chapped, red hand and smiled,

her face crumpling inwards a little. Could she possibly be missing teeth? According to the file in Frances's bag, Sheena Henry worked as a cleaner at Argos at night, took a computer course in the morning, and spent the rest of her day in electronic thrall to a tattooed and steel-toothed inmate called Les. But this couldn't be Sheena, because Sheena was forty-one, only ten years older than Frances. This woman, despite the optimism of freshly dyed hair, had the wizened look of an apple left outside all winter.

"Sheena?" Frances said weakly.

The woman took her arm and began leading her toward a block of flats. "Let's get inside before we've froze." She nodded toward the boy, who was throwing bits of cinder block at his pet. "Miserable little bastard," she sniffed. "Should be in school, 'stead of faffing about with that bloody dog."

Once inside her flat and fortified with hot tea, Sheena scattered stories like an upended purse—a cascade of blighted hopes, useless children, men who had stuck around long enough only to fatten themselves on her cooking and then take up with a neighbour. She was remarkably cheery as she went over the details of her sciatica, her daughter's gastric-band surgery, her son's truancy. It was this zesty air of defiance that had distinguished her voicemail from the hundreds recorded every week at the offices of *Under the Skin*.

If the story were published, Sheena would pocket £400 and Frances would have wedged a toe in the magazine's door. So she sat across the tiny kitchen table and watched Sheena's face relax as she unburdened herself. There was a picture of a pretty blonde girl in a school uniform on the fridge and a stack of *Under the Skins* on the kitchen counter. Frances was on her fourth Hobnob and her third cup of tea. She felt no nearer to plucking out the heart of Sheena's mystery, but much closer to needing the toilet, a circumstance she tried to avoid during an interview. It seemed so unprofessional.

"What exactly attracted you to Les in the first place?"

"My mate Sandra's dating his friend Terry. Can you call it dating if they've never actually met without a piece of glass between 'em? Anyway. She tells me about this bloke, Les, and texts me his picture, and—" Sheena fanned herself. "He's well fit. I thought, might be nice to have a fella who's with you, but not with you, you know? Not underfoot all the time causing trouble."

"But he was in prison. Did you really need a man so badly?" Frances cursed the words as they left her mouth, and felt a hot flush spread to her face.

For a moment Sheena concentrated on pulling a Rizla from its package and filling it with tobacco. "I don't imagine you'd understand. You're a pretty thing. And young enough. Maybe things are different here to what you know. Where are you from, anyway?"

"California," Frances said.

"Well," said Sheena, "there's no Brad Pitt 'round here. We make do with what we've got." Picking up the teapot, she reached over to fill Frances's cup, which had a bite-sized chip in the rim. Frances crossed her legs, but didn't protest.

Her phone beeped, and Frances glanced at the screen. It would be deeply unprofessional to check her messages during an interview—something she'd never consider—but she snatched the phone up when she saw the email address: *Stanley*. Sheena's voice faded as Frances stared at the brief message, which radiated a forced jauntiness: **Frances, have you heard? We've somehow been nominated for a Well Done London Award. Do you fancy putting on a frock and joining your old friends? Moaning and crap food guaranteed.** There was a postscript after his name: **If anyone deserves to be there, it's you.**

The sheer presumption of it. Was she supposed to sit and watch while the people who'd rejected her celebrated their success? Frances's pride battled with her desire to be among them again, to be part of their miserable, wonderful circle. Her phone clattered to the table and Sheena stopped, mid-sentence, to stare at her.

Frances dragged herself back to Les, the monster. "You would visit him? And you kept up contact through phone calls? He became threatening over the phone?"

Sheena's fingers strayed to the little gold cross at her throat. "He became horrible, really. Told me his mate Terry was keeping an eye on me, saw me down the pub acting like a slag. Which I was not." She drew a long breath. "Then it got worse. Les said he knew I was shagging some bloke I work with at Argos. Which I was not. But he called me one day, said horrible things. That he'd do to me and my kids when he got out." A tiny rivulet of blue eyeliner began migrating down her cheek. "I had no idea he was such a bastard, or I would never have taken up with him in the first place."

"You're worried about what will happen when he gets out?" *God, it's boiling in here*, Frances thought, and shrugged off her cardigan. *Does heat increase the urge to urinate?* She needed the bathroom quite badly now.

"When he gets out? Oh, no—"

A sound at the front door made Sheena turn, and a tall dark shape moved through the hallway followed by a small squat one.

"Oi, you," Sheena bellowed. "Come in here and say hello to our guest."

From the explosive sigh and the sound of dragging feet, Frances knew it would be a teenager even before she saw him framed in the kitchen door. The boy from the playground. His fleshy dog squatted, pink-eyed and panting, at his feet.

"Hello, guest," he said.

"This here's Michael, my oldest." Sheena grabbed the sleeve of the boy's parka. "Who is still not too old to turn over my knee if he doesn't start going to school." The boy grunted and began to leave, but Sheena held him firm. "And this is Frances, from that magazine I told you about. In London. She's going to write a story about Les and what a monster he is."

"Well, maybe," Frances muttered. "It's not really up to me—"

"And how he threatened us with violence. How we're terrified."

Michael burst out laughing, the dog echoing with a series of sharp barks. "You are fucking joking me. I'm not scared of that twat." He turned his pale, narrow face to Frances. "Did she tell you what he was in for?"

"She doesn't need to know that," his mother said quickly.

"This fucking monster that's giving her nightmares?" Michael moved into the tiny kitchen, and the dog followed. *Damn*, thought Frances, *now I'm going to have to squeeze past him to get to the toilet.*

"It's not important, Michael—"

"You think maybe he's banged up for rape? For doing someone with a knife?"

Sheena smiled apologetically at Frances and tugged harder at her son's sleeve. The dog growled low in its throat. Dragging her son closer, Sheena whispered, "Four hundred quid."

"Awright then," the boy said, shrugging her off. "He's Charles fucking Manson. He's the Yorkshire Ripper. He's not some little pisshead in the nick 'cause he didn't pay for his fucking TV."

Frances stared at Sheena, her urgent need momentarily forgotten. She imagined her new career, not yet built, crumbling before her eyes.

"Is that true, Sheena? Is he in jail for not paying the licence fee?" She'd always thought it was an urban myth that people would be thrown in jail for not paying their television licences.

"Wasn't just the licence fee," said Sheena with indignation. "He hadn't paid his council tax neither. And you should have seen what he done to the bailiff that come for him."

Suddenly Frances felt sick—for herself, for this skiving boy, for this kindly, deluded woman.

"I need to use the bathroom, if you don't mind," she said, pushing back her chair.

At that moment, the mobile at Sheena's elbow went off, the opening notes of Katy Perry's "Hot N Cold" echoing around the kitchen. The dog began a series of frenzied leaps for the phone while Michael cursed and yanked on its lead.

"Jesus and Mary," Sheena whispered, staring at the number. Her mouth sagged into a pink oval. "It's like he can hear us."

Frances, edging sideways out of the kitchen, said, "Why? Who is it?"

"It's him," whimpered Sheena. The phone sang, in a tinny voice, that someone was kissing and making up. The dog made another lunge and let out a strangled howl as Sheena planted her foot in its chest.

"He's calling from jail?" Frances said.

Both mother and son turned to look at her.

"I tried to tell you, love," said Sheena as she reached for the phone. "He's out now. Lives the next estate over."

"Excuse me," Frances said as she stumbled past the boy, breathing in a cold layer of cider and cigarettes.

"Toilet's just there," he said, and yanked on the chain as the dog, demented now, tried to follow her, snapping and snarling.

She scurried across the hall and slammed the door on the dog's snout, not caring if she hurt the stupid thing. Fumbling with the knob, she found the little button in the centre stiff with disuse.

"I don't believe it," she muttered, trying to pinch the lock closed with her forefinger and thumb. The rattling sounded ridiculously loud in her ears, though not, by some degree, as loud as the combined howling of Sheena and the dog.

"You just scared the shit out of her!" Sheena screamed, presumably to the sinister Les. "You actually did! Poor girl just had to run to the toilet."

"No!" Frances called desperately through the door, as she struggled to get her jeans down. "No, it wasn't him."

She noted just before bare bottom hit cold water that the toilet seat—clear plastic embedded with a strand of barbed wire—had been left up. With one hand she yanked it down, and collapsed with relief.

"I wasn't frightened," she said to the poster of Rihanna that covered the inside of the bathroom door. "I just needed to pee."

She couldn't find a towel, so after washing her hands with a cracked bit of soap she wiped them dry on her jeans. For a desperate minute she was gripped with the desire to call her parents, to swallow the dry crumbs of her pride and ask for a plane ticket home.

If she'd had £400 she would have given it to Sheena herself, just to spare her all the shame. She could hear the woman's voice, now reduced to a rolling sob, in the spaces between the dog's thudding attempts on the door.

"Uh, Michael?" Frances called. "Michael, can you control the dog? I'm coming out now."

Deep breath. She reached down to the knob, but it refused to turn in her hands. Maybe they were still wet. Frances rubbed them on her jeans and tried again, but it was no use. The tiny lock was resistant in her hands. It refused to move a millimetre. She knelt, desperate now, grabbed the knob and began fiercely rattling it back and forth.

"What you doing in there? You didn't lock the door?" It sounded suspiciously like the boy was trying not to laugh. "Fuck's sake, that thing hasn't worked in years."

That's what they'll say about me one day, she thought, and put her cheek against the cool of the door, in the shelter of Rihanna's gleaming legs. *Maybe it isn't too late to go to law school.*

nine

The boy stopped at Augusta's table and poked at the untouched stack of eight-by-ten photographs. They had been taken just after she'd been cast in *The Blood Bank*, and showed her in full vampire surgeon garb: mouth a red target, stethoscope draped over her tight vest top. As if she might visit the gym after a tracheotomy and a blood cocktail.

"What was you in?" the boy asked. He had narrow green eyes and dark hair that grew long to cover jug ears. She had a sudden desire to push his hair back and tell him to wear his impediment with pride.

"What was I in?" she said. "Trouble, mostly. Also some programs that your parents might remember."

He nodded, picked up a photo from the top of the pile. "How much to sign this one?"

"My autographed bosom will set you back ten quid, darling. A bargain to rival the Louisiana Purchase."

The boy nodded again and put the photo back on the pile. With a nervous half-smile he wandered off to join the queue at the next table, which snaked into the middle of the ballroom. At least fifty people waited patiently for the autograph of an American astronaut who'd orbited the earth three times and nearly drowned when he couldn't get out of his landing capsule. His signature fetched ten times what hers did.

Augusta sighed and, scanning the room, reached into her purse. Her fingers closed around the tiny bottle she'd bought at the off-licence when Alma disappeared to use the loo. With a sweet crack, the metal lid gave beneath her fingers. Hiding the bottle in her palm, she brought it to the table and quickly dumped the vodka in her coffee. Such a ridiculously small bottle, the kind they gave out in airplanes. The kind you might slip into a Christmas stocking.

She was taking her first sip when Alma returned, hobbling on her stick, a look of determined cheerfulness on her powdered face. "Any business?"

Augusta shook her head. "It's been quieter than a nun's knickers. But Uncle Sam over there—" she indicated the retired astronaut, who sat under a giant photo of himself in space-helmeted glory, "has been drawing them like flies. Even though he barely set a toe in space."

Alma set down her enormous vinyl bag with a thump. "World's largest autograph show, my arse," she said. "I was just over talking to Phyllida, do you remember her?"

"The raddled old tart who was in *Doctor Who* with you?"

"It was a classic episode," Alma said with dignity.

"You played a monster covered in licorice allsorts."

"A metaphor for the horror that lies beneath an appealing façade," Alma sniffed. "Not that I'd expect you to understand. In any case, Phyllida's got a bigger queue than the post office. She's preening like she's Judi bloody Dench when the truth is she can't even get a Hovis advert."

Against her better judgement, Augusta asked: "How much is she charging?"

Alma, rooting around in her bag, looked up with a scowl. "Thirty pounds."

"Never!"

They sat, avoiding each other's gaze, trying not ponder the algebra of their humiliation. After a moment, Alma pulled out her phone and aimed it at Augusta, who automatically smoothed her hair. "What in God's name are you doing, darling?"

"I'm putting us on Twitter. Someone must bait the trap."

Half an hour later, Alma had sold eight autographs, and Augusta two. She sat morosely over her empty coffee cup, plotting another trip to the off-licence. Alma had scrawled, "Meet the Dynamic Duo of Canals!" on a piece of paper and affixed it to the front of the table. In its heyday, *Canals* had been the best loved of night-time soaps, its popularity due in large part to the rapport between Alma's shrewish pub landlady, Doris, and Augusta's dim barmaid, Kit. A few nostalgic autograph hunters wandered over. For the most part, though, they lost business to a set of Hungarian twins who had once nearly murdered James Bond under a circus tent.

A familiar tide of self-pity washed over Augusta. Was this the sum of her life, this fetid ballroom in Leeds, which smelled of old carpet and Boots perfume? Her only stage the world's largest autograph show? She'd told the American girl from the *Advance* that she had two meaty roles lined up, and the girl had printed it. Maybe she'd even wanted to believe it.

Grudgingly, Augusta admitted to herself once again that the article hadn't been badly done, and was not nearly as vicious as it might have been in more waspish hands. The girl—Frances, that was her name—had some flair.

With Alma's help, she had looked up Frances's past writing. The articles in the *Advance* were lively, sometimes silly, but told with dash. A long story about a Russian spy who'd been poisoned at a London hotel had moved Augusta to unexpected tears. But there had been no stories for the past month, which seemed to indicate the girl and the newspaper had gone separate ways.

A dark thought had begun to take shape in Augusta's mind. The girl would be a most useful tool; she seemed to know something about the idiots in California who were publishing Deller's book.

The mere thought was an irritant. Augusta said, "Did you know Deller's writing a book about me?" There was no answer from Alma, and she looked over to see that her friend had fallen asleep, her sparse eyelashes gummed together. To think that one spent one's life in pursuit of pleasure and acclaim, only to have it end in a relentless trudge from nap to tea. It hardly seemed worth it. She jammed her elbow into Alma's ribs and the old woman jumped. "I said, did you know Deller's writing a book about me?"

Alma rubbed a paper-white hand across her mouth. "Kenneth Deller," she said finally. "Is he still carrying a torch for you? You'd think he'd have burned his arm to a stump by now." She sat up straight, yawned. "He was always so lovely to me." At the look in Augusta's eyes, she added hastily, "Though he's a complete shit, of course. By all known measures."

"He intends to spread lies about me, Alma. About a past that exists only in his twisted imagination." Augusta picked up the coffee cup, drained the last few drops. "But I'm not going to let it happen. I have a plan."

Alma shook her head, her lips drawn tight. "I don't know, my dear. I once heard Reggie Kray say 'I have a plan' in exactly that tone. Sometimes it's best to let—Oh, hello."

A woman had approached their table, carrying a canvas shopping bag loaded with books and magazines. She was in the canyon of middle age, suspended somewhere between Augusta and Alma, and she wore a dark-purple beret pulled flirtatiously over one eye. Her broad smile took in both of them.

"My two favourites," she said, setting her bag on the table. "You don't know how happy I was to read you'd be here. *Canals* hasn't been the same with Kit and Doris gone."

"You are too kind," murmured Alma.

"And you, Mrs. Partridge, oh how I'd looked forward—"

"Miss," said Alma.

"I beg your pardon?"

"It's Miss, not Mrs. Like 'Miss Havisham.'"

"Ah-ha, yes, that's good," said the woman, but she seemed momentarily thrown. She fished in her bag and brought out an ancient, plastic-wrapped copy of the *Yorkshire Evening Post*, its pages the colour of weak tea. She pulled the newspaper out of its wrapper, carefully opened it, and slid one of the inside sections across the table toward Alma.

A theatre review spread over a half-page, a huge photo anchoring it in the centre: Alma playing Eleanor of Aquitaine in a provincial production of *The Lion in Winter*. She ran a thin finger over the photograph that showed her face clenched in rage under a medieval wimple. "It was an abysmal production," she said fondly. "The fellow playing Henry was blotto at every curtain, couldn't remember a single line. We only realized later that it was the beginning of dementia. We played to empty houses."

"Yes," said Augusta, "but at least you had a full set of teeth."

Alma slapped her lightly with one hand and picked up a pen to sign the newspaper. The woman took it back and slid it into its wrapper. She put a twenty-pound note across the table.

"Ah, so you would like the full deal," Augusta said.

The woman leaned down, her beret dipping across one shining eye. "I have something special for you. I've been saving it for years."

Augusta felt a curious lurch in the pit of her stomach. From within her bag, the woman took out a magazine, the kind that featured photos of celebrities' improbably perfect weddings and Christmases. The cover of the magazine stirred no memory. She noticed the date in the top right corner: December 1993.

The woman was beaming with excitement. "I kept it because I know how rare it is, to find family pictures of you…" Augusta wanted to get up and walk away, but she felt pinned to her seat. She tried to reach out and push the magazine away, but the woman had already opened it to a dog-eared page.

Don't look, she thought, *don't look.* But of course she looked, and there she was, in front of a Christmas tree, with Charlie on her lap. She remembered the *Blue Peter* pyjamas that Ken had bought him. She pulled the magazine closer, as if the little-boy scent of him would lift off the page. How old would he have been? She did the math in her head: four. He would have been four years old. She scanned the image for clues, but she had absolutely no memory of the picture being taken. It was like looking at a stranger's photo album.

Next to her, she heard Alma draw in a quick breath and then the woman's bright voice: "What an adorable little boy. Where is he now?"

ten

The little gang of punks clustered on the towpath, Camden refugees in twenty-hole Doc Martens and with grommets the size of bath plugs stretching their earlobes. Augusta, leaning out her window, did not need to see her reflection to know that her forehead was a creased map of contempt.

Every day brought a different configuration of punks, but the one constant was a knobby-domed goon who spent his days fishing small plastic bags from the recesses of his bondage trousers. Their Artful Dodger. They'd strayed from their natural habitat, the market stalls and noodle shops of Camden, just out of sight around a bend in the canal. Downstream was King's Cross, where the prostitutes and drug dealers had been driven from their once-rich hunting grounds by encroaching ciabatta peddlers and pilates studios.

Augusta had bought the flat in a moment of chemically assisted mysticism. *It's on the canal*, she had thought when the estate agent first walked her through the empty, sun-drenched rooms, *and I'm in* Canals. The handful of

Percocets she'd taken earlier had taken the edge off the morning and become her partner in crime: *Buy the flat, Kit. You deserve it.*

And Kit did deserve it, poor thing. After that string of husbands—the one who'd set fire to his scooter under her front window, the other who hadn't mentioned he was wanted for war crimes—even the pluckiest barmaid in England was starting to feel the drag. Unfortunately, Kit was soon to meet her bloody end in front of a rack of cookery magazines at WH Smith, the victim of a desperate act of violence and, more importantly, the producers' equally desperate desire never to work with Augusta again. Two years after she'd bought the flat, Kit was dead, and Augusta was left with a mortgage, the mere spectre of future work, and no painkillers to ease her passage into the day.

The punks huddled closer, and Augusta strained to see what they were busy with. A spliff? A bag of pills? She felt a spasm of envy as she imagined what they would soon share: a magic carpet of fellow-feeling, insulation from the chatter of the crowd and the voices in their own heads.

A wintry breeze blew through the open window, carrying the scent of the canal, diesel, and weed entwined. The old England and the new. The afternoon stretched before her, Siberian in its emptiness.

With a last glance out the window, Augusta picked up her coffee and moved to her desk. As she set down her mug, she ran her finger over the surface, scarred with rings from more glamorous drinks. She picked up the picture of Charlie that sat beside her computer. It was taken when he was—nine? Ten? She didn't remember much about that school holiday, except that Kenneth had brought the boy to meet her down by Tower Bridge. He had left them, backing away down the Thames path as if he were afraid to let the boy out of his sight.

Augusta and her son had sat on a bench watching the tourist boats on the river, and she'd whispered that maybe, if they were very lucky, a sailing ship would come by and the bridge would be raised, its two vast blue arms creaking slowly to the sky.

The boy looked at her politely but didn't say anything, and she tried to think, for the thousandth time, who he reminded her of. Caramel hair, eyes almost the same colour, freckles matching those, and a ridiculously small nose. But didn't all children have noses that size? It was adulthood that brought the giant honker, the misshapen hooter, the syphilitic proboscis.

Charlie had accepted her offer of an ice cream, and sat eating it with neat deliberation, his eyes on the river. She kept one hand in her purse, her fingers touching a flask of whisky.

"We're studying the river at school," he said. "Do you know how many bodies they pull out a week?"

"What, now?" she asked, startled.

"Yes. There are special river police—do you know how many bodies they pull out?"

She shrugged, thinking that if she'd known children were this morbid, she might have been more interested in having one.

"One a week. Fifty-two a year. On average."

They'd sat for at least an hour, hardly speaking, but content. At least she was. Being with her son gave her a strange, electric thrill. She'd imagined that passersby were staring at him, handsome in his school blazer. The bridge never went up and no police boats went by. As the sun set Kenneth came to find them, astonished they hadn't moved.

Perhaps that silence presaged this one. Seven years. What kind of son doesn't speak to his mother for seven years? She opened the lid of her computer and laboriously punched in an address she knew by heart. The book shop's web site was designed to look like it had been produced on a typewriter, the letters black and wavy-edged. Hell Yes Books, West Third Street, Los Angeles.

She placed her cursor above the tab that said Who We Are, held her breath, and clicked. Charles Price, events manager. As always, she was grateful for the tiny concession he'd made by keeping her name. Well, her adopted name. She squinted at his photo. He was beautiful, her boy, but he looked sinewy, almost gaunt. Augusta thought: *If he's on a raw food diet I'll kill him.*

She felt the familiar indignation rise. He couldn't pick up the phone? Admittedly, she might have made more of an effort. But she had been busy. A woman on her own, trying to make her way in the world. Irritation drew Augusta up a little higher. The boy sold books in a Los Angeles shop. Part-time. Which of them had more time for maintaining bridges?

Some people preferred burning bridges. She imagined Kenneth Deller, tight polyester trousers aflame, plummeting from a great height. Augusta closed the bookstore's page and typed in a new address. A lurid web page sprang up, flame-orange and hope-pink, and she squinted against the glow. "Are You in a Love Rut? Stuck with a Love Rat? Mr. Romance Can Help You Through!" Happy couples, glued together like conjoined twins, offered testimonials to Mr. Romance's prowess in matchmaking, but nowhere on the web site was there a picture of the man himself. Because then people would see that he was a fat bastard with lying crocodile eyes.

Under the section labelled Upcoming, there was a note about the date of Mr. Romance's next radio show. Below that was a promise—or a threat—that Mr. Romance's self-help manual for overcoming heartbreak would be in stores soon. A pain pierced her chest as she saw the title of the book: *The Heart Is an Egg (It Can Be Broken, But Never Beaten)*. Underneath, it read: "Drawing on painful personal experience as well as years as relationship counsellor, the author will explore the ways that lies and self-deception can curdle even the strongest bonds." There was no more information forthcoming. Whatever that fucker was writing about her, it was, for the moment, sealed in his brain's soft yolk.

Drawing on painful personal experience. He was sitting in Los Angeles at that moment, redrawing their past. His lies would become her truth. She moved the cursor over the little tab that said "Contact." Perhaps she should send him another email. He was too pig-headed to have absorbed the threat in the first one.

She sat back, letting the rage buoy her. It would not stand. From down the hall, she heard one of her neighbours' doors opening. The first human sound she'd heard all day. She could die in here, and no one would know. Only Alma, who might be dead herself any day.

With a sudden start, Augusta reached for the bin by the desk and started to rifle through it. There was a mountain of detritus inside, most of it paper: a flyer from the local Italian advertising its latest abomination, curry pizza. A handout from the council explaining recycling protocols. And bills, God, so many bills, all of them still sealed in their envelopes. Frantic now, she dug deeper. Apple core (when had she bought apples?). A dead mouse, or something like it. No bottles; those she carefully placed in the communal bin downstairs.

Finally, near the bottom, her fingers found a bit of thick paper. She had been impressed by the rich, pebbled stock when the letter arrived. It had landed with the rest of the post, and when she saw that the return address was Los Angeles, her heart had thumped madly. But once she'd glanced at the contents and realized it wasn't from Charlie, she'd chucked it out with the other rubbish.

Now she carefully wiped a bit of ash off one corner and sat back with the letter in her hands.

Dear Ms. Price,

Please let me introduce myself. I'm Tyson Benn, the Talent Liaison Manager for Fantasmagoria™, which you might know is the Largest Fan-Based Multi-Media Entertainment Gathering™ in the Los Angeles area (Orange County excluded).

I am currently organizing the schedule for this year's event, and I would like to extend an invitation to you to appear in our panel discussion, "Type-A Personalities: The Evolution of the Vampire Medical Drama."

Your iconic role as Dr. Helen Mount in *The Blood Bank* would make you an ideal participant on this panel, and we are hoping you might consider our offer to visit Los Angeles and meet some of your most devoted fans at the 12th annual Fantasmagoria™. Of course we would like to extend our hospitality, and would provide all flights, transfers, accommodation, and a per diem to be used at your discretion.

Please do let me know at your earliest convenience if this might be of interest, and I can provide you with further details.

With warmest (Type O) regards,
Tyson Benn

eleven

Mr. Romance leaned over a low white wall on the crest of Mount Hollywood. A thousand feet below, the lights of Los Angeles glowed like circuits on a computer board.

I should really try to conjure a more tender image, he thought. *How about this: at night, seen from above, the city looked like the cover of a greatest hits album by a country rock band. Like fireflies pinned in a case, slowly dying. Like the spark of hope snuffed out in a thousand silent rooms...*

He would have to work a bit harder.

"It's so beautiful up here," said the young woman beside him, who was nestled in the crook of her boyfriend's arm. "I can't believe I've lived in this city all my life and I've never been to the observatory." She clutched her boyfriend's hand, brought it up to her cheek in an old-fashioned gesture. "Did you know about it, Asad?"

"Yes, moron," Asad said, playfully. "Some of us look up when we're driving." Taking her shoulders, Asad turned her toward the domed white building to their left, luminous against the purple sky. "I can't believe you've never seen *Rebel Without a Cause*, Tay. I know what we're watching next movie night."

"Anything's better than *Hostel Part 15*," the girl said, but she was smiling. "Or whatever you made us watch last time." Taylor slid closer to her fiancé, pressed her face to his shoulder.

Kenneth Deller felt an unaccustomed lurch: he hoped they would make it. He'd been working with them for two weeks, and the bafflement he felt when they first contacted him hadn't diminished a bit. They'd chosen one of his mid-price packages, From Friend to Forever, which usually attracted a lesser class of lover. Taylor and Asad seemed as plump with good fortune as any two people he'd ever met, blemish-free from skin to soul. She was studying to be a doctor, while he, on the same campus, trained as a pharmacist. They seldom interrupted each other, and their glances were filled with affection as well as hunger. They were already luckier in love than he had ever been.

Even these two, however, were not immune to the American desire to quantify self-improvement. What had drawn them to From Friend to Forever was its promise: "Five steps to long-lasting love, tailored to suit your particular relationship, based on the romantic history we'll discover at some of the city's most iconic landmarks." He loathed the word iconic, but this was a small price to pay in the quest for clients.

Deller beckoned them across the lawn where a few couples strolled, post-dinner and pre-coital.

"Here," he said, "is Colonel Griffith J. Griffith's monument to his sorrow."

"Isn't it an observatory?" Asad asked.

"It is, or it was once. But it's also a temple to one man's folly, his failure to grasp the ineffable power of love."

He worried for a moment that he'd over-egged the pudding, but Taylor said dreamily, "The ineffable power of love. You know, Ken, I do love your accent."

He hid a smile. The Manchester in his voice had lured scores of posh London girls to his bed, and horrified an equal number of their parents. But it carried no subtle class codes here. He was merely English, and thus a sophisticate.

Taylor stared at the building, which was lit as carefully as a movie star, its three darkened copper domes shadowy against the sky, its name picked out in Art Deco type above the front doors: Griffith Observatory.

"Griffith J. Griffith was a scoundrel, a pint-sized chancer from the Welsh Valleys," Deller continued. He walked toward the path that separated the building from the mountain's edge, and they followed. "He was no more a soldier than I am. But he climbed Los Angeles society as if it were a ladder, and on the way up, he—a good Episcopalian—found himself a beautiful Catholic wife."

They'd walked around the corner of the observatory, and a wide, white plaza stretched before them, its ramp curving around the hill like the train of a bridal gown.

"Oh," said Taylor softly.

The smell of scorched chapparal drifted up from the slope below, a reminder of the previous month's wildfires. Ken stopped by the low white wall and continued: "They were happy for a while, the phony colonel and his papist bride. Slowly, though, a worm of paranoia burrowed in his brain, and he became convinced that his lovely wife was conspiring with the Pope to steal his riches and siphon them off to Rome." He lowered his voice: "A paranoia that culminated in the bloody events of 1903."

"What bloody events?" whispered Taylor. Asad took the opportunity to clutch his fiancée tighter.

Ken let his voice drop. "On holiday with his wife by the seaside, Griffith J. Griffith snatched up a pistol and—" his voice cracked through the air "—shot her in the head!"

Taylor gasped and drew back against her boyfriend.

"Fortunately," said Ken, "she didn't die. And when Griffith got out of San Quentin, he was a changed man. Full of sorrow for what he'd done. Desperate to atone. He convinced the city to take his money, and this—" he swept a hand toward the observatory "—is what they built with it."

He paused and leaned back against the wall, quite pleased with himself. Then he noticed that the posture made his belly stick out, and stood up straight.

Taylor and Asad were looking at him as if they expected more. Finally, Taylor shot a glance at her boyfriend and said, slowly, "I think I see why you brought us here, Ken. Yes, I'm sure of it. You're warning us about the dangers of interfaith marriage, right?"

People who study science, he thought sourly, *have a restricted sense of wonder.* "It wasn't necessarily what I was getting at, Taylor, no. Obviously, that is something that you and Asad have already discussed, and I understand both your families are quite supportive."

"'Course that's not it, baby," Asad said with a patronizing smile. "He's warning us about money issues. He's saying there should be a prenup. Is that it, then? That's the lesson: we should have a prenup."

Why did he even bother taking them on these magical journeys? It was like reading poetry to sponges. He began walking back to the road, and they followed at his heels.

"Was that it?" Asad asked, trotting behind. "Because my dad thinks we should have a prenup, too."

"What?" Taylor gasped. "Your father thinks so? Oh, that is rich…"

He stepped between them, put an arm around each of their shoulders. They'd stopped in front of the white obelisk of the Astronomers Monument. Johannes Kepler gazed into the night with pitiless stone eyes.

"Look up," Ken said. As usual, no stars were visible; there was a price to be paid for the glow of the lights below. The last few couples wandered back to their cars through the soft darkness. "I was trying to tell you…about forgiveness. About compassion."

It's about biting your tongue, he wanted to add, *about keeping the live wire in your hand rather than shocking the person in front of you.* He watched their bright, hopeful, blank faces and sighed. They could figure it out for themselves.

Driving down the winding road that led from Mount Hollywood through the dark valleys of the park, Kenneth turned on the radio, pleasantly surprised to hear the Hollies singing about bus stops and wet days. He wasn't the first lad to flee the steel-grey skies of Manchester for California. Best not to think in terms of portents, though, not when he was this tired and already seeing ghosts.

As he approached Los Feliz, he knew he should move

over to the right-hand lane to make the turn, but instead, after a shamefully brief mental tussle, continued to drive down Vermont.

His eye caught a movement inside a parked car, two shadows shifting, merging into one solid lump. Maybe, somewhere, Taylor and Asad were making the beast with two gym-sculpted backs. More likely they were drinking decaf Nespresso, poring over the bridal registry at Barneys.

He would post their wedding pictures on his web site; it would be good for business. Maybe he'd include a bit about them in his book — the anxieties that bubbled beneath their flawless façade. He shuddered at the thought of the manuscript sitting unfinished on his computer. If he didn't hand it in soon, he'd have to pay back his advance. The emails from the office of Middle Way Books were growing less Zen by the day.

The mere thought made him weary, and there was only one cure for his malaise. A right turn took him into a parking lot under a neon sign that read HOUSE OF PIES. Truly he did not need House of Pies when he already had a stomach full of pies, but logic held no sway at the end of a very long day.

He slid into one of the vinyl booths, smiling at the waitress as she came over.

"Peach pie, two scoops of vanilla, and black coffee, please," he said, not bothering to look at the menu.

He watched the couples at nearby tables, fascinated, as always, by their behaviour. Busman's holiday. The younger women nursed whimsically flavoured teas, staring with famished eyes at their boyfriends' desserts, making occasional darting sorties with their forks. The older couples sat in companionable silence, a single plate between them.

It must be nearly thirty years since that afternoon when he and Augusta sat in the Little Chef on the A46 near Binley, sodden with Southern Comfort. Or was it brandy and ginger? He had been reading *The Loved One* to her, the little paperback spread open between a bottle of HP Sauce and a full ashtray. He wished the novel were longer. She roared with laughter at Evelyn Waugh's satire about failed Englishmen in California. He loved her laughter, the rolling-barrel sound of it. When she laughed he could see into the pink cave of her mouth, the sharp little teeth, the talented tongue. The sight made him giddy with hunger.

He read to Augusta as she ate, pausing for her laughter. Under a flowered, floppy hat she bent her head to her plate and worked through a jacket potato with beans and sweetcorn—"It looks like vomit on a pillow, but it's quite delicious"—a piece of gammon, and apple crumble to finish. The memory of happiness lingered, a flavour barely remembered.

In those days, he'd thought nothing about her drinking. Everyone he knew drank too much. The drink made Augusta wanton—it made her want him. It was only after the boy came and she retreated to her bedroom, meanly clutching clinking bags, or disappeared for days on end, that he began to despair. Even then—and this was something he tried not to admit to himself, though it was the truth—he would have said nothing, so long as she would have him around.

A line of doggerel from the Waugh novel drifted into his thoughts: "I wept as I remembered how often you and

I / Had laughed about Los Angeles and now 'tis here you'll lie…" Well, here he lay, in a bed of his own making. And a cold bed it was.

"Peach, two scoops." The waitress had arrived silently on thick rubber soles and placed the plate in front of him, warm and redolent of summer. The fruits of August. He laughed out loud at the idiot machinery of his own subconscious.

twelve

"Meet the new boss," said Stanley Pfeffer, aiming his cigarette at a man in evening dress leaving the back seat of a
Range Rover. "Same as the old boss."

"Fresh from Tbilisi," said Sue. "Oil money to burn, and
he decides to buy our little rag." She took a long haul of red
wine. "Probably should have just set fire to his roubles and
saved himself some time."

"Not roubles," said Frances. "Georgians use lari."

Stanley looked at her and shook his head in wonder.
"The nooks and crannies of your mind never fail to aston-
ish me, Frances."

It was silly to take pleasure from a tiny compliment,
but her larder of praise was not particularly well stocked
these days. Frances felt heat rise to her face. They stood,
shoulders almost touching, and watched the Georgian join
the stream of tuxedoed guests arriving at the hotel for the
Well Done London Awards. At the newspaper he had just
bought, where his real name was considered unpronounce-
able, he had been dubbed Oli Gark.

A tall blonde, equal parts sinew and diamond, towered over the *Advance*'s new proprietor. Solicitously, he held a hand over her perfect bottom and steered her through the hotel's doors. Frances had seen the shoes she was wearing in the window of Selfridges. They did not carry a price tag.

"His daughter's pretty," she said.

Stanley gave a tubercular laugh. "He doesn't have any daughters."

Frances stole a sideways glance. Stanley was already half in his cups, grey hair wild against the sea of black. *Men should always wear tuxedos*, she thought. Even the bottom-heavy had their geometry corrected by the stiff weight of jacket and trousers.

She tore her eyes away and scanned the crowd: Augusta Price was meant to be receiving an award tonight. Frances had seen her name near the bottom of the press release, where the Survivor of the Year prize was listed. She had no desire to run into Augusta again. For a week, she'd debated whether to accept Stanley's invitation, and the threat of Augusta's presence had almost been enough to keep her at home. One morning, though, she realized she hadn't spoken to another human being in four days. Spurred by panic, she stumbled from bed to write Stanley a note: **I'll be there.** Loneliness was a stronger goad than fear.

The Georgian turned to glare at Stanley through the glass doors, then disappeared into the crowd. "I think he loathes me," Stanley said. "He saw me in my office this morning and didn't say a word, just cleared his throat. I thought he was going to spit on the floor."

"Maybe," said Sue, "that's a sign of affection in Georgia." She ground out her cigarette. "If we win an award tonight, you'll be golden, Stan." Draining the last of her wine, she attempted a wink at Frances that convulsed half her face. "I'll see you both inside. Eventually."

"Order us something crippling," Stanley called after her.

A silence hung between them as they watched tawny-orange soap stars and firefighters, awkward in formal wear, arrive for the dinner. Neither of them made a move to go inside. They watched as three-quarters of London's journalists and all of its B-list celebrities walked a carpet that had once been red and was now the colour of Mateus.

He looked down at her and smiled. Frances caught her breath, acutely aware that the dress she'd chosen, bought for half-price in the Christmas sale, offered a rich landscape of cleavage. Stanley had noticed too. They both looked away at the same moment.

"The scene of our greatest triumph," he said finally. "This ridiculous hotel."

She looked up at him in disbelief. "Our greatest triumph? You nearly got me killed."

He reached into his pocket for a second cigarette, which she recognized as a rare luxury. *Or maybe the luxury is standing here talking to me*, Frances thought. He snapped his lighter open and blew smoke up into the sky.

"Don't be an idiot. It was a great story. You did a cracking job with it."

The spy. The poor, dead spy. A year before, a Russian spy had swallowed a cocktail spiked with Polonium 210 in the hotel bar. The next day, Stanley had dispatched her to the bar, armed with a Geiger counter, to write a story about the cancerous hazards that lay in wait for London's business tycoons, oligarchs, Gulf State princes, and their unsuspecting paid company.

On the day her story ran in the *Advance*, the spy had died—alone, suffering, friendless—in a sealed-off hospital ward. Frances had to remind herself not to look for parallels in everything she wrote.

She'd woken every morning for a month feeling under her arms for swollen glands, searching for blood in her urine. Stanley had found her hunched over her screen Googling "symptoms of radiation poisoning." An hour later, when she'd come back from lunch, there was a bottle of vitamin C on her desk and a note that read, "Don't say I never give you anything."

A raucous group of partygoers passed by and Stanley bent closer so he could speak in her ear. "I've been worried about you, Frances. You probably think I've been ignoring you, but I've been putting out calls. Seeing what's available. It's a crime that you're not writing."

She thought about all the time they'd spent at the pub, or in his office, dreaming up ideas: Why don't you take a white cane down the Tube and see how bad it is for the blind? God, she missed that feeling: the thrill of the chase, the pleasure Stanley took in her stories. It was only rarely that he'd actually risked her life.

"Do you miss me?" she asked. "Or do you miss having a willing slave?"

He looked down at her, blew a plume of smoke over her head. "Is that what you were? My slave? I wish I'd taken time to enjoy that a bit more."

Their eyes locked and for a moment Frances felt she'd shed something weighty, cumbersome. The relationship that had tied them was gone, and she was just a woman standing with a man whose company she enjoyed.

"Frances," he said, and stopped. He appeared to be fishing for sober wisdom from deep within. She noticed that he'd missed a patch of stubble under his chin, dark grey against the paler grey of his skin. *I could reach up and kiss him right now*, she thought, dizzy, *and he wouldn't stop me...*

"Frances," he started again. "There is something I wanted to say. About the day you left." She caught her breath, expectant, and he leaned down: "You left an awful pile of crap behind."

Or I could stab him with the nail file in my bag. One thrust, right through the eye. He was still looming over her, expectant, like he hadn't just thrown a glass of cold water in her face.

"I...I need a drink, Stanley." Shaking her head, she turned and walked away, leaving him standing by the driveway, hands open, as if waiting for something to fall into his grasp.

Frances stormed into the ballroom and snatched a glass of wine from a waiter's tray with such haste that it swayed in his hands. He glared at her, but she didn't notice. She'd spotted something alarming at the bar: a small figure perched on ludicrous heels, cinched into a low-cut black dress, crowned with an abundance of red hair.

Her first and only instinct told her to run in the other direction. But it was too late: Augusta had seen her, and began making her way over, parting the crowd like a vindictive and half-dressed Moses.

When Augusta reached her, Frances blurted, "I'm sorry."

"Most people are, at one time or other," Augusta said.

"It means nothing, in the end."

She stood watching Frances coolly, as if she'd been expecting this exact conversation. Strangely, of all the people at the party, she seemed the most sober.

"I'm sorry about that story. It didn't turn out as well as I'd hoped it would."

"The headline," Augusta said, "was 'Washed-Up Tales from a Soap Flake.'"

Frances laughed, a slightly maniacal bleat. "Yes, well, that's the sub-editor. Most of the time I don't think they actually read the stories. The picture of you was good, didn't you think?"

"The caption said, 'Augusta Price was once famous for drug addiction and being killed off for ratings.'"

"They're not big on nuance, it's true."

"And they spelled 'addicton' wrong. You might want to let them know."

For the first time, the girl smiled, but it was the kind of smile that preceded tears. "I would, but I don't work there anymore. They sacked me."

"Because you called me an old bag?"

"I did not, and no, that's not why. Look, can I buy you a drink? A peace offering." Frances cocked her head, a mute plea for Augusta to follow, and apologized her way through the crowd. Augusta squeezed in next to her at the bar, elbowing aside an elderly quiz-show presenter.

"As it happens, I'm not drinking."

Frances couldn't keep the shock from her voice: "Forever?"

Augusta threw back her head to laugh, and the barman stopped, mid-pour, to take in an eyeful of décolletage.

"We're not supposed to talk about forever. Only today. And today I choose not to drink. To add to my woes, I must attend a funeral tomorrow. Being hungover at a funeral just reminds you how close you are to the grave." She reached for the bowl of cashews on the bar. "You cannot imagine how boring it is. To be sober among these dullards."

"It's pretty bad being drunk among the drunks," Frances said. She gathered her courage. "Look, I am truly sorry about the article." She took a business card from her bag; she'd scratched out "*London Advance*" and written "freelance journalist," beside her mobile number. "I've struck out on my own," she said.

"Because you struck out."

Frances felt the ominous tremble in her lower lip. "I suppose that's one way of putting it."

Augusta looked at her through mascara-crusted eyes. She waved at the barman, who poured a glass of wine. With one purple-tipped finger, she slid the glass over to Frances.

"Here," she said. "This is what you take for disappointment."

As she raised the glass, Frances felt a warm finger tapping the curve where her neck and shoulder met and, cursing herself, turned around. Stanley stood, bleary-eyed, thrusting a glass of wine in her direction.

"I already have a drink, thank you."

He bent to whisper in her ear: "Yes, but you should always have an extra, for emergencies." He reached over her to offer his hand to Augusta.

"Stanley Pfeffer," he said. "I understand you're getting a gong. Congratulations."

"Yes," she said. "The 'I'm Still Alive' award for beating

the bookies' odds. They thought I'd be at the bottom of a swimming pool by now."

Stanley's laugh cut across the crowd, and Frances saw the *Advance*'s new owner glaring at them from the other side of the bar, brows stitched together in an angry furrow. She tugged on Stanley's arm.

"I think we'd better take our seats." She smiled at Augusta, as sweetly as she could. They found their table, at the back of the room, and Stanley pulled out her chair. The *Advance*'s new owner presided over a much better table near the front. He sat and stared at his new employees with fish-hook eyes.

An hour later, between an award given to two firefighters for rescuing a child from a smoky basement and one to a dog that had detected its owner's cancerous tumour, Augusta received her honour. She came to the stage, thanked Keith Richards for making her look good by comparison, and left with a wave.

Stan pushed away his dessert and leaned heavily toward Frances. "There's a reason I never called you, Frances. Everything I say comes out wrong. I was trying to tell you that the things you left behind made me realize...what I was missing, I suppose." Shoving himself away from the table, he gestured to the waiter again. His arm, in Frances's increasingly blurry vision, seemed about a mile away.

"Another bottle, Stan?" Sue said. "Look, I'm not complaining, but you saw the memo we got last week about cutting costs. We're not even supposed to be expensing muffins and coffee, never mind cases of pinot."

"Who cares?" slurred Stan. "Who cares? We might never all be together again, like this." He raised his glass at the Georgian. Frances suddenly knew what it meant to be alone in a foxhole, surrounded by enemies.

"Where were we?" Stanley turned back to Frances, aimed his arm for the back of her chair, missed. "Ah, yes. The future."

She'd already poured out a stream of misery as he listened intently. She held nothing back, not even the humiliation of her aborted stint at *Under the Skin*. "I even thought of going home," she whispered. "Phoning my parents and getting them to send me a ticket. Admitting failure. What's worse? Going home a loser, or staying here where nobody cares if I live or die, like that poor Russian spy?"

Stan leaned in closer, beckoned her to do the same. Frances bent toward him. When they were only inches apart he whispered, "Can you keep a secret? It's kind of what I thought you might do. After I had to let you go."

She yanked herself away from him, and said in a small, deadly voice: "What?"

Stan hesitated, as if trying to gauge where the landmines lay in his path. "For God's sake, Frances. I thought I was doing you a favour."

"A favour?"

"So you could go back home. And you wouldn't have to work for me anymore." His voice rose to a shout. "I mean, who leaves California to come work in a complete shithole, anyway?"

"Are you calling my newspaper shithole?"

The *Advance*'s new owner stood behind Stanley's chair, wearing an interrogator's smile. Frances shivered. The blonde companion slouched beside him, bored, smoothing the skirt of her white dress.

"Ah, Nikolaz," said Stan. "No, of course not. I would never call the *Advance* a shithole." He ran a napkin across his forehead. "I might call it a toilet on some days, but only with great affection."

The Georgian smiled without using many muscles. Frances wondered if he really had once been KGB, and if so, how many prisoners had soiled their drawers at the appearance of that smile.

"Is very funny, Mr. Pfeffer. Is English funny, I think." He bowed his head slightly. "I see you at office."

thirteen

The vicar walked slowly back to the church through a scattering of mourners, his surplice a flash of white in a shoal of black wool. Above a mound of freshly dug earth, Alma stood with her head bowed—whether in prayer or as a result of osteoporosis was unclear.

Drawing a shaky hand to her eyes, Alma dabbed delicately. "Goodbye, Barry," she whispered. "You dreadful old cunt."

"Miss P," came a hiss from the bulky figure holding her elbow. "You can't say 'cunt' in a churchyard."

"Why, my dear? Because this is a holy place?" Alma pointed to an empty bottle nestled at the bottom of a headstone. "The abundance of Babycham bottles would suggest otherwise."

Deb, Alma's carer, had worked at the Ellen Terry Home for Theatrical Professionals long enough to know not to step on a punchline. She shook her head.

"It's just not right, is it?" Deb said. "Maybe his spirit is still here."

"Well, if Barry is still floating around, he's trying to find some way to bugger the vicar. The man was randy as a goat in May."

Alma shivered and drew her coat around her. Augusta reached out to fasten the buttons across Alma's chest, but the older woman batted her away. She pivoted on her stick, began taking small steps away from the grave. "It's not that I didn't like Barry," she said. "One very cold night in February I took the train to Bristol to see his Malvolio at the Old Vic. He was magnificent—of course, he never let you forget it. Especially," she stopped and peered up at Deb, "he never let you forget what a hot piece he'd been in his youth. Do you know he told me he'd once been the filling in a Danny Kaye–Laurence Olivier sandwich?" She set off again. "I cannot abide a braggart."

For a moment Augusta stood and watched the peaceful scene below. The Church of England knew how to build a gateway to the afterlife: moss glowed green on the headstones, the branches of chestnut trees were laced like penitent hands above. The church, pale Bath limestone rubbed smooth by the years, looked more like a bed and breakfast than the dark temples of recrimination she'd visited every Sunday of her childhood.

Her mother hadn't even been Catholic, and yet the three of them had trudged off to Mass every weekend. If it had been a particularly naughty week—and most of them were—Augusta would drag her feet as they approached the gothic doorway, her mind racing with counterfeit sins to which she might admit. If she fidgeted too much during the service, her father would point to a low, arched door near the altar and whisper: "The Other Place." He told her that the Other Place was where you went after you were dead, and all the relatives who hated you in life gathered to torment you through eternity.

A dozen of Barry's ancient friends stood in a small knot, the men willing themselves straight, the women with bright powder caught in the creases of their cheeks.

"Alma Partridge!" cried a stooped man in a club tie. "How long has it been, my girl?" A clutch of teetering elderlies drew her into its fold.

Augusta handed Deb a cigarette, then lit one for herself. "She's happier than I've seen her in ages."

Deb nodded. "Funerals are just Facebook for old people."

In the taxi back, Deb provided a commentary on the current events in *Canals*, assuming that the show's two former stars pined for news of the viruses, miscarriages, and divorces that plagued their lost landscape.

"Chad, you remember, what killed Kit…"

"I've had no luck forgetting," murmured Augusta.

"So now he's taken up with Iqbal down the chippy. Iqbal's mum's not too happy, you can imagine, what with him being gay and Islam—"

"Muslim."

"Right, so his brother's beat him within an inch of his life…"

Augusta felt the inconsequential weight of Alma on her shoulder, heard the small, rattling breath as she slept. She put a finger to her lips and Deb, with a frown, fell silent.

At the Ellen Terry Home for Retired Theatre Professionals, Deb helped Alma out of the heavy fur coat. It was like seeing a child emerge from a suit of armour. The room was growing dark, though it was only mid-afternoon. From the window of Alma's room on the second floor, Augusta could see joggers puffing on the common below. *What if I started running?* she thought. *More absurd things have happened. Maybe I could run all the way to California, and rip out his bloody throat and stuff the hole with pages of his book.*

She should have gone to Hollywood when she had the chance, when she was ripe for the plucking. That bird had long since flown. California meant nothing to her now apart from death and oranges. The place that had stolen her son. Suddenly she remembered a day long forgotten, when she sat with Deller in a café by the motorway, and he read to her from *The Loved One*. The idea of Los Angeles had seemed utterly foreign to them, descent into failure even more so. "I wept as I remembered how often you and I / Had laughed about Los Angeles and now 'tis here you'll lie…"

Augusta mouthed the words, smiling. She caught herself and snuffed the spark of memory before it had a chance to kindle. Behind her, Alma gave a sigh as she settled into a worn armchair, lighting a cigarette in defiance of the house rules. Every time one of the nurses chastised her, she pleaded dementia.

The wall above her head was covered in framed photographs: Alma taller, Alma with dark hair instead of grey, wigged and pancaked as Medea, as Nora, as Rosalind. A virgin sacrifice in a Christopher Lee film, she ran toward the camera sobbing, blood trailing from her throat to the ripped collar of a gossamer negligee. Not a single personal picture graced the walls—not a dog, a child, a lover.

Deb excused herself to check on some of her other wards, or "clients," as she preferred to call them. Augusta drew a deep breath, began to speak, but found herself drawn to the activity on the common below: in the near-darkness a woman knelt by her child's side, placing his feet in plastic carrier bags, tying them tightly above his ankles. What enigma of modern parenting was this? When the woman stood up, her son ran joyfully down the path, jumped with both feet into a wide puddle and stomped like a demented elf. Augusta imagined the spray from the child's frenzied feet, saw the mother's shoulders shaking.

She wondered if it took a special skill to care for things, a gene that she'd been born without, the same way she'd always been terrible at maths. Perhaps this disconnect wasn't such a bad thing. It allowed her to see what was good for people when they couldn't see it themselves. Frances, for example. She had taken one look at the poor girl at the awards ceremony and knew what she needed. A bit of adventure. A sense of purpose in her life. Frances had seemed wild-eyed, expectant, a rabbit who could be lured easily into a trap. *Not a trap*, Augusta corrected herself. *A safe harbour.*

"—and did I tell you about the old girls down the hall who have taken up together? Laura and Corinne, they were in rep in Edinburgh, known each other for years, but only in their ninth decades have they decided to walk the path of Sappho. I suppose it's no wonder, considering they'll get no cock from the old boys around here. My dear, are you even listening?"

Augusta drew herself away from the scene outside. "I was going to ask your advice."

Alma leaned forward, blue eyes wide. "You're not back on the opium?"

"No, darling, there's no opium involved."

"Is it work, then? I fear it's a desert out there, for women like us. Though of course you're still lovely as ever, my dear."

Augusta raised an eyebrow. "I do own a mirror, you know. Anyway, it's been worse. There are enough odds and ends to keep me in fags." There was nothing more dreary than tales from the coal face of middle-aged anxiety. She lied smoothly: "I'm doing some worthy thing for Channel 4. I'm the wife of a Q.C. who's secretly running an Albanian sex-trafficking ring from the garden shed."

Alma sniffed. "Not exactly *Middlemarch*, is it? Still, you need to keep your oar in."

Augusta shifted in her chair. Why were old people's homes so hot? She fanned herself with an ancient copy of *The Stage*.

After a minute she said, "I suppose I'm asking about the past. Family, you know. Those things."

"Oh, my dear," Alma said, putting out her cigarette in a saucer at her elbow. "I'm not sure I'm the one to ask about family. You might have better advice from a cat."

"That's exactly the reason I wanted to talk to you." Augusta stood, and put her palms against the cool window. She could barely make out the figures on the common now; the mother and child were gone. "I'd get a sermon from anyone else. Some treacly nonsense about the importance of keeping people close. You, darling," she put a hand on Alma's shoulder, "you're my vinegar."

"I shall take that as a compliment. All right; I'm prepared to cleanse."

Augusta turned to the window again. "I'm thinking about taking a trip to California."

"Ah."

"You do know why I need to go?"

"Of course I know."

"Well, for God's sake then, help me. A good idea or no?"

Alma regarded her for a moment. "At the risk of sounding gnomic, my dear, I should think you won't know till you get there. Possibly not even then."

Or possibly not ever, Augusta thought. "All right," she said, and bent toward her old friend to cup her face. "I'll think about it. If I go, I'll drop you a line."

"Drop me a line?" said Alma, pushing her away. "My dear, I'm on Skype."

fourteen

Across the street, two drunks throttled each other in the doorway of the Twelve Pins. Once the scene would have filled Frances with horror, but now she watched from her kitchen table, numb. She could call the police, but she only had a few pounds' credit left on her mobile. BT had cut off her landline the week before.

It was freezing in her flat. Every time she approached the thermostat she pictured a heap of pound notes, merrily burning. Her computer sat open on the table, displaying a list of bills the bank wanted her to pay at her earliest convenience. Frances had added the column again and again, but each time she'd arrived at a figure that defied the laws of arithmetic.

The nights were drawing in; the light was gone by four p.m.; misery arrived with the dusk. She couldn't remember what it felt like to be warm. Forty years earlier, her father had fled Coventry for the California sun and never looked back. At times like this she cursed her decision to make the opposite journey.

Best not to think of her father, trapped in the big house overlooking the Pacific. She glanced out the window. One of the drunks collapsed to the ground, succumbing to a particularly vicious head-butt. Frances turned back to her numbers.

Ping. The sound was so rare that for a moment it startled her: Doorbell? Smoke detector? Then she remembered. It was the sound of an email arriving on her phone, a noise that used to drive her mad with its frequency.

Frances reached for her mobile and stopped; her breath caught. She read the message again. Then she burst out laughing, which seemed the only proper response to a job offer received by email from a crazy alcoholic. *Former alcoholic*, she reminded herself. It was not in her nature to be uncharitable.

The message from Augusta Price said simply, **I have an adventure in mind, and I believe you are exactly the woman for the job. Would you care to join me to discuss Plan Z?**

From across the street she heard police officers arrive to subdue the combatants at the Twelve Pins. Frances sat in the shadows, thinking. It was true that she had nothing left to lose. Dignity gone, job gone, romantic prospect gone, if he had ever existed at all. Stanley had fallen silent in the wake of the awards-show debacle. Sue had sent a text saying he'd gone AWOL from the newsroom. The Georgian owner had ordered Stanley's office repainted.

In her ample spare time, Frances found herself reading about Augusta. In her story for the *Advance*, she'd noted how the historical record and Augusta's had diverged, but she hadn't realized how wide the gap actually was. She found interviews that Augusta had given over the years, and the facts of her life shifted, merged, disappeared. Charles was mentioned rarely as a child, almost never as a young man. It was like seeing a chalk drawing slowly disappear on a wet pavement. Deller appeared even less frequently. Why was Augusta so keen to erase her past and to ensure that no one added new details? Frances's curiosity, dormant this past month, began to stir.

The room had grown dark, but she knew the contours of the little flat well enough that she didn't need light. It had seemed depressing when she'd first moved in, hardly bigger than her childhood bedroom, with a bathroom light that sparked and fizzed every time she pulled the cord. But now that she was about to lose it the flat achieved a shabby, romantic grandeur. She got up to switch on a desk light— a vintage French jeweller's lamp, a gift from her parents. She stood for a moment and then moved over to the bookshelf, where her fingers ran across the titles until she came to a spine printed in a particularly lurid green. She took the book down, its pages still stiff with the Post-it notes she'd scribbled when she'd gone to interview Augusta. Her thoughts scattered, pinballs bouncing and deflecting off all the possibilities. She sat down at her desk, adjusted the lamp, and opened the book:

The Shaman of Notting Hill

The moment we heard a new drug was making the rounds, we all wanted to give it a try. You have to understand, it was a more liberal age. You'd come home on the bus at four in the morning and find yourself next to a builder from Essex, in a pirate blouse, eyeliner running down his face, snogging another bloke. Things were more fluid then.

I'd had a little success on television, a few promising small parts in film, and my agent wanted me to try Los Angeles. The great pink castle in the sky. But, being a rebellious sort—or "idiot," if you prefer—I decided instead to spend that spring in thrall to a radical group of actors in London. Radically averse to bathing or picking up the tab, as it turned out.

They preferred to style themselves performance activists, taking over derelict buildings to torment audiences with blood- and snot-drenched productions of Edward Bond and Samuel Beckett. They ate and drank Brecht and Boal: "liberation through theatre." In fact, they were liberating their todgers: the four actresses in the company were meant to inspire creativity in a variety of ways, none of which required clothes. We were meant to be grateful for such offerings: so many other girls waited in the wings.

I was insecure about my own talents, tainted with the stain of television success. So I was perversely happy to be told that everything I had done, to that point, was shit. It was a relief to shut my mouth and follow someone else's bad decisions for a change.

Did I mention they had great drugs? That might have been part of the lure. I was still an amateur at this point— a bit of speed, a bit of hash, a few lines of coke at the beginning of the night and a Valium at the end. But these guys were serious. The Edmund Hillarys of mind expansion. They were on the frontiers, at the summit, always looking ahead for new and better ways to claw through the barriers around their imaginations.

This is how I came, one warm night in May, to be sitting in a decrepit flat in Notting Hill with a wizened creature who called himself a shaman, drinking a brew that tasted of cat litter, which was supposed to blow my mind open forever. Only after I'd taken the first rancid sip did it occur to me: I was probably better off with my mind sealed against draughts.

To start at the beginning, though. Danny was our troupe's leader—as an anarchist collective, we shunned hierarchies, but Danny always got his choice of roles and women. He'd been to Peru, shooting a small role in a Werner Herzog movie, and there he'd got wind of a powerful hallucinogen used by Quechua Indians in their rituals: *ayahuasca*. It translated to "vine of spirits" or "vine of life" or "vine of death"; Danny wasn't sure which.

Somehow, Danny blagged his way into an *ayahuasca* ceremony—using his beautiful voice or his luscious bottom or perhaps both—and came back to London a new man. While he was tripping, all knowledge in the world became available to him. For weeks he droned on about how we needed to take this drug together, to fly as one through the cosmos. The world's first *ayahuasca* bore. To shut him up, we agreed. This is the thing about druggies: they're always looking for the new best high. Why not a potion brewed from an Amazonian weed?

That was our first problem. It grew in the Amazon, and the only fellow capable of administering it was also in the Amazon, having his jaguar visions at the end of an impassable dirt track. Danny was adamant that we needed to take the trip properly, and that meant having a shaman as our navigator. He put all his energies into bringing the vine and the man to London, a highly illegal and fraught proposition. The troupe's meagre resources were marshalled toward this purpose. It meant the end of our plans for a black-light version of *No Exit*, to be staged in an abandoned post office in Pimlico. The world somehow survived its absence.

Finally Danny had pulled sufficient strings, bribing a baggage handler at Heathrow and a cousin who worked at the Foreign and Commonwealth Office. The date was set. The setting was crucial—a hut in the jungle would have been ideal, but we didn't know anyone who lived outside the M25. So we settled for a flat in Notting Hill, the next best thing.

You must remember that in those days Notting Hill was a jungle, a different country, a no man's land. Today it's where you buy eggs with pedigrees stretching back to Noah, but back then it was a criminal's playground. A place to score drugs and run.

Despite Danny's enthusiasm for *ayahuasca*—or perhaps because of it—I had misgivings. Hallucinogens had never been my favourite form of escape; I don't like riding in a car that has no brakes.

I turned for wisdom to my dear friend Alma Partridge, whom you have already encountered in these pages, and whom you will recognize as the Sage of Swindon.

"My dear," she said, "if you wish to leave your body behind, why don't we just take a ferry to Calais and buy a bottle of absinthe? I am sure it will be more hygienic."

But I was young and rash (one of those conditions I outgrew) and brushed aside her concerns. Alma convinced me that she should at least wait for me outside the flat lest

anything go wrong. And she did, sitting for hours in a diabolical café in Ladbroke Grove while all manner of fleshly
and chemical transactions went down around her. Never
was there a truer friend.

On the appointed evening, we arrived at the flat, lent
to us by Danny's friend, who was either in prison or in
Aberdeen. Eight of us made the trip; there was only one
other woman, Bea, a pretty, slightly vacant actress who
specialized in distressed damsels and was even more likely
than I to offer unclothed succour.

We entered the flat—high ceilings, cobwebs, and a
floor entirely covered in an elegant mosaic of black-and-
white tiles. A tripper's nightmare, those tiles.

Unaccountably, there were bowls lined up along
the edges of the floor. In the centre was a pile of what
appeared to be, and yet could not possibly be, cloth nap-
pies. We gathered around this heap and stared.

I will not lie to you, reader: the afternoon had been
spent at the pub and by the time we reached Notting Hill
we were quite drunk. Yet there's something about a pile of
children's shit rags that cuts through even the densest fog.

While we stood gawping, Danny said, "I might have
forgotten to mention this one thing about *ayahuasca*. It's
a bit of an emetic. Also perhaps a laxative."

And then, like a general leading the charge from the
front, he proceeded to drop his trousers—no under-
wear, of course—and pick up a nappy, which he fastened
around his pelvis, as if he were Jesus and these his swad-
dling clothes.

At that, I turned to leave. I was quite happy for
my self-knowledge and my knickers to remain in their

untroubled natural state. But just as I was preparing my exit, the door opened: Enter the shaman.

I'm not sure what I'd been expecting, but it was not this tiny, weathered creature, with rheumy eyes that moved calmly from me, fully clothed, to Danny, trousers around his ankles and nappy drooping sadly between his hairy thighs. The shaman (I never knew his name) wore blindingly white trainers and a leather jacket advertising Billy Joel's 1982 world tour. I was much more impressed with the handsome dark boy at his side, who whispered something to the old man in Spanish. This was the son, we soon discovered, on hand to facilitate the ritual and the financial transaction that preceded it.

While the shaman wandered over to look out the window, the son took Danny aside for negotiations, speaking English this time.

"My father needs a bottle of rum to aid the arrival of the spirit guide. Also £500, a gift for our rainforest foundation. And he would like tickets to a West Ham match."

Danny nodded; he had half a nappy sticking out of the top of his trousers and was hardly in a position to negotiate.

Before the ritual began, I tucked myself in next to this lovely boy. A graduate of the University of Leeds, as it turned out, he went by the extraordinary name of Lenin. When I expressed my concerns about the *ayahuasca* ritual, he reassured me with a hand on my knee.

"You will be fine," he whispered. "You will be free, and empty yourself."

"That's what I'm worried about," I said, but I'm not sure he shared my little joke. He wanted to share something, though; the hand slid north from my knee.

In the kitchen, the shaman prepared the brew in a battered kettle. I could hear him humming to himself, a hypnotic sound. I saw the others wince as they drank, and when it came to my turn I held my nose and fought to keep the mucky stuff down.

The details thereafter become fuzzy, though not the visions themselves. I remember Danny putting some dire Andean music on the stereo—"El Cóndor Pasa," perhaps—and Lenin rolling his eyes. I remember the shaman, shirtless, kneeling before me and his voice keening in the dark.

I don't know how much time passed; I was concentrating on the reassuring presence of Lenin. Then I heard someone—or many someones; it sounded like a legion—breaking away from the circle, crawling off, retching and moaning. Danny had dragged himself into the hall, where I could see him peering at one of the black tiles by the dim glow of his cigarette.

He bellowed into the silence: "How can I find five pence in this hexagon?"

But by this time I was above it all; I had left my body. I had left the room. I was outside, in winter, on a beautiful snow-covered hill; the trees were draped in ice, each shard bright in the moonlight. On either side of me, great ice horses formed from the snow and leapt off the crown of the hill, their manes flowing, hooves leaving trails of sparks in the air. They came in waves, forming and leaping and evaporating, like a vast surf of silver light. A small part of me was aware of the room, the sounds of distress, but it seemed a galaxy away.

Reaching out, I grasped the silver tail of one of the horses. It was silken and warm under my hand. I was pulled, soaring off the mountaintop, and we flew through a tunnel of pulsing colour, the faces of everyone I'd ever known smiling at me—really beaming with love—from within glowing bands of blue and purple and green.

Tumbling slowly, I fell into a warm, dark room, a room from an earlier century, lit by a fire in the hearth. I was watching another me in that room; a more beautiful version of myself, my hair less tangled and my eyes more kindly, standing in front of an easel. And I was drawing like Raphael: rapidly, confidently, perfectly proportioned figures and animated faces. Keep in mind I'd never been able to draw a stick figure, and yet here I was, a prodigy, producing these sketches that looked like they belonged in the Uffizi. And I knew, somehow, that the Augusta in that room could dance or sing or play piano with equal facility, speak Greek or Latin, understand quantum physics, catch a shark with her bare hands.

People who have never taken drugs think of them as a contraction, as something that pulls you away from yourself and your friends, your responsibilities and dreams. They think that drugs diminish the drug-taker in some profound way. But the truth is completely the opposite. When used properly—assuming you haven't stolen your son's milk money to buy speed, or walked home covered in sick that may or may not be human—drugs are a gift of expansion. The accordion of your life unpleated. That night in Notting Hill I felt I was wandering the familiar house of my mind, discovering rooms I'd never known existed.

I sat in the flat and dreamed of the best incarnations

of myself, and in the morning they were gone. I was first to wake, unpeeling eyelids that felt like they'd been stuck together with Blu Tack. We were jumbled in a bed—how many of us, I don't know—our limbs and hands and feet tangled together like the tails in a nest of rats. Lenin was shirtless beside me, and I was naked next to a woman who hadn't been there when I'd last visited this astral plane. Above the bed rose a vapour of rum and last night's pot smoke. A vapour in my head, too, though there was a pain in the centre of it as sharp as a knife.

Despite the pain, and the scream that sounded as I stepped on someone's hand on my way out of the bedroom, I felt…well, I felt new. As I left the flat, I saw that during the night someone had scrawled a message on the door: *It's best if you don't know.*

I went to find Alma. A come-down crowd filled the café. I wasn't sure she'd have braved the whole night, but there she sat at the table where I'd left her. She was drinking coffee with a pair of Corsican gangsters she'd befriended over the course of the evening. I joined them and together we watched the sun rise over the city.

fifteen

"Of course, it didn't happen exactly like that," Augusta said. "It was perhaps slightly less spiritual than I've let on." She paused, an expression of horror crossing her face. Frances turned to see what monstrosity had caught her attention. "Has it come to this?" Her voice cut through the din at the champagne bar of St. Pancras rail station. Her gaze was locked on a corner table, where a young woman with glossy dark hair was transferring a baby from its pram to her lap. "Must people bring their infants everywhere?"

"I once wrote a story about a woman who'd forgotten her baby in the Brighton casino," said Frances.

Augusta gave her a glance that wasn't softened by two glasses of champagne. "Do you want children, Frances?"

"Me? No. God, no." *With a ten percent chance of yes,* thought Frances. But it didn't seem the right time to test their fragile entente.

"Hmm. Perhaps I should tell you about another small matter I may have neglected to mention in my book." Augusta picked up her empty glass and waved it at the barman, holding up two fingers. "By the end of the *aya-huasca* evening, or at least some time over the following week, I'd fallen pregnant." She frowned. "Within the next two weeks, certainly. I wasn't exactly keeping a diary." She pulled up the collar of her coat so that it framed her face like an Elizabethan ruff.

"Also I left poor Alma sitting in that dreadful café. I just never showed up. The bit about the Corsicans is true, though. They fell in love with her once they found out she'd played a copper's wife on *The Sweeney*. They offered to come get me out of that flat, drag me away, kicking and screaming if necessary. They told Alma that what I lacked in my life was a man telling me what to do." The bartender arrived and set down fresh glasses. Augusta tipped hers up. "What they didn't know was that I already had too many."

Maybe this is what hallucinogens feel like, Frances thought. Sitting in a train station drinking champagne with a woman who had recently wanted her dead and was now proposing a business partnership. The world was turning too fast.

A flattened electronic voice announced, in French and English, that the 12:57 Eurostar for Brussels would shortly be leaving from Platform 1. Another voice, male and brusque, reminded passengers to keep their luggage with them at all times and report any suspicious activity. A few feet away from where they sat, the train let out a subdued hiss.

Augusta reached into her bag to retrieve a small white blister pack and poked out two capsules with a dark finger-nail. Seeing Frances's look, she cocked her head to one side.

"It's just codeine. You get them in Boots, for God's sake."

"Should you be mixing them with, you know, drink?"

"It's champagne," Augusta said, tossing her head back in a practiced motion. "Hardly drink."

Eyes closed, she kept her face turned up to the weak winter light that filtered through the glass vault above them. Frances couldn't take her eyes away: the pale face, skin falling ever so slightly away from the bones, the sweep of lash and brow, the fine mesh of lines at the corners of the eyes. What was it about some faces, some gestures, that was so hypnotizing?

Augusta spoke without opening her eyes. "Are you bored, Frances?"

Frances was startled from her reverie. "Am I what?"

"Are you bored, darling? Does your life lack zing?"

The thin light that fell on them from above offered no warmth. Frances was freezing.

She said, "Augusta, I live in a flat the size of a shoebox that I can no longer afford. I've lost the only job I ever loved. My sole entertainment is watching drunks fight across the street." She took a sip of her champagne, savouring it. "At this point zing seems like the light from a distant planet."

Augusta laughed. "Then you'll think about my proposal?"

Frances watched the passengers boarding the Eurostar. They were headed for Brussels, yet they still seemed happy.

"You want me to write an outline for your new book on overcoming adversity."

"Yes, although I forbid you from using that phrase."

"And then I'd ghost write the book?"

Augusta fixed her with a deadly stare. "You would assist me in summoning the muse."

"Fine, I'm good with muses." The champagne was making her bold. "Will I be, you know, remunerated?"

"My dear," said Augusta, leaning in so that Frances felt herself mesmerized by the pulsing brown pupils. "*Richly* remunerated." She turned back to her drink. "There's one last thing."

"Mmm?"

"We shall begin in California."

Frances felt the ground move under her, and realized with a start that the train was rolling away. "We'll do what?"

"I've accepted a short, expense-free sojourn in the Golden State. Land of your birth, I believe, and outlet malls. I'm quite excited by the malls." Augusta spread her hand to study her nails, a languid gesture that Frances was sure she recognized from television. "I imagine we could have all the fun the law allows. And, of course, you might guide me in the art of storytelling. I found it quite draining the last time."

Augusta slid her gaze sideways, the way a cat watches a mousehole. "Did I mention there will be a free hotel? And a stipend?" It occurred to Frances that she always felt like a pathetic animal in Augusta's company: magician's rabbit, seeing-eye dog, pack mule. Dead duck.

California. She hadn't been home in two years. She thought of her mother, alone with her father in the giant, echoing house overlooking the ocean, overseeing the installation of the wheelchair ramp and the chairlift. Guilt gripped her.

And yet…California. The place of fresh starts. She imagined her name on the spine of a book, or at least at the end of the acknowledgements. To be in Augusta's company for a few days would be maddening, yes, but possibly enlightening. She needed to remember how to live. She was barely into her thirties—too young to lie down and wait for death.

"I'll do it," she said.

They had just finished clinking their glasses when a group of tightly suited young men took a table nearby, bringing with them the unmistakable hilarity of the expense-account lunch. One of them, tall and ginger, held up a hand and shouted for the waitress in boarding-school French. His friends brayed with laughter. The waitress stiffened, rolled her eyes, and slowly came over.

Augusta watched their table through half-closed eyes: "How old do you think they are?"

Frances turned bleary eyes on them: "I don't know. Old enough to know not to be rude to people who earn one-tenth what they do."

"Exactly," said Augusta. "I fear they've been brought up under a terrible influence." She appeared to be on the verge of saying something, but stopped, and slid off her stool. "I'm off to the loo, darling. Order us another round, and whatever you do, don't leave the bar. Beyond here be cocksuckers."

Frances and the barman both watched her go, swaying gently as if she were taking a turn on a ship's deck. *If I leave London now*, Frances thought, *I leave behind what I've built, and the chance to find another job I love. And the man I love.* She shook her head, hoping her thoughts would fall into some orderly pattern. Could you love someone you'd never kissed?

There had been a night at the pub when Stanley, astonished that she'd never been to Paris, had drawn a map of the city in the crisp crumbs on the table. "That's St. Sulpice there, you must see it," he'd said, and pressed her forefinger into the centre of the pile. "I'll show it to you." He blew the crumbs off the tip of her finger, turned red, and stumbled off to the bar.

I'll never see Paris now, she thought as Augusta returned. *But maybe I don't need Paris, or London. Maybe what I need is home.*

Augusta slid onto her stool. "There was a reason I wanted to talk to you about the bit of the book involving the shaman." She scowled at her empty glass. Lifting her hand to the barman, she said, without looking at Frances, "Darling, if we are to travel together, you're going to have to be less of an amateur."

"You mean I'll have to get better at ordering drinks?"

Augusta laughed, and said, "There is an art to it. There needs to be one glass in your hand, and another waiting on the bar. Kenneth had the knack. I suppose everyone must have one talent."

"Kenneth?" Frances mumbled. She'd had three glasses of champagne and no food. She tried not to think about who would pay.

"Try to keep up, darling. Kenneth was there that night. The night of the *ayahuasca*. Possibly also for the nights that followed; I'm not sure. Those few days were…well, a defining time in my life. Unfortunately, they also appear to have been ripped from my memory."

"Kenneth?" said Frances stupidly, and feared from the look in Augusta's eyes that there might be sharp words in her immediate future.

"Kenneth Deller," Augusta said slowly. "I told you

about him the first time we met. A reporter, or at least he was when I met him. More pertinent to this story, he was a barnacle. A barnacle on the ship of my life."

"Oh," said Frances, as if a hole had cleared in the fog. "He's the one you didn't want to include in your book."

"Well," said Augusta. "Yes." From her purse she'd pulled a pack of cigarettes and a silver lighter, cunningly designed to look like a miniature pistol. She began spinning it on the bar.

"Are you trying to tell me," Frances said, dropping her voice, "that he was there the night your son was conceived? That he's the father?"

"I never said any such thing." Fiercely, she turned on Frances. "Why, what have you heard?"

"What have I…" Frances shook her head. Would this make more sense if she were sober? "Augusta, I don't understand. What are you talking about?"

Two young women, chatting, slid up to the bar and sat next to them, tucking shopping bags at their feet. Augusta beckoned Frances closer.

"It's true I didn't include him in my book, but apparently he's writing one of his own. I would very much like to know what he is writing about me. What lies."

Up close, Augusta's dark irises contained a dozen shades, brown and amber and purple. *No wonder men become lost*, Frances thought. Cobra in a snake charmer's basket. Fly in the spider's web.

Augusta took a cigarette from the pack and, with an unsteady hand, pulled the trigger on the lighter so a spurt of flame shot out the end. "You see, he thinks he knows about me. About certain things that transpired." She blew a stream of smoke. "But he does not." *That's the earth shifting under my feet again*, Frances thought. But it was only another Eurostar train, rumbling to a stop beside them. The barman hurried toward them, flapping hands in panic.

"Augusta," said Frances, as calmly as she could. "Are we going to California so I can help you write a proposal for this new book—"

"Of course we are, darling."

"—or are we going because you want us to spy on this Kenneth fellow?"

"Now you're being ridiculous."

"Or are we going because there's some weird unfinished business with your kid?"

Augusta slid off the stool, and Frances edged backwards, thinking: *This could go either way. This could go any way.*

"You'll have to put that out," the barman called. "There's no smoking, miss."

Taking a long final haul, Augusta dropped her cigarette into her glass, watched it expire with a hiss. She turned back to Frances, her face impassive. "I haven't spoken to my son in seven years."

Lamb to the slaughter.

sixteen

When people asked why he stayed in Los Angeles, he would say this: where else can you see a movie in a cemetery filled with dead movie stars? On the wall of the Abbey of the Psalms mausoleum it was 1944, and two men were in love with a ghost.

The movie was *Laura*, the ghost was played by Gene Tierney, and she wasn't dead after all. When she appeared like a sculpture made of light the audience on the lawn of the Hollywood Forever Cemetery shifted and gasped: had anyone ever been so beautiful? Even Kenneth, who had seen *Laura* half a dozen times, sighed and sank a little further into the arms folded behind his head.

Charles was unmoved by the film. He sat hunched over, hands cupping his chin, watching Laura ensnare her prey. He shook his head as the final soliloquy carried over the silent crowd: "Love is stronger than life. It reaches beyond the dark shadow of death…"

"What utter horseshit," Charles said, loudly enough that the young women on the blanket next to them turned in anger, suddenly ashamed of their tears.

They were still glaring twenty minutes later when the film ended. Charles placed the remnants of their dinner in the picnic basket, wiping each fork before placing it in its proper slot. Kenneth poured the last of the white rioja into his plastic cup. A little warm now, but still drinkable.

"The next one's at Valentino's crypt, if you want to go," Charles said.

Around them, people picked up their blankets, older couples arguing good-naturedly about where they'd left the car, young men rubbing their girlfriends' arms.

Kenneth scraped the last bit of Reblochon off its waxed paper and balanced it on a cracker. Not as good as Carr's water biscuits. The things they'd left behind. He opened his mouth to say something and shut it abruptly.

"Ken," said the boy, "you're catching flies. And you've been strange all night."

The older man shook out one leg, then the other, knees popping like twigs in a fire.

"We may have a visitor," he said finally. "I noticed that Augusta's coming to town. Some fan convention. There was a Google Alert yesterday."

Charles didn't look up from the picnic basket. "You're still stalking her online, then."

He frowned at the boy. "Not stalking. Following at a respectful distance."

"Has she been in touch with you?"

Kenneth's laugh threatened the button on his trousers. "Hardly," he said. "As I recall, 'traitorous cunt' was the last thing she said to me. And there was also that moment when she tried to cut off one of my fingers."

"Well," said Charles, "she always was a bit of a romantic."

When Charles smiled, he showed wolfish fangs. *Whose teeth are those?* Ken wondered, for the thousandth time. *Nobody else in my family has teeth like that. But those definitely could be Deller ears, poor lad.*

"I wondered if she might be coming through your book shop," he said. "You know, for her memoir." He made air quotes around the word memoir, but his hands froze in mid-air when he realized how ridiculous this looked.

"That book was full of shit," the boy said, suddenly fierce. A security guard standing nearby turned to look at them. "She's full of shit. I can't believe you don't know that. Or are you still making excuses?"

It may be my only skill, thought Kenneth. He bent his head back. Above, there were no stars, just a milky cataract that gave the sky its glow. Nothing like the black nights you got in London, in winter, when the dark started to close in as soon as you'd finished lunch.

He remembered being in a car, boxed in between snow-topped hedgerows, Augusta irritatingly mute in the seat beside him as he drove, faster than he should, because they were late, as usual. The headmaster's smile grew cooler by several degrees each time they missed the beginning of Charlie's concerts. After the first visit, when he'd written "guardian" on the school's entrance form, there were no more questions about his relationship to Augusta, or Charlie. The other boys were sure to taunt him about it, though: How's Charlie like a stray dog? Bitch for a mother and no idea who his dad is.

As they'd entered the auditorium, winded after a fast walk past the rugby pitch and the library and the cabbage-scented dining hall, the school orchestra was already in place, the boys shuffling and giggling and scraping their chairs. All except Charlie, whose eyes scanned the crowd. He relaxed visibly when he saw them, and put his trumpet to his lips.

Augusta ignored the stares of the other parents, but Kenneth knew she was taut as a violin string, finely tuned to each breath and whisper. They were always the subject of curiosity, because no one could quite fathom the workings of their relationship—Kenneth least of all.

Her silence on the drive did not bode well for the evening. Kenneth watched as her eyes skimmed the crowd and came to rest on a boy from Charlie's class, sitting a few rows ahead, legs splayed into the aisle. He had the mutinous air of a trainee delinquent. The boy turned and caught Augusta's eye, smirked. Then he saw Kenneth and shrank back into himself

Augusta's thrumming nerves made him twitch. He put a calming hand on her arm and whispered, "I think Charlie's trying to say hello."

Augusta looked away from the baby thug to smile and wave at her son. Charlie's face broke into such a huge grin that Kenneth had to close his eyes against it. As the lights dimmed, he whispered to Augusta to switch seats with him. That way, she'd be seated behind the giant banker in the row ahead and hidden from Charlie's anxious gaze if she happened to doze off. And she'd be out of the sightline of the gleaming-eyed little punk.

After two carols, he wished she *would* fall asleep. Instead, she shuffled, coughed, and sighed loudly every time the headmaster spoke between songs to expound on the ecumenical nature of the season: the joy of the moment, he said, was in the brotherhood of all students, whether they were Hindu or Jew or Muslim, or indeed, "alternatively faithed." Augusta failed to hide a laugh behind her hand.

As the last note sounded before the interval—a ragged start had built to a perfectly respectable "O Holy Night"—Augusta was on her feet before he could stop her. Kenneth reached to grab her sleeve between his fingers, but he was left holding her coat, a dry and empty chrysalis. *Sometimes I could kill you*, he thought as he watched her saunter over to the surly boy, tap his shoulder, and beckon him toward the exit.

Charlie had left the stage, trumpet still in hand. He walked up to Ken, his eyes darting around the room in a fruitless search.

"Hello, lad," Kenneth said, bluff and hearty. Around them, boys were enfolded in their mothers' perfumed embraces, their fathers' humorous congratulations. "I think your mum's just gone to the loo." But the boy's expression said: You're full of shit.

In fifteen minutes Augusta had returned, and they watched her bounce down the centre aisle, dropping a hand on the shoulders of the few parents she knew, waving to others. She rubbed the tip of her nose, which was red and running, Kenneth noted, and not from the cold. The jubilation on her face was as familiar as the deep silence that had come before, and equally unnerving. Eyes bright, lips freshly glossed, she came to Charlie and gathered him up. By that age he already towered over her by half a head. At first he remained stiff in her arms and then, as if his strings had been cut, sagged against her, his head on her shoulder.

"What a little genius up there," Augusta said, the words running into each other. "I couldn't believe it was you. My little light under a bushel! My baby Miles Davis."

"Don't want to be Miles Davis," the boy mumbled.

"Of course you don't, darling. Look at how that man ended up. Now, you want to pick up another instrument, while you still can, while your brain is flexible, you could be Stevie Wonder..." She was still babbling as the lights went down.

Gently, or at least without actual violence, Kenneth pulled her to her chair. "Augusta, be quiet. And let the lad go. They're starting up again."

She drew herself away, and picked up her coat. "Actually, I'm dying for a fag. I'll just nip out for a bit." She cupped her son's cheek. On stage the violinists were tuning their instruments. "Don't worry, love. I'll be back to hear you bastardize 'Silent Night.'"

With that she walked away, and the man and the boy watched her go, not knowing what to say.

A Sussex public school's not so far from a Hollywood graveyard, Kenneth thought, as he watched the security guard crouch and shine his flashlight at the perfectly groomed underside of a boxwood hedge. Lawns trimmed with manicure scissors. Families dragooned into visiting once a year. The professionally sombre recruited to run the place.

Charles had somehow survived it all, slim and graceful and contained, nothing like him. Nothing like either of them.

"When was the last time you had a date, lad?" he asked. "You're a rare commodity. You're straight, reasonably attractive, and you don't smoke crack. You're like a bloody ten-kilo white truffle!"

The boy shook his head. "That is completely random, Ken."

Random. He was so American. "Seriously, now."

"Seriously, Ken. When was the last time you went on a date?"

"You know I don't date," said Kenneth, yanking the picnic basket from the boy. He found three grapes in the bottom and put them in his mouth. Waste was the sin they forgot to put in the Bible, his mother liked to say. He handed the basket back to the boy and said, "It's an occupational hazard. Do you know many chefs who like to cook at home? Doctors who perform surgery on the coffee table?"

The boy made no attempt to keep the scorn from his voice. "Really, Ken? That's why you don't date?"

Kenneth wanted to reach for the lad's shoulder, the way he would have years ago after another broken promise, another school holiday spent by themselves in the flat. *I love you enough for ten people*, he thought. *I wish I had twenty arms to hold you. But it's not enough.*

He put his hand on Charles's shoulder, and tried to keep his voice light. "She broke us, I'm afraid."

At last the boy turned to look up at him, and it must have been the lights hidden in the bushes that made his eyes shine like that.

"We're not broken," he said. "We're together."

seventeen

They'd arrived at Heathrow three hours before their flight, which was precisely enough time for Augusta to reveal that only one of them would be flying business class, and to strike up a friendship with a Japanese tuna exporter at the caviar bar. She drank three glasses of champagne in quick succession, and left the tuna man with an autograph he didn't recognize and a bill for more than a hundred pounds.

"Our flight," Frances whispered, tugging at Augusta's arm. "They just called our flight. Let's go."

Blotting her lips on a napkin, Augusta slid off the stool. "You are already proving to be a goddess of efficiency." She reached up to put her arm around Frances's shoulder. "Have I already told you how glad I am that we're embarking on this little adventure together?"

Frances felt a warm flush. She was useful once again, essential to purpose. She hadn't realized how much she craved the feeling. It was a sign of trust that Augusta had given Frances her bag to tow while she strode toward the gates.

"There's just the one thing," Augusta said as they joined the end of the security queue. Ahead, business passengers were invited to enjoy Fast Track Boarding. A much longer line, twitching like an irate snake, coiled off to the other side. Grim-faced travellers clutched their shoes in one hand and their intimate lotions in the other.

"A tiny thing, darling," Augusta added, and, grasping Frances's hand, pushed a small plastic vial into it. There was no label on the jar, merely a dozen or so lozenge-shaped white pills rattling around under a childproof lid.

Frances stared down at the container in her hand, frozen, until she felt the hot-breathed impatience of the person behind her in line.

"Come along, walk, everything normal," Augusta said in a low voice. "Just tuck them in your bag. You'll have no problem getting those through, and I would. They like to search me. I fear they can't keep their hands off my tits, though it might also be the residual effects of certain... well, there were one or two rules I tried to bend in the old days."

Augusta's manacle grip on her wrist propelled her forward in the line. Finally Frances found her voice: "What are these, Augusta?"

"Nothing illegal, my dear. Nothing like that. I just don't happen to have a prescription for them. They're merely... mood stabilizers." The couple in front of them shuffled ahead, and Augusta dragged her forward to fill the gap. "I'm a bit of a nervous flyer, you see. That's why I needed a drink. If there's turbulence, or if someone objectionable sits near me—I might require something of a medicinal nature."

"No," Frances spoke more loudly than she intended, and a security guard handing out plastic bags stopped to glance their way. "No, I won't do it."

But Augusta had already peeled away toward the Fast Track queue, which was moving rapidly through the security gate.

Frances made a last desperate grab, caught her by the elbow. "Augusta," she hissed. "They're going to stop me. People always know when I'm lying."

At this, Augusta turned and cast an eye up and down. "You could not be more innocuous. You look like a bloody communion wafer." And then she was gone, slinging her bag onto the conveyor belt, stripping off her bracelets before stalking, hands above head, through the metal detector.

In the glass dividing the two streams of passengers Frances caught a glimpse of herself: oatmeal-coloured sweater, biscuit-coloured skirt, mushroom-coloured tights. Beige was the best way to travel dirt-free, her mother had always said.

Impatient shuffling behind Frances told her she needed to move, or she'd draw attention to herself. As unobtrusively as possible, she slipped her hand into her purse, dropped the pills into a side compartment and zipped it up. Her bladder threatened to empty of its own volition. She seemed to have ceased breathing. The guard with the plastic bags was still watching her, and she thought: *Oh my God, they're trained to spot drug smugglers, and that's what I am. A drug smuggler. What if there are dogs? Could dogs smell pills? Oh God, I'm going to jail. In England. I'm going to Wormwood Scrubs.*

Slowly, she shuffled along. She placed her handbag in the plastic tray provided and nearly screamed when another security guard jabbed a finger at her carry-on.

"I'm sorry?" Frances whispered.

"Laptop, love," said the security guard, who looked like she'd been doing this job since the Luftwaffe roared overhead. "Turn on your laptop."

Sweat pooled between her shoulder blades, at the tops of her thighs. She watched her bag slide toward the black cave to be X-rayed. Cruelly, it stopped, and with an electronic bleep was spat out backwards, only to slowly enter the cave again.

Her thighs were glued damply together. Frances came out of her daze when a child behind poked her with a Barbie's pointed plastic foot. A security guard stood on the other side of the metal detector, gesturing impatiently. She passed through unremarked and felt her legs go limp with relief. Maybe it was all going to be okay, after all.

"Is this your bag, love?" It was the Second World War veteran valued for her bloodhound tenacity, peering at her over reading glasses. *She's fried bigger fish than me*, thought Frances. *She's sent hundreds of perps away to the big house.*

She whispered, "Yes. That is my bag."

"Mmm. May I open it?"

Her moment's bravado was gone. She tried to marshal her panicked thoughts: *I've never seen those before, they're not mine, what are they anyway?* The drug mule's mantra.

The battleaxe rummaged around for a moment and said, "Ah, here. This is what I saw."

Frances clutched the edge of the table, aware that

around her people were watching as they did up their belts and shoes. She closed her eyes.

"Yes, this. Is this yours?"

Frances opened her eyes. The lovely old guard was holding up a pair of manicure scissors, an inquisitive look on her dear old face.

"You do know this is a forbidden item, don't you?"

When Frances stumbled into her seat on the airplane, her heart playing "Flight of the Bumblebee," she sat for a moment, eyes closed, sweaty hands fixed on her purse straps. On one side, a man the size of a refrigerator was methodically working through a bag of pretzels, his eyes fixed on the seat ahead. On the other, a tiny old woman in a sari had a copy of *Hello!* magazine in her lap. She looked up from a story about the Duchess of York's new weight-loss program and smiled with such serenity that Frances felt some of her anxiety leaking away.

Which still left her with enough adrenaline in her body to kill a horse. *Breathe*, she thought, *breathe. You're on the plane now. You'll be up in the air soon, then two salty meals and a couple of bad movies and you'll be home.* Home. At the thought, the blood began thudding in her ears again.

"We'll be pushing back in just a minute," the pilot said over the PA, and advised passengers that they'd be in the air for ten hours.

A flight attendant came up the aisle, her face a kabuki mask of eyeshadow and lipstick, and said, "You'll need to put that bag under the seat in front of you or in the overhead bin."

I'd prefer to chuck it at Augusta, Frances thought. She took out her bottle of water, and her fingers brushed the bag's zippered compartment, where the jar of pills lay stashed. *Once we're up I'll flush them.*

Bending down, she struggled to shove the bag under the seat in front, and vaguely heard the grunt of the refrigerator of a man next to her as her shoulder jostled his knee. It was tempting to stay down there, with the sock smells and odd clankings from the plane's belly. It was especially tempting when she heard a voice from above.

"Darling, I believe you have something of mine." Augusta stood in the aisle, wearing a satin blouse she'd forgotten to button to the top.

Refrigerator man stared up at her, hand halfway to his open mouth. Leaning over him to hiss at Frances, Augusta had placed her cleavage mere inches from his face, the intersection of black lace and creamy flesh filling his line of vision.

His lips worked. "It's Kit Gallagher, innit?"

Augusta's face transformed instantly from fury to pleasure.

"Kit Gallagher as was, I'm afraid. She's gone to that great brewery in the sky." She raised her eyebrow at Frances. "My…property? Perhaps you'd be so good as to find it for me."

The flight attendant, slamming the bins closed down the aisle, had reached them. "I'm afraid you'll have to take your seat now, ma'am."

Augusta drew herself up and wasted her best smile. "I just need to get something from my friend here."

"You'll have to get it once we're in the air, ma'am."

"Really," said Augusta, "it will only take a minute."

"Ma'am," said the flight attendant, at the edge of her professional patience. "We are about to take off. You have to take your seat."

Fascinated, Frances watched them face off, two women sure of their power. Even the old lady in the sari had traded the manufactured drama of *Hello!* for the possibility of a real-life catfight.

Finally, Augusta drew a deep breath. "Of course, I wouldn't want to inconvenience anyone."

With a final smile at the refrigerator man, who dribbled several pretzels on his crotch, she turned for the business cabin.

Frances jolted awake as something heavy hit her ankle. The plane was banking to the right, and her bag slid out from under the seat ahead. With a small groan she sat up, noticing other passengers waking as the plane bucked and whined beneath them. Only the nervous ones, so far. The pathetic flyers—and she was one of them—could smell each other's fear. The darting stares, saucer eyes meeting over the seat backs.

Thump. The plane dropped suddenly like a pickup coming too fast over a hill, and somebody ahead of Frances yelled, "Whoa!" On one side, the lady in the sari slept neatly, straight up and down, while the giant man to her right was fixed on the screen in front of him, where Jennifer Aniston adjusted her bikini.

This time the plane lurched from front to back and dropped suddenly, its engine whining. Frances closed her eyes. *We weren't meant to fly.* The screen showing the Jennifer Aniston movie suddenly flashed Announcement and the pilot's voice came on.

"Hello, folks," he said, "It's Captain Hawkins on the flight deck. There's a bit of weather ahead, so I'm requesting permission to climb a little. Should smooth out shortly. I'll keep you posted."

As he finished, the plane skittered from side to side as if it had hit a patch of ice. The flight attendant who had confronted Augusta passed down the aisle and gave Frances a reassuring smile.

Frances undid her seatbelt and tugged her bag free of the seat in front. She nearly fell on the refrigerator man as the plane shimmied, and he grunted as he let her pass. In the toilet, she rested her cheek on the cold wall. She felt an overwhelming urge to vomit, but that would mean putting her face near the toilet seat, which glistened wetly in the dim light, a sodden wad of tissue clinging to its hinges. The plane bucked again and she was thrown against the door. A tiny hum of panic rose in her throat.

The flight attendant's voice on the PA made her jump: "The captain's put on the seatbelt sign, so we're asking everyone to please return to their seats."

There was no time to debate. She reached into her bag and pulled out the vial Augusta had given her: a dozen white pills, oval, the size of two grains of rice stuck together. In case of emergency, Augusta had said. Well, plunging to your death into the side of the Rocky Mountains was a pretty fucking dire emergency.

But what if I take one and I'm allergic, Frances thought. She gasped, looked up at her white face in the mirror. *What*

*if I take one and I'm hooked? Hooked on pills! Then I'd
have to go to rehab, and Dad and Mom will know, because
they'll have to pay for it —*

The plane made a precipitous yaw to the right. Frances
popped open the lid and poured the pills onto her palm.
How many? She tipped ten back into the bottle and
dry-swallowed two. Too late now. As she put the bottle
back into her bag, the flight attendant thumped on the toilet door: "Excuse me, you'll need to take your seat now,
please."

Frances picked up her bag and lurched out the door.
She'd rather be dead of an allergic reaction than dead in
a smoking wreck, with only her expensive orthodontistry
separating her from the next corpse over.

On either side of the aisle, passengers tightened their
belts, whispered calming words to their children, tipped up
the dregs of their miniature wine bottles. An unfathomable
few continued to sleep or work on their computers.

She was almost at her seat when, over the roar and
bump of the plane's engines, she heard the curtain of the
business-class cabin sliding back. Augusta stood framed in
the doorway, two spots of colour high on her cheeks, with
the flight attendant behind her like a farmer intent on an
escaped bull.

"Holy crap," Frances whispered and scrambled over the
refrigerator, elbows and heels sinking into tender places.
She buckled herself into her seat as Augusta staggered
down the aisle. There was a red-wine stain, almost the
shape of Africa, on the front of her blouse.

"Frances!" she barked. "There, Frances! My things,
please!"

The flight attendant was right behind her, and had the advantage of sobriety. "Sit down now, please ma'am."

"I just need," said Augusta, forming her words with care, "to get something from my friend. A medication, if you must know. For an ailment. Which I have."

"Now, ma'am. For your own safety."

"I would have come to collect my things earlier," said Augusta, "but I seem to have drifted off." The airplane lurched sideways and Augusta, with a screech, clutched the flight attendant's arm.

"I'm taking you back to your seat, ma'am," said the flight attendant, and began tugging Augusta toward the front of the cabin.

Now the other passengers were craning to look, whispering and reaching for their camera phones.

Frances's seatmate nudged her. "Are you friends with Kit Gallagher, then? What do you reckon her and the stewardess get in a scrap? Maybe tear some clothes?"

Augusta batted the flight attendant's hand away, knocking a man's reading glasses off his head. "I will return to my seat," she said, "when I have what I need."

"Ma'am," the flight attendant said in a voice perfected through several Dealing With Difficult Passengers seminars, "I will only ask you once more. You are posing a hazard to yourself and to the security of this flight. Resume your seat."

Her colleagues scurried to her aid, surrounding Augusta like a ring of sheepdogs around an angry bull. One of them carried a handful of plastic restraints.

Augusta had reached down to autograph a man's arm, although from his terrified expression it seemed he hadn't requested the service. As the plane lurched once again, she fell, laughing, onto his lap.

"Christ's sake, darling!" Frances heard her screech. "You're well upholstered."

"That's it," the flight attendant said, and reached down to take Augusta's arm.

"Hands off, you mad bitch!" Augusta's voice was muffled by the man's lap, her pointed toes kicking out at anyone within reach. "I know my rights! I am a British citizen! You just want to fondle my…" The words were lost as the other the flight attendants descended to form a protective circle. "Get your hands off…sue you…Sober as a judge, I tell you. As a judge!"

"Miss Bleeker? Ma'am?"

With a great effort, Frances unpeeled her eyes. The police officer was standing before her, arms crossed over a barrel chest. Was it the same one who'd escorted her past all the open-mouthed passengers? Nothing was clear at the moment; she was looking at him through a veil of fog.

"Yes," she managed. Had she been eating peanut butter? She could barely get the words through her dry lips. She coughed, pulled herself upright on the plastic chair. "Yes, officer."

Lodged in the crevice between his chest and one beefy bicep was a gold badge: POLICE OFFICER, it said in purple script above the words AIRPORT POLICE. LAX was embroidered on his uniform, above the badge. Lax? There was nothing lax about his grip. *Oh.* The clouds in her brain parted slightly, and she remembered where she was. Home.

"I wanted to return this to you, Ma'am." The officer held out her bag, which she'd left behind in the chaos.

Frances reached out, but there was an odd disconnect in her brain, and the bag wasn't where her hand thought it should be. She pawed the air for a moment until, with a sigh, he bent down and placed it in her lap. A curled piece of paper had come unstuck from the wall behind his head: PLEASE ASSIST LOS ANGELES WORLD AIRPORTS POLICE IN THEIR ENQUIRIES. INCIVILITY AND ABUSE WILL NOT BE TOLERATED. She giggled, but it sounded very far away. "Thank you, officer," Frances said carefully. "Am I three to go? Free to go, I mean? With my friend?"

"My colleague is still questioning your associate, ma'am." The officer frowned at her, and Frances felt that in an earlier age he would have wagged a finger, or worse. "Disrupting a flight is a serious offence, especially these days. A federal offence."

"Absolutely, yes, I understand," said Frances. "I appreciate the seriousness of the situation, officer." She added weakly, "I'm American. British people sometimes don't understand our rules."

He watched for a minute as Frances tried to rub feeling back into her face. "I'll keep you apprised of our progress. Meantime, there's a water cooler over there."

She waited for a moment, not trusting her feet. Sure enough, when she stood, one knee buckled and she sat back down with a graceless thump, her chair screeching against the linoleum. Two agents, huddled over a printout, turned to look her way.

Frances closed her eyes again, giving in to the pull of sleep. There was something unfamiliar about this tumble into darkness, a hallucinatory quality she'd never felt before. At the edge of her consciousness people who only wanted the best for her gathered: her father, her mother, Stanley. Oddly, Augusta was there, gazing at her with concern.

Frances jerked awake and felt for her purse. It had slid from her lap onto the next seat over, lodged against an elderly man in a cherry-red suit, whose shirt was open to reveal a profusion of white chest hair. He turned to her and slung an arm over the back of her chair, smiling appreciatively. "How you doing?"

Slowly, Frances managed to unpeel her lids. The police officers at the end of the hallway were gone. She realized, with a start, that the old man in the red suit was standing in front of her.

"Would you like to join me for a coffee, my dear?"

Someone had poured grit in her eyes while she slept. How long had it been? The hallway was still filled with sunlight streaming from the mesh-covered windows.

"I'm fine, thanks," she said, though her voice was rusty. "I don't think we're meant to leave this...station, or whatever it is."

He shrugged, and walked down the corridor. Still no sign of Augusta or the two cops who had ushered her off the plane. Frances found she didn't much care; she was wrapped in a delicious blanket of calm. Somewhere in her head a tiny voice urged her to be furious with Augusta, but it was coming from another room.

A female police officer walked by, escorting a man whose face was surly under a baseball cap: "Sir, it is illegal to have a loaded firearm in your car when you come to the airport." Her voice rose as they passed Frances. "I understand that, sir, but the law does not make exception for birthday presents."

"Here you are, young lady." The man in the red suit had returned, and he was bending over, solicitous. "You looked like you could use this."

It was a plastic cup of water, warm and slightly murky. Frances felt a prick at the back of her eyes. When would she ever stop misjudging people, and crying when she did?

"Thanks," she said, and smiled up at him. "It's very kind of you."

"It's my pleasure," said the old man, with a half-bow. "Maybe you'd like to give me your number?"

Frances sighed. "I don't think so."

She closed her eyes again, but it was only a moment before she heard a door opening at the end of the hall. Augusta emerged, her hair a wild cloud, the wine stain like a wound over her left breast.

Frances stared. She'd been expecting a diminished Augusta, worn down by exhaustion, drink, and an abrading conflict with American security. Instead she radiated satisfaction, as if she'd just read the critics' reviews of her latest performance and they were all in awe. Behind her, one of the police officers rubbed dark-ringed eyes.

Augusta sailed toward her with the two cops in her wake. "How kind of you to wait, Frances, while this misunderstanding was sorted out."

As if I had a choice, Frances thought.

"Once I explained to Officer Cruz," she indicated the

younger of the two, "about the mixup over my medication, they were most understanding."

"Your medication," Frances repeated.

"My epilepsy medication," Augusta nodded. "And how distraught I was when I thought I'd left it at home. How I had perhaps one more glass of wine than I ought. For my nerves."

"Absolutely," said Frances.

"And when I explained to Officer Cruz that I was here to meet fans of my show...well, it turns out he has seen *The Blood Bank*. On the Internet." She turned to the younger officer, put a hand on his forearm. "I will be sure to have all of the episodes sent to you."

Seeing his partner's scowl, Officer Cruz cleared his throat.

The older officer glared at Augusta over his half-rims. "You are free to go with a warning this time, Miss Price." As Augusta nodded meekly, his frown deepened. "This time. We take all disruptions in federal air space very, very seriously, whether they constitute a security threat or not. It remains the airline's prerogative to lodge a formal complaint against you for defamatory remarks."

Augusta nodded, eyes to the floor.

"Well, then," said the older man. "We have your contact details. We'll be in touch if there are further developments."

He turned to leave. His partner raised his fingers in a half-wave at Augusta, and followed.

As soon as they were gone, Augusta rolled her eyes and flopped onto the seat next to Frances. "Dear God, now I know why you moved from this place. These people are so...officious."

"Maybe that's because they're officials." It sounded to Frances as if she was speaking from the bottom of a deep pool.

Augusta leaned back in her chair, gave Frances a long, hard stare. Finally, she said, "How many did you take?"

She had no energy to waste on a lie. "Two," she said.

Augusta made a sound that was half cough and half laugh. The old man in the red suit joined in with a high cackle of his own.

"Four milligrams of Ativan and you're still conscious," she said, and slung Frances's bag over her shoulder. "Maybe we're meant to be together after all."

eighteen

The flowered sheet that hung across the apartment, dividing the warring combatants, was laundered to almost transparent delicacy. It carried Deller back forty years to his grandmother's kitchen, where wet linen lay draped over a wooden rack in one corner, drying as stiff as cardboard.

The elderly woman sitting on one side of the sheet, though, belonged to a different species from his nan, who was a champion of stoicism, her mouth grimly clamped shut in the face of joy and sorrow. Ken's grandmother could suffer for Britain. Myra Rosen, now sitting in front of him, eyes glittering under hoods of powder-blue shadow, seemed never to have let a grievance pass unspoken.

"And so I asked him, 'If you're going to use the bathroom when it's not your time on the schedule'—and I understand, these things happen, I'm not a monster—I said to him, 'Could you please at least give me some warning?'—so maybe I can find my way to the bedroom and not have to witness him tramping across my floor." She leaned across the table, pushing aside a plate of cherry Danishes, and whispered: "It's his prostate, you know how it is with old men, the *shvantz* is the first thing that goes—"

"I can hear you! My ears are still working, thank you very much!"

The aggrieved bellow came from the other side of the sheet. Kenneth could hear Mr. Rosen shuffling around in the hidden kitchen, emitting an operatic chorus of groans and sighs to accompany his wife's narrative.

Estranged wife, Kenneth corrected himself. But were they estranged when they still shared an apartment, if not a life? A bulletin board was nailed to the wall. It laid out, in ten-minute slices, precisely when Myra was allowed on her husband's side of the curtain to access the kitchen, and when he was allowed on her side to relieve his overburdened bladder.

"Well," Kenneth said, with false brightness, "it's a bit like *It Happened One Night*."

Myra Rosen reared back in her chair so that her golden chandelier earrings tinkled. "Are you suggesting that one is Clark Gable?" She jabbed a thumb at the curtain.

There was a snarl from the other side: "And the man in the grocery store mistakes you for Claudette Colbert?"

"Maybe once I did look like Claudette Colbert," said Myra, gazing at herself in the polished surface of the table, "till Mr. Vampire sucked my youth away."

"There's a good place to start," Kenneth said hastily. "Tell me how it began."

He couldn't look at his watch, but he was acutely aware of the time slipping away, of the thousand things that were swirling around in his brain: Augusta in the same city and Charles pretending it meant nothing; and his publisher's latest email inquiring about the state of his book, which had strayed from passive-aggressive into purely aggressive.

"It was when I heard you on the radio," Myra continued, "and you were talking to a lady whose husband was a useless lump—" (behind the curtain, a bitter laugh) "and your advice made me think. So I had my neighbour look you up on the cyberspace."

"No," said Kenneth, "I mean your beginning, as a couple. You and Mr. Rosen."

"Oh," she said. "So long ago, really." Her eyes were unfocused, lost in the past. There were no family photos on the walls, Kenneth noted, unless Paul Robeson and Cesar Chavez counted as family. "My cousin and I were at an SWP meeting in Long Beach—"

"That's the Socialist Workers Party," Martin Rosen called over.

"Yes, I know," said Kenneth. "I'm from Manchester."

"Anyway," Mrs. Rosen continued, "I saw him arguing with Ben Faber across the room. Jabbing him in the chest like this." She leaned forward to stab Ken with her scarlet talon. "My cousin thought Marty was too short, but I liked the way he was yelling at Faber about the Hungarians. So it was 1956, I guess."

"It was after," Mr. Rosen yelled through the sheet.

"I'm the one doing the telling!" Mrs. Rosen yelled back. "So I talked to him when he came over, even though he was clearly a Trotskyite. More fool me."

"Look who's talking!" A pot slammed hard on the stovetop. "You never even believed in the revolution."

As they bickered about which faction had betrayed the proletariat fifty years ago, Kenneth looked at his watch.

He cast his eye around the apartment; sometimes there were clues buried in the silt that gave some hint about the roots of a marital dispute. Sometimes there was just a lot of detritus.

"Okay," he said, his voice rising to be heard above theirs. "Okay, Mr. and Mrs. Rosen!" More quietly, he said, "I'm not actually a therapist. And I think that you both may benefit from counselling. Obviously, you'd have to leave the apartment and go together."

"Never."

"Not in this lifetime."

Where to begin? He reached for a cherry Danish, his second. Really, he shouldn't, but they were astonishingly delicious—and chewing always helped him think. He brushed some crumbs off his shirt and said, "What I usually ask couples when they come to me is this: What would you like to achieve from our time together?"

There was silence from the other side of the curtain. Mrs. Rosen stared at him as if he'd spoken gibberish, and finally spread her hands wide. "We just want what you give other couples. What you say you can deliver."

"Which is …?"

Now she was looking at him like he really was crazy. "To rekindle the romance, of course."

Kenneth nearly spat out his Danish. Quickly he took a gulp of coffee to wash it down. The kohl around Mrs. Rosen's dark eyes was starting to smudge and he realized, with a heavy heart, that she had begun to cry. Crying he could handle, though; intractable disputes based on age-old grievances he could not.

"Mrs. Rosen." He leaned over to take her warm, lined

hand, feeling the heavy weight of her rings against his palm. He spoke in his soothing-nervous-brides voice, pitched only for her ears: "May I be frank?"

She nodded, her lips trembling. On the other side of the sheet there was expectant silence. "There are...issues at the heart of your marriage."

"Issues?" she whispered.

"Yes, Mrs. Rosen, issues. I think you need more help than I can provide. Perhaps the way forward"—he really was ninety percent American these days—"is along the professional route."

Mrs. Rosen pulled back, her dark eyes suspicious. "You're not a professional?"

"I'm..." He thought for a moment. "I'm a paramedic, not a heart surgeon. You might be better off in an operating room."

She leaned back in her chair and looked over at the fabric wall dividing her life. Her voice dropped to a whisper. "Let me ask you something," she said. "You've been in love?"

They always wanted to know this. Was he married? For how long? Why not? The taint of bachelorhood hung over him.

"We've all been in love, Mrs. Rosen."

"But have you been in love here," she thumped her fist against her chest, the other hand clamped to his wrist, "so that it hurts? Even when you know you shouldn't? Even when you know it's over? And only one of you is still in love?" The rivulet of tears was a full stream now.

From the other side of the sheet Martin Rosen called, "What are you saying over there? Are you bothering that poor man, Myra?"

But neither one of them answered him. They sat in silence, staring at each other, and in her crumpled face Kenneth saw a mirror of his own.

At the bottom of the hill below the Rosens' apartment building he found a bench by the curb and sank onto it. A public service ad covering the backrest told him, under a photo of a grim-faced man, that cases of syphilis had skyrocketed. Someone had spray-painted the man's crotch green. Who would pose for a syphilis ad, anyway? You'd have to be on your last pint of milk.

The same kind of desperation, he thought, *that drives people to abandon semi-respectable careers in broadcasting in order to reinvent themselves in utterly absurd ways far from home.* Sweat plastered his shirt to his chest, and he shrugged off his corduroy jacket. Even this close to winter, the sun refused to relent.

In the strip mall across la Cienaga a dusty-windowed gym was sandwiched between an Arby's and a 7-Eleven. YOU DON'T PAY TILL IT DROPS AWAY said the bright-yellow sign on the door. YOUR LOSS IS OUR GAIN. His stomach grumbled, and Kenneth hauled himself to his feet and began walking down the hill to his car.

Perhaps when he got home he'd reward himself with a few minutes on YouTube. Just a few, no more: viewed too often, the images became stale and lost the power to stop his heart. When he was being good, he'd restrict himself to only reading about Augusta. The Google Alert he'd set up to follow her made him feel like a dirty-trousered old pervert, but shame had less power than desire. He'd been walking to the radio studio, idly scrolling through emails, when an alert informed him that Augusta would be coming to town to speak at Fantasmagoria™. He'd had to sit down for a minute, staring at his phone in joy and disbelief.

One night, after hours of bored searching, following Augusta's name deeper and deeper into the bowels of recorded information like Theseus in the labyrinth, he'd found a clip. Clicking on a link, he was suddenly confronted with a young Augusta on the rust-and-brown set of the BBC chat show *West Country Now*. His breath had caught. He remembered every flower on Augusta's short tunic, every dirty throaty laugh, as if he'd been there. Because he *had* been there.

In those days, his pride had been a malleable thing. When she rang after weeks of silence to ask for a drive to Bristol, he did not give voice to his first thoughts—*Piss off, where have you been, some of us have to work, you lazy cow.*

Instead, he said: "When should I collect you?"

In those days before she had Charles, her mood was reliably buoyant, so long as she knew pleasure was guaranteed. They stopped off in Notting Hill on the way, and he slipped out of the car to pick up her tiny package from a sullen bloke in a greengrocer's in Lancaster Road. She sat with one foot on the dash and the window open as he drove, her tiny dress swirling and dancing so that several times he'd nearly gone off the road.

With one hand she'd rummage in the little paper bag and with the other she would reach out to touch his hair— but not often enough, not nearly often enough. *Still,* he thought, *maybe, maybe.* At one point she reached over and she put something smooth and round against his lips, and he opened his mouth, not caring what entered his body as long as he could feel her fingers on him.

They'd found the BBC studio on the edge of Bristol and she'd dragged him toward the doors, her little hand damp in his. The producer, a safety-pin-pierced anomaly in exile from London, greeted Augusta with something like worship: she'd recently starred in a production of *The Cherry Orchard* set on a council estate in Brixton. It had closed after two weeks, but not before every tabloid in the country had denounced its depravity.

"Please come with me, Miss Price," the producer simpered. "Not you," he said to Kenneth. "Guests only. You can wait in the lobby."

The producer put his hand up as warning, a wee white smudge against Ken's barrel chest, and for a minute Ken considered taking it and bending the fingers back until they snapped. The blood roared in his head, and elsewhere. What had she given him in the car?

"Darling," said Augusta, slipping between them and curling her arm around Kenneth's waist, "this is my navigator. He goes where I go. *E pluribus unum.* Besides, he's one of you. He works for the BBC." When the producer continued to scowl at Kenneth, she added imperiously: "In London."

"Fine, then." He turned to wag a finger in Kenneth's face. "But no talking to the other guests."

"I shall try to restrain myself," Kenneth said.

The producer flounced ahead of them down a series of corridors lined with posters of steamships and finally came to a stop before a green door. He held it open.

"You're the final guest, Ms. Price," he said, beaming at her. "That was my idea. It's like Christmas lunch—saving the best for last."

"You are too kind, darling. Just one thing. It's been a long journey: Loo?"

"Oh!" He pointed down the corridor. "The ladies' is just there. I'll come back for you in about twenty minutes."

Once he was gone, they turned to greet the other chat-show guests, seated on a nubbly orange sofa: a local rugby champion who appeared to be missing most of one ear and the lower half of the other, and an ancient, wizened Cornish farmer who had grown a potato that looked like Ted Heath.

"I am in exalted company," Augusta whispered, as the rugby player stood to offer her a seat, or a drink, or something more.

"Thank you, love, no," she said. "It's been a very dusty ride in from London, and I fear I've got something in my eye. Ken, do you think you could help me remove this fearsome speck, before I go out there and terrify the good people of Bristol?"

She lifted a hand to the rugby player and the ancient Cornishman, and with the other dragged Kenneth out the door and into the corridor.

"Augusta, wh—" But he didn't have time to speak before she had shoved him against the wall and pulled his face down to hers. He felt her lift onto her toes to reach him. For some reason, he always found this tiny action thrilling: as if in this one way, he had power over her; it was the only time she ever exerted herself for him. He pulled her tight, one hand cupping her bottom.

At the end of the corridor came the dull clap of a door shutting and he pushed her away, though it nearly killed him.

"Augusta," he whispered. "That little prat is going to come looking for you in just a few minutes."

"Just enough minutes," she whispered, and rocking forward she lifted up to gently bite his lower lip.

He was sure the rugby player and the old codger could hear his groan through the wall. Augusta hooked a finger in his belt loop and began creeping backwards, beckoning him with her other hand like a crone in a fairy tale.

With her back she opened the door of the loo and pulled him in. He glanced around nervously. Was it a firing offence to be caught in the ladies' room of BBC Bristol? But then she was on him again, her warm hands sliding under his shirt.

"The door," she whispered. "Lock the door."

And of course he did as she ordered. Then he reached for her, sliding his hands under her arms, his nose in her hair.

"Wait," she whispered, and put her bag on the ledge by the mirror.

There was a plastic vase filled with plastic irises, and she swept them off into the bin. Opening the bag from the greengrocer's, she took a little wrap of paper from inside. She'd seemed happy before, but now she positively glowed.

"Augusta," he said, as she laid out a tiny heap of cocaine. His voice sounded half-hearted even in his ears.

"Credit card," she whispered.

"Augusta."

"Credit card."

What he should have said was: I'm not your chauffeur, your drug buddy, your mule, your lackey. I'm not any of those things. You won't let me be any of the things I want to be in your life. But he couldn't think beyond the fact that he was going to shag her. Reaching for his wallet, he handed over a credit card on which the numbers were barely visible.

It took less than a minute for her to lay out four lines. Taking the ten-pound note he handed her, she inhaled two of them deeply and tilted her head back. He watched the line of her throat as she swallowed, her breasts rising underneath the ridiculously tiny flowered dress, and it was all he could do not to pull her to him. Instead, he took the ten-pound note she offered, and bent over the two remaining lines.

The icy blast hit the back of his throat, his teeth, his brain. Everything he needed was there, in the ladies' toilet in BBC Bristol. He turned to Augusta and she was looking at him with such wolfish hunger that he thought: *I'm not going to last thirty seconds.*

Then her mouth was on his, and he could feel the sink at the back of his thighs. As she unzipped his trousers he tried to turn and lift her onto the sink and they nearly fell, giggling.

"I missed you," she murmured against his neck.

"Bloody liar," he said, pulling her hair away from her face, harder than he'd intended. "Fucking little liar."

And then he didn't care, at least for the next five minutes. He had her hands up above her head, clapped flat against the mirror, and she was moving frantically against him when they heard a knock at the door.

"Miss Price? Are you in there? You're on in five."

nineteen

It was painful to gaze upon people who were half her age and twice as successful. *They don't even look old enough to drive*, Frances thought. She sat at a table by the hotel's rooftop pool, watching pods of glossy teenagers nestle together on red velvet beds.

The poolside was designed to look like an opium den, each bed outfitted with a blackened but non-functioning pipe. No one swam, although the morning sun was already searing. She'd forgotten how oppressive constant sunshine could be.

At least she remembered how to speak Californian: "I'll have an egg-white omelette, tempeh sausage, and a glass of pomelo juice," she told the waitress.

She hadn't even looked at the price. Let the people from Fantasmagoria™ pay $30 for her conversion to health. Frances felt a fleeting sense of peace: a breakfast that contained neither alcohol nor anything fried. She was home.

Why, then, did she feel like an imposter? One of the girls on the opium bed squealed, and Frances pulled down her sunglasses to watch. She recognized the young woman, star of a Disney sitcom who'd gone badly off the rails. After a successful stint in a Miami clinic, the starlet had emerged and returned to her Idaho hometown. There she methodically apologized to every schoolmate who had ever been the subject of her cruelty. *The Sorry Tour*, as it was called, became a popular reality show on the Healing Network. Frances had a bit of an addiction to *The Sorry Tour*, which she watched on her computer late at night. Not a single popular girl from school had ever apologized to her.

Frances turned back to her computer, shielding its screen from the sun's glare. She had three tabs open: the outline of Augusta's new book, her Facebook page, and a web site titled How to Tell If Your Loved One Is Back on Drugs.

On the addiction page, each warning sign was written in lurid pink:

Number 3: Erratic or thoughtless behaviour.
Number 7: Borrowing or stealing money.
Number 8: Self-obsession to the exclusion of all others.

She sighed and closed the page.

With one tentative finger she opened Stanley's Facebook page. It felt as if she were spying on him, as if she were lurking in a doorway across the road from the *Advance*. He had changed his profile picture; instead of the scowling photo he'd had taken one lunch hour at Snappy Snaps, there was a tabby cat. Puzzled, she clicked on his profile. She sat back, pushed the computer away. Under "Work," where it once listed his editor's job, it now said: "Accepting suggestions."

So he'd been sacked, too. She felt a heaviness settle over her. In a way, this was worse than her own firing. It was over, officially. The curtain had fallen on their adventure. Perhaps she could go back to the *Bakersfield Californian*. Frances pictured the glorious vista of her future stretching from town-council meeting to tractor-sales report.

Her breakfast arrived and she murmured "thanks" to the waitress. It looked less like food than a sculpture of food. She poked at the omelette with a fork. Overhead, a helicopter beat the air — police or news channel, it was difficult to tell. This was another thing she'd forgotten about Los Angeles: there was almost as much traffic in the sky as on the streets below.

She pulled her computer back and called up her own Facebook page.

She hadn't updated her status in weeks. After a minute, she typed on Stanley's wall: "I'm home, wherever that is." Message in a bottle.

twenty

"I wish someone would turn off that ungodly sun, just for a day."

Augusta sat huddled on the passenger seat of the rental car, shrinking from a beam of midday light. She wore a diaphanous orange kaftan and last night's mascara. Both hands clutched a water bottle.

"Everyone in this city is the wrong colour," she grumbled. "Shades of nut and tangerine. Only I am the colour God intended."

Frances fought to conceal a grin. Outside, the streets of Burbank baked. Gym, taco shop, dollar store, gym, taco shop. There was one office tower on the block, and they'd parked outside. It was the first time she'd found something funny in two days. At the rental car desk, she'd crossed her fingers behind her back as she handed the clerk her credit card.

"This is why my career never advanced in America," Augusta said, and took a swig from her water bottle. "I refused to tan."

"Ah."

"Do you know," Augusta continued, "that I was once offered quite a plum role on *Dynasty*? I was meant to play Joan's sister. Her much younger sister. It stretched credulity, but there you are."

Frances frowned. "I don't remember Joan Collins having a sister on *Dynasty*."

Augusta took another sip of water. After a moment, she said: "It might not have been *Dynasty*. It might have been *The Love Boat*." Frances bit her lip, and Augusta glared: "It was a two-part special. At Christmas. I was meant to bring a certain grandeur to the high seas. But there was an unfortunate incident with the purser on the Lido Deck, and my role was recast." She took a swig from her water bottle. "I have loathed the sea ever since."

They sat in silence, the only sound the car's air conditioner. Frances's phone emitted a tiny beep. Her thumb hovered over the responses to her new Facebook post. Her mother, never more than thirty seconds from "Like," had responded: "I don't get it, sweetheart. Where are you? Call!" There was one other new post. Frances's breath caught as she read Stanley's message: "So that's where you've washed up, mysterious creature. Remember you've got another home."

She read the message over and over, trying to distill the essence of its meaning.

She turned to Augusta: "Can I have a sip of water?"

Augusta clutched the bottle more firmly. "The question is may I. And the answer is no. I have…germs."

As Frances watched Augusta tuck the bottle carefully into the bag at her feet, a sudden thought hit her: she'd never seen Augusta drink water before. It seemed a bit late to begin. She was tempted to snatch the bottle and give it a sniff, but instead let out a small huff of exasperation. This was her life, for the moment: baby sitter and designated driver.

"What are we doing here, Augusta? We should be working on the book."

"I've told you. We're waiting for an old friend of mine. I'd like to surprise him. He should be coming out any time now."

A small cluster of people stood outside the revolving doors of the office tower.

"And what does this mystery man look like?"

"Well, I haven't seen him in years," Augusta said. She took out her compact, and dabbed at her nose. "Tall, but likely running to fat. He'll be wearing a suit if I know him—bespoke suit, the vain prick. Face like a crushed meringue."

Vain prick. A series of calculations slowly fell into place in Frances's mind, the tumblers of a lock clicking open.

"Wait a minute, Augusta. Are we stalking—"

"There is no stalking, darling. I am not the Countess of Fuckland hunting deer with the Queen."

"But —"

"Shh!" Augusta clapped a hand over Frances's mouth, and Frances noticed, through her irritation, that it tasted like a martini. "That's him."

Frances craned her neck. "Which one?"

But Augusta was silent, her eyes locked on a man who strode down the street toward them. Immediately, Frances knew he was foreign. Unlike most middle-aged men in Los Angeles, he wasn't dressed like a high school student.

Despite the heat, he wore a dark suit and brogues. The sun caught strands of thinning blond hair. He had a slightly bashed handsomeness that reminded Frances, for some reason, of Stanley.

"I'd give him a second look," she said without thinking.

Augusta sat bolt upright and whipped around with a furious glare. The movement caught the man's eye and he paused on the sidewalk, squinting against the light.

"Mother of God," Augusta whispered, and slid down in her seat. She peered at the man over the dashboard as he stood on the sidewalk, caught in indecision.

"Get down," she hissed at Frances. "Get down before he sees you!"

"That would really attract his attention, Augusta," Frances said.

Their prey took a step toward the car and Augusta, huddled under the dashboard in a cocoon of orange chiffon, hissed: "He's seen us! Drive, for the love of God. Drive!"

As Frances turned the key in the ignition, she wondered exactly how badly this would end. The feeling of powerlessness was familiar; in middle school, she'd never defied the girls who wanted to copy her homework. She pulled out into traffic. In the rear-view mirror, she saw the man staring after them, eyebrows knit together.

"So," she said. "That's Mr. Romance."

twenty-one

It was the work of a moment to unscrew the Smirnoff bottle. The crack of the cap coming free was lost in the shouting from the front of the store, where Frances stood, fists clenched, dark hair in disarray.

"There's no way it could be declined."

The only other customer in the shop pretended to read a magazine, but secretly feasted on the drama at the cash register. Augusta saw Frances swallow, make a deliberate effort to control herself.

"Please try again. There's plenty of credit left on that card."

With a sigh, the clerk swiped again.

Calmly, Augusta unscrewed the cap and guided a stream of vodka into her water bottle. For a moment, she was a stranger watching herself: a middle-aged Englishwoman stealing vodka from a corner shop in Hollywood. At one time the image would have shocked her, but she'd long since realized there was always another step down.

The shop door slammed. Hastily she slid the water

bottle into her bag and waggled three fingers at the clerk on the way out.

Frances paced outside, jabbing at her phone, and Augusta considered, for a moment, whether to give the girl some privacy. She sidled closer.

"Hey Mom, it's me." Augusta watched the girl's shoulders hunch. The irritation she felt at Frances's feebleness was diluted by a less familiar sensation, something like pity. Maybe Frances's mother would know what to do with the child.

Augusta crept closer. If she eavesdropped, she might even learn a thing or two about this mothering business. It couldn't be too late. But Frances saw her, frowned, cupped the phone with her other hand.

Augusta wandered to the curb. Across the boulevard, two businesses nestled in the derelict shell of a theatre, their competing services advertised with neon signs. JESU-CRISTO ES EL SEÑOR, read the larger and more garish one. The other invited passersby to EAT SKOOBY'S HOT DOGS.

"The blood of Christ and the sausage of Christ," muttered Augusta, "together at last."

Frances stood looking at the phone in her hand. It was unpleasantly clear to Augusta what would come next. She took a quick swig from her bottle and walked back to the girl. How did one offer comfort in a situation like this?

She reached into her bag. "Cigarette?"

The girl's face crumpled.

"Oh no, darling," Augusta said. "No tears before lunch. Please. I'm not properly fortified." She reached for Frances's hand, patting it awkwardly. "We'll work on the book today, shall we? That will make you feel better. Our path from ruin."

"I'm not about to cry," Frances said. She began walking back toward the car. Under their feet, dusty gilt stars of the Walk of Fame named celebrities of the past and present. "I wish that I could phone my parents with good news, that's all. Just once." She stopped, seeming to steel herself. "Augusta, when do you think we might see that advance from the publisher? We could put it toward the bills we're piling up."

Augusta scuttled ahead, suddenly very interested in the star below. Rhonda Fleming. Who in God's name was Rhonda Fleming? At one point she must have shone brightly indeed. She turned to Frances. "Any moment now, darling. I've just had a call from them this morning. Apparently there was some tangle over the international bank transfer, but it's sorted now." She was pleased with how plausible this sounded. Indeed, there were messages on her phone; none was from her publisher, however.

Frances's eyes were red in the bright light, and Augusta led her over to a bench. She dropped her cigarette, noticing with some regret that it had fallen, sizzling, on Boris Karloff's star. From her bag she pulled a pair of giant sunglasses that had come free with a magazine.

"Here," she said, shoving them at Frances. "These will help."

Frances sat unmoving while Augusta slid the glasses onto her face, adjusting them so they sat just so.

"There you are, darling. Very alluring. One should always choose mystery over mucous."

"You mean I look great with my face half covered." But Frances gave her a grateful smile.

For a moment they sat and watched the parade of pilgrims paying obeisance to the sidewalk.

"My father was utterly disgusted that I wanted to be an actress," Augusta said. "He said I would bring shame on the family. I might as well be a streetwalker, he said. Do you know what he wanted me to be?"

Frances shook her head.

"An accountant."

"He did not!"

"No word of a lie. The man thought I should be in charge of other people's money. Which is one of the reasons I was always convinced that he wasn't really my father."

Frances dissolved into hopeless giggles on the bench beside her. Augusta patted her knee.

"You should get used to it now or you'll be in tears from here until death. You will often disappoint your parents." Augusta took a swig from her bottle. "And sometimes your children, too."

twenty-two

A girl ran by them up the hill, turning to smile at Charles as he moved closer to the edge of the path to let her by. The boy's eyes followed her as she disappeared around a bend.

Kenneth put a hand over his side to ease the pain of a stitch. "You know what my father used to say when he saw an arse like that? 'Two cats fighting in a pillowcase.'"

"You are a terrible pervert, Ken."

Kenneth stopped, dropped his hands to his knees, let his head hang down. So this is what it felt like to have a heart attack. He saw a bead of sweat fall from his forehead onto the cement path and sizzle there. When it felt like he could breathe again, he stood up and glared at the boy who stood above him on the steep path, unmelted.

He gasped, "Nice thing to say to your old man on his deathbed."

He hadn't changed from the suit he'd worn to the radio station that morning, and now it hung from him like a sodden sail. He wore handmade loafers from Lobbs of St. James's, which had not gone out of style once in twenty years. Passing joggers gaped at the indecency of his dress.

"I thought," he said when he'd caught his breath, "that we were going for a drink."

Wordlessly, Charles thrust a bottle into his hand and Ken held it at arm's length, squinting.

"Goji berry and kale smoothie. Now I know you're trying to kill me."

There was a bench at the edge of the path and he collapsed onto it with a grunt of relief. With a professional eye, he watched the hikers trundling up the canyon: dog-walkers and incognito actors, baseball caps pulled low over their eyes, couples with liver-spotted hands and ageless foreheads.

The boy had come to sit next to him. "How's your book coming, anyway? Sorry. I know you're never supposed to ask a writer that."

Kenneth closed his eyes against the setting sun. "It's not coming. They're ready to kill me, though in a completely non-violent Buddhist way." He squinted over at the boy. "They want it to be more personal. Stories of love and loss."

"Well, you'd be good at the loss part."

"Have I ever mentioned you're a miserable little twat?"

They sat for a minute, quietly, until Kenneth no longer felt he needed CPR. He knew he probably shouldn't say anything.

"I think I saw your mother," he said.

Charles stared at him for a moment, mouth open. "Augusta?"

"Yes, your mother," Ken said testily. "Augusta."

"Here?"

"In Burbank." The ridiculousness of the idea struck him, and he began to laugh. "Your mother, in a hire car, in Burbank." His laughter turned into a roar. "Now that's humiliating."

The boy slumped against the back of the bench. The setting sun turned his hair gold. Ken thought, for the thousandth time, how beautiful he was, how unmarked by everything that had happened. How was the lad still single? The failure felt like a weight on his chest. Mr. Romance can't find a girlfriend for his son, what a joke. But the truth was, the boy had never been interested in love.

Gingerly, he said, "Maybe we could try to see her."

Charles was watching a hawk wheeling overhead. He said nothing, but after a minute he took out his phone and began checking his messages.

"To see how she's doing." Kenneth reached over and covered the phone's screen. "Charles," he said. "It's been such a long time."

Finally the boy turned to look at him. "You go if you want, Ken. You're the family exorcist. I've no interest."

twenty-three

She was alone in the airless dark. Why was there no one else on the Tube? And why was the train stopped at the station with the doors closed? Frances pressed herself against the glass, peered out onto the empty platform: Tooting Bec. She was going to die alone and friendless at Tooting Bec.

It would be in her obituary, the final indignity of her life. Except her obituary would never be printed, because obituaries were reserved for people who'd actually done something memorable with their time on earth. In the sinister hush of the train something stirred and Frances shrieked, slamming her fist against the train door.

"Open up," she cried, pressing her face to the small area of glass not covered in alien grime. "Can anyone hear me? Open up!"

There was an echo: "For God's sake, open up!"

Something grabbed her legs. Terrified, she kicked out, and then heard the voice again: "Don't make us use force!" A burst of laughter in the dark.

Frances sat up, heart hammering, and reached for the

light by her bed. She wasn't at Tooting Bec Tube station; she was in a hotel in Los Angeles. She kicked at the sheet that trapped her legs. At her door there was a renewed pounding.

"We know you're in there. Open up!"

Grabbing her bathrobe where she'd dropped it, Frances stumbled the few feet to the door.

"Augusta," she whispered, "I'm sleeping."

"I would expect nothing less. Open the door, darling."

Frances did as she was told. Augusta stood in the doorway, blue suede stilettos in one hand, a light sheen of sweat on her face. Behind her, slumped against the wall, was a stocky young man, eyes closed, arms folded across a Dark Knight T-shirt. There appeared to be a tiny cocktail umbrella woven into his beard. He may have been snoring.

"I want you to meet a friend of mine…Tony."

"Thane," the boy muttered, without opening his eyes.

Augusta swung to face him, putting a hand on the wall for support. "You can say that as many times as you like. I'm still not going to believe you."

Shoving her way past Frances, she flopped down in the room's one armchair. Thane, roused, followed her, and as he smiled apologetically at Frances she noted he was dragging an orange traffic cone behind him.

"Good night?" she said, though the sarcasm drifted over their heads.

Augusta half-fell from the chair to crouch in front of Frances's minibar.

"Dear God," she muttered. "Untouched. Mine, for some reason, is empty as Old Mother Hubbard's cupboard."

She reached in and grabbed two tiny bottles of Johnnie

Walker Red. She held one out to Thane, but he shook his head. The movement seemed to unbalance him and he fell backward on Frances's bed like a giant redwood axed at the roots. He lay there, burbling.

"Join me?" asked Augusta.

"I'm not sure that's such a good idea," Frances said. "Tomorrow's your big day…"

"Nonsense. It's the evenings that are big."

Frances was still shaken by the residual terror of the nightmare. She sat on the edge of the bed and took the bottle of whisky from Augusta, wrestling with its tiny, stubborn cap. Augusta's was already half gone, and she sat with her eyes closed, the bottle resting in her cleavage.

"This your new boyfriend, then?" Thane's jaw hung open, revealing a liverish purple tongue, and Frances reached over with two fingers to push his head to the side. She plucked the tiny yellow cocktail umbrella from his beard and left it on the bedside table. "He can't be more than seventeen, Augusta."

"Don't be ridiculous, darling. I made him show me his driver's licence. He was twenty last week. I'm not making that mistake again."

"Which mistake was that?"

But Augusta was looking at the sleeping boy. "One forgets how beautiful they are at this age. Even the unfortunate ones. How fragile."

She reached behind her into the fridge, groped blindly for a bottle, and held it up to her eyes: tequila. "The truth is, there was something rather sweet about him that reminded me just a bit…" She sat staring at the bottle, and then, abruptly tipped its contents into her mouth.

The clock said 4:47 a.m. Not sanity's best hour. All hope of sleep faded. All Frances wanted was to fall back into bed, into Stanley Pfeffer's dream arms, and here she was, watching Augusta pull an envelope the size of a postage stamp from her bag.

"A flat surface, darling…this will do."

Frances watched as she tapped the edge of the doll-sized envelope on the tabletop. She had been in enough late-night pubs to recognize the sight of a cocaine wrap. How on earth had Augusta managed to find drugs in such a short period of time? Then she remembered the web site she'd consulted: Never underestimate the resourcefulness of the addict.

Augusta squeezed the edges of the envelope and tipped a small pile of white powder onto the cover of the hotel's in-house magazine. It drifted like a beard of snow onto Tori Spelling's chin. Frances's eyes darted to the ceiling. What if they had cameras in the room? Could she be arrested merely for watching someone take drugs?

Augusta had rolled a bill, and held it out to Frances. "You?"

"It's almost morning, Augusta. You have to be ready for your Fantasmagoria™ panel in a few hours."

Augusta glared. "All the more reason, darling."

She bent over the magazine, a curtain of hair obscuring her face, and sprang back up with a small sound of contentment. *Why hasn't she passed out yet?* Frances thought. Thane was at least twice her size, and he'd gone down like a six-year-old girl.

"He'll be there when we arrive." Augusta's speech was sharp-edged again. "He'll get there early. I know he'll want to see me for as long as possible, even though he'll be lurking in the back row. Coward."

She seemed to have forgotten Frances was there, lost in a monologue that required no audience. Rooting in the fridge again, she retrieved a bottle that looked like chocolate milk. Baileys Irish Cream. The alcohol of last resort.

"Who, exactly?" Frances asked, and immediately regretted asking.

"Mr. Romance," Augusta sneered, and poured the creamy liquid into a tea cup. "What a goddamned fraud. I suppose if a takeaway followed by a pimply white arse pumping away in the bins behind Tesco is your idea of romance, then fine."

"Maybe," said Frances, as she tried to crawl under the duvet, "he just wants to say hello."

"The last time we met," Augusta said, "I tried to cut off his finger with a steak knife." Her head dipped over the magazine again. "He was jabbing it at me. 'You don't deserve to be anyone's mother,' he says."

Somehow, Augusta had leveraged herself to her feet and tottered back to the window. The sky had brightened to violet.

If I close my eyes, Frances thought, *maybe she won't notice I've fallen asleep and she'll just go on talking.* Thane rumbled like a beached whale alongside.

"My maternal failings. Well. He wasn't entirely wrong for once." She turned over her shoulder to speak to Frances. "Do you know when I first realized I wasn't meant to be a mother?" She was a dark silhouette against the brightening window. "It was too late, of course. Charlie must have been five or six. He was in Year 1, and his class was studying dinosaurs or planets or something that interests small children. I'd agreed to go on one of those dreadful school trips. He'd been pestering me for ages. It was the first and last time."

Frances thought, *She's forgotten I'm here.*

"We took a bus to the dinosaur museum. The whole place smelled of cheese sandwiches and sick. The other mothers avoided me the entire time, which was a small mercy. At the end, we'd stopped at the fountain in the courtyard, thirty children screaming for pennies to throw in, you can't imagine the noise. It did my head in. I remember my wish very clearly. I threw in a coin and I closed my eyes and I thought, *I hope I've got enough Valium to see me through the week.*

"One of the other mums chucked her coin in, and she turned to me. I can still see the smile on her face. She said, 'Do you think there will ever come a day when we'll make a wish that's about ourselves, and not about our kids?'"

Augusta drained the tea cup, set it on the desk. She walked over to the door and stood with her hand on the knob. "I'd never made a wish for Charlie before, not once. It had never occurred to me. But by the time I got home it hardly mattered, because my own wish had come true, and I slept like the dead."

She opened the door and looked back at Frances, huddled on one side of the bed. "I've never told anyone that story before. I think I'd forgotten it."

The door closed and she was gone.

twenty-four

"And joining us from London, the star of *The Blood Bank* — Augusta Price."

Augusta nodded at the audience, narrowing her eyes against the glare of the stagelights. A bottle of orange juice sat on the table next to her and she took a sip, grimacing. Horrid, pulpy stuff. Her hangover hurled itself at the walls of her skull.

Tyson Benn, Fantasmagoria™ host, held out a hand in her direction. A ripple of applause — a smattering, truth be told — greeted his introduction. He smiled encouragingly at her. He had a round, angelic face that he'd tried to make sinister with a pointed Vandyke beard.

"I'd like to welcome everyone to 'Type-A Personalities: The Evolution of the Vampire Medical Drama.'"

In the darkness, the audience settled itself. Frances was out there somewhere, still miffed about the Thane incident. She'd been deliberately frosty in the taxi on the way over. More important, *he* was out there somewhere. Augusta strained to see into the gloom, but all the faces were one blur. All she could see were the glowing red eyes of count-less cameras. He was there, though. She could smell his treachery.

From the centre of the stage, Tyson Benn introduced the last of the actors on the panel: "I'm sure he needs no intro-duction to you folks here today. For ten years he was the star of *Koenig*, which one critic called 'the *Berlin Alexan-derplatz* of the vampire drama.' All the way from Germany, please welcome Christoph Frank."

Herr Frank smiled in gratitude as the audience roared a welcome. Augusta had never met the actor, indeed had never seen *Koenig*, but what she saw now astonished her: Frank, a wiry man in his early fifties with tattoos blan-keting both arms, had a vampire's smile. His canine teeth, glistening on his lower lip, had been filed to sharp points. *The fucker's actually got fangs*, she thought. She had once succumbed to a barbaric haircut to play Saint Joan, but to disfigure one's self permanently seemed an act of madness. Then she noticed, as the actor brushed a hand along his bottom lip, that his fangs wiggled. She shook her head in disbelief. Poseur.

There were three other actors who'd played vampire doctors on the panel, two of them balding. All wore read-ing glasses. Only Herr Frank had maintained a commit-ment to undead gauntness. Each one of them spoke about what had drawn them to the vampire medical drama. When it was Augusta's turn, she said simply, "I was craving blood," drawing an uneasy laugh from the audience.

The other actors droned on interminably, responding to questions from Benn and the audience. Augusta muttered an occasional response, but her attention was directed out into the dark, undifferentiated mass of the audience. The sound of the other actors was a muted buzzing in her ear.

"Perhaps you can explain to us," Tyson Benn was saying to the star of *Koenig*, "why the vampire metaphor was so powerful for you, growing up in East Germany?"

Christoph Frank began explaining the motivations behind his character, a Nosferatu doctor who'd assisted the Nazis with their deadly experiments. The sibilants whistled through his sham fangs and she tried to tune him out. Her threshold for bullshit was perilously low; one drink would have sorted her out. But she'd chosen to face the day cold, wanting to feel the full force of her rage.

Of course he was out there. Sitting in the audience, watching her, imagining the lies he would tell...

"Don't you agree, Augusta?" Tyson Benn's question shook her from the reverie. The entire panel had turned to look at her. Herr Frank's winged brow was raised expectantly.

"Possibly," she said. She had to unstick her lips to speak. "About what?"

Herr Frank spread his pale hands. "That *Koenig*, and the programs that emulated it—even your show, for example—work best at the level of the unconscious. But for the richness of the subtext, they would never have lasted more than one week."

God, if she had a stake she'd do him herself. The other panellists were nodding, waiting for her reaction. Augusta tore her eyes away from the audience. Had she heard a familiar cough?

"I don't know, darling. Maybe things are different in Berlin, but in Newcastle I think people watch because they want to forget work for an hour. A bit of sex, a bit of terror, a bit of a cuddle on the sofa."

Herr Frank frowned at her, his eyebrows drawn together. "But surely we demean an entire genre if we think it is merely…"—his narrow shoulders shrugged—"escapism. Where we connect with our audience is in the power of this uniting metaphor."

"Most people watching television don't give a sailor's weeping cock about metaphor," Augusta said.

Tyson Benn drew a breath in sharply and consulted his question cards. Underlying the nervous titters in the audience, she heard a low bass laugh, a familiar sound. *There you are.*

A hand had shot up in the audience, and the moderator, glad for the distraction, nodded.

"This is a question for you, Miss Price." A man's nasal voice, about halfway up the auditorium. He was invisible in the gloom. Augusta rubbed her temple against the throbbing. "I've not seen *The Blood Bank*, so I can't talk about it. But *Koenig* is a masterpiece. It shattered perceptions." Out of the corner of her aching eye, she saw Christoph Frank bow his head in humble thanks. "I guess I just want to know why you wanted to act in a genre that you're clearly so dismissive of?"

People in the audience began to stir, roused at the scent of hostility.

Augusta had been scanning the crowd, but snapped to attention: "I beg your pardon?"

"It's just that Mr. Frank is clearly committed to his role, and to his fans. I mean, you only have to look at the physical transformation he's been prepared to undergo—"

"Do you mean the teeth?" Augusta said, astonished. "They're not real, darling. Fake as a tranny's tits."

Now there was a genuine hubbub. Frank whipped around to her and said something furious in German. A ripple of laughter swept through the audience, and the moderator tried to interrupt.

"This is what I mean," the questioner continued from the floor of the auditorium, his voice rising. "Why would you insult a respected actor like that? Especially since… well, what are you? Like, a soap star."

Augusta felt the hot blood rush to her face, but before she could say anything, her tormentor disappeared, yanked back into his chair as quickly as if his legs had been kicked out from under him. And she heard a familiar voice in the audience, as clear as if it were in her ear: "I think it's time you shut your gob."

He stood in the empty front row, looking up at her. Augusta was still on stage, unwilling to surrender her advantage. He'd always towered over her, and she hated it.

"My knight in shining armour," she said.

He said nothing, and for once she couldn't read what was in his face. Disappointingly, he didn't look quite as shit as she'd hoped. At least he hadn't succumbed to the witch doctors—there was no sign of a needle's work, no plumping or peeling. A cracked delta of lines fanned from the corners of his blue eyes, and two deep grooves ran from nose to mouth. The nose remained bent at an awkward angle; she'd always thought he was one punch away from handsome. There was no escaping the pull of genetics, though, and the extra weight around his chest and belly was only somewhat contained by a narrow-cut navy suit.

The rest of the panellists had filed off the stage, Herr Frank with a bitter glance in her direction. Tyson Benn was gesturing at her, his tiny beard quivering in fury, but she ignored him.

"You've turned into your dad," she said.

"Yes," Kenneth said. "But you haven't."

"Hmmm. You wouldn't believe."

"No, really, Augusta." He moved toward her, resting his hands on the lip of the stage. Looking up her skirt, cheeky fucker. "How wonderful you look."

From up here, she caught a glimpse of pink scalp through his wild yellow hair, and she felt a prick at the back of her eyes. *Dear God*, she thought. *I'm as bad as Frances.*

She was tempted to step on his hand to regain control of herself, but instead she said harshly, "I hear you're keeping busy, Ken. Perhaps you fancy yourself a writer."

"You hear such things, Augusta." He rocked back playfully on his heels, hands gripping the stage, like a boy at the top of a climbing frame. Enjoying himself. Flirting. The phosphorescence of her rage was blinding; she could melt him with her eye-beams. But he seemed oblivious.

"You," she hissed, aiming one trembling finger, "are not to write about me."

"The same way you didn't write about me?" He was laughing at her. She should have cut off his fingers when she'd had the chance. "I was hardly mentioned in your book. Nor the boy. As if we never existed."

They regarded each other for a moment.

"Are you going to see your son?" Kenneth asked. "He knows you're in town."

She felt drained, limp as an old sock, her mouth dirt-dry. If he'd offered to take her out for a drink, she would have accepted. Pathetic. "I can't imagine Charlie wants to see me."

"I think you'd be surprised," he said. "Charles is a young man now. He's put away childish things. But I haven't." Kenneth smiled up at her, and it was as if she was seeing him in an old, half-remembered dream. "Come to lunch with me, Augusta. You can tell me off then. You always used to enjoy that."

In the darkness, a throat was ostentatiously cleared. Augusta strained to see who it was, and Frances came into the light, a reluctant witness if ever there were one. She gave a stiff little wave.

"Hey, Augusta. That was…well, at least it's over. Now you can relax." She gave Kenneth a fleeting smile and stuck out her hand. "Frances Bleeker."

"Ken Deller."

Frances had already begun backing up the aisle. She lifted a hand to Augusta. "Well, I'll leave you and your friend. See you back at the hotel."

"*You're* my friend," Augusta called after her, but the girl had disappeared into the dark.

"You have a friend?" Kenneth said, and she could hear the mockery in his voice.

"That is Frances. My amanuensis, you could say. A charming girl, if a bit teary. She's helping me with my second book." Augusta put her hands on her hips, the spotlight warming her to her task. "Because the first was such a great success."

"Ah," he said. "I shall look forward to a second book in which I fail to appear."

Now he was laughing at her. She felt her fists ball in rage. Nothing was going as planned. At this point he should be wailing like a whipped dog, begging her forgiveness. Not giving her that infuriating grin, like the past hadn't happened, like they hadn't burned each other's houses down. Her leg tensed and she thought, *One good kick and I can at least smash in those teeth, the dental bill alone will send him to the poorhouse...*

"So," he said. "Can I buy you lunch?"

"Fine," she said.

twenty-five

She had always liked the way Kenneth walked. There had been times when it was the only thing she did like about him. Now Augusta scurried to keep up as he strode down Wilshire Boulevard with his long, loose gait, eyes locked on a point in the far distance. He walked as if no one was watching.

The pain in her head was alive. "Are we nearly there?" she panted.

He pointed to a white building in the distance, its roof ridged like a hedgehog's back. "Just there," he said. "We'll have lunch at the art gallery."

Would there be wine at the art gallery? Surely there had to be. Even the Americans weren't as barbaric as that. Augusta hurried on, determined not to give him the satisfaction of asking for a slower pace. Her feet hurt, but her pride was even more bruised. What a debacle! Kenneth had hurried her out of the convention centre, ignoring Tyson Benn's angry demand that Augusta stop and apologize to her fellow panellists.

"I'll have her right back," Ken called over his shoulder as he guided her to the car park.

As he drove, the messages from Benn flooded in on her phone: she had offended Christoph Frank and missed her autograph session. There was an equally frantic message from Frances saying that Fantasmagoria™ would no longer extend the hand of hospitality to those who had bitten it. They were being kicked out of their rooms. Augusta considered tossing the phone out the car window, but settled for shoving it to the bottom of her bag.

She felt a stitch in her side and slowed. An ornate green fence ran along one edge of the pavement, and she grasped it, breathing hard. The sun was warm on her face and for once she was grateful, and looked up to welcome it. A strange smell hung in the air: vegetal, dark, slightly bitter. She opened her eyes, blinked. Kenneth had realized she'd stopped and walked back toward her.

On the other side of the fence was a wide, grassy park. Schoolchildren played on the steps of a museum set on a little hill back from the street. Here and there, the beautiful lawn was marred by dark and greasy pools that seemed to shift and bubble in the sun.

"Ken," she said, "where the hell are we?"

"La Brea tar pits," he answered. He'd come to stand next to her, closer than a stranger should.

Augusta squinted through the fence. There was something odd going on. To the right, a giant elephant statue stood on the shore of a tar pit. It had the wrong proportions for an elephant, though, its shoulders too high and its tusks too long. The word for the prehistoric creature came into her head suddenly: mammoth. Next to the statue of the mammoth was a smaller one. A baby. Its trunk was raised in distress, and it appeared to be calling to a third mammoth, half-sunk and floundering in the sticky goo. Its mother.

Augusta stared at the dreadful tableau, the baby mammoth agonizing over its lost mother, the mother sinking in the tar, and felt the morning's rage rush back. Her fingers tightened on the fence.

She hissed, "You are a miserable bastard."

Ken turned sharply to look at her. "What?"

"This—" her hand flapped at the immobile mammoths. "This little domestic tableau. The abandoned baby. You brought me here to see this."

He stared at her for a moment, and she realized, to her fury, that he was trying not to laugh.

"Augusta," he said, when he'd managed to control his face. "You're as mad as a box of frogs."

He ordered a bottle of wine for them, and, as if sensing her need, filled her glass almost to the top. He gave himself a much smaller measure. She forced herself to wait before snatching up the glass. Instead she studied the other diners in the gallery's courtyard, all of them looking as if they'd stepped, lineless and creaseless, from some celestial factory. Everyone in London looked unkempt most of the time. Only here did she realize the word had an opposite.

"Do they really need help with love, these pretty robots?" Now she could reach for her glass. The wine slipped down her throat, and immediately she felt her mood lift.

Kenneth shrugged. "Doesn't everyone?"

"I suppose I find it odd that you're here, of all places. Such a rough pebble amid all the glossy stones."

If it stung, he wasn't about to show it. "I like Americans," he said. "You know where you stand with them. There's no incessant digging for meaning."

Augusta set her glass down with a clang, and the couple at the next table looked over. "Is that a jab?"

He leaned closer, and for a moment she saw him as a young man, the swagger that had taken her breath away.

"If I'd meant to jab," he said softly, "you would have felt it."

She sat back in her seat. So. A declaration of war. Strangely, it was a relief to have his feelings out in the open. That little stunt with the sad elephants had been deliberate. *If I'd meant to jab.* Well, he did mean to jab, didn't he? He would have his revenge on her, in print, in his idiot book. She took a gulp of wine. Did he really think she'd let him ruin her future by lying about their past? He was a bigger fool than she remembered.

"So that's what you want," she said. "To hurt me."

He looked at her, genuine confusion in his eyes. She noticed that he still had the tiny scar in the arch of his right brow where she'd winged him with an ashtray. She remembered the ashtray, shaped like a Sputnik satellite, but not the reason for the fight.

"I don't want to hurt you, Augusta. I just wanted to take you to lunch." He returned to studying his menu, so she barely heard his next words: "And perhaps stare at your legs."

She searched for a suitably acid retort but the wine was an alkaline bath for her anger. "I'll be back in a moment," she said, gathering her bag. "Order me something delicious, would you? No arsenic." She found the waitress and asked directions to the loo. She turned suddenly back to the table, hoping to catch him staring at her, but he was gazing away from her. She fumed all the way down the white marble staircase.

It was only when she climbed back up the stairs and saw him still gazing in the opposite direction that it struck her: he was watching her reflection in the gallery's tall windows. He wanted to stare at her without being caught staring. She felt an odd spasm in her centre, unrooted to any emotion she could name.

"I've remembered what we were arguing about that time," she said, as she slid back into her seat. He'd refilled her wineglass.

"Which time was that?"

Augusta waved a finger toward him. "The time your head got in the way of the ashtray."

"Ah."

"It is rather a large head, you have to admit."

"Rather a large ashtray, too." The waiter arrived and set down their plates. Ken had ordered lamb shanks for both of them, pale bones upright in a glossy, rich heap of meat. Augusta inhaled greedily; she hadn't realized how hungry she was.

"I remember that row clearly," he said, spearing a chunk of lamb on his fork. "You wanted to miss the school holiday in order to film some dreadful movie in Cardiff." He chewed placidly, ignoring the clang as Augusta's fork clattered to her plate.

In a deadly quiet voice, she said, "That is not why we rowed."

"And you wanted me to tell Charles that you were in hospital having your appendix out. To explain why you couldn't see him." He picked up his wine glass, watching her over the rim. *He's enjoying this*, Augusta thought. Sitting here, sparring with her, was the highlight of his week. His year.

Taking a deep breath, she said, "I think you might have the beginnings of Alzheimer's, Ken, since the events of your life seem lost in some kind of fog. But I recall that day clearly: you told me you wanted us all to spend the school holidays in a caravan park..." she leaned toward him and hissed, "*in Skegness*." She picked up her knife and fork. "This is why you cannot be trusted with the past. Your memory is a colander with extremely large holes."

He stared at her, and to her irritation she realized, once again, that he was trying not to laugh. "You do know the story of the pot and the kettle, don't you, Augusta?" Before she could say anything, he said, "There's an easy way to solve this. We'll just ask the lad what happened."

She reached for her wineglass and turned to the windows, where the afternoon sun was a solid block of light. She could take her knife and cut it, she thought; slice it into pieces and take it home with her. Her eyes felt sore in the glare, and she closed them for a minute.

When he spoke his voice had changed. There was no mockery in it now, just gentleness. A voice she'd once welcomed in the dark. "You are going to see him, aren't you?"

She turned back to her plate, but the lamb had cooled and sat jellied and unappetizing. The chatter rose around them, bouncing off the walls, and suddenly all she wanted was to be in bed, enrobed in silence. She didn't trust herself to look at him. *It's just been a crap day*, she thought. *A crap day that began with a hangover and went downhill from there.*

A finger nudged the back of her hand and she looked up at him. Under the tiny scar, his blue eyes were coaxing. "I still have that ashtray, if you'd like to see it. One of the few things you left behind. I always imagined you might want to throw it at me again one day."

twenty-six

The sign above the cracked carport indicated that they had arrived at the St. Tropez Motel.

"That," said Augusta, pointing to the sign, "is the triumph of hope over evidence."

The taxi dropped them at an inglorious delta between the rapids of the 101 freeway and the sluggish current of Hollywood Boulevard. Frances, thoroughly beaten, reached for her flat wallet. Augusta left the cab and stood on the sidewalk, watching the wind turn over a used condom in the gutter.

"My God," she said when Frances joined her, "I love the glamour of Hollywood."

They dragged their bags past an empty swimming pool where the paint sloughed off in great psoriatic flakes. Frances's shoulder dipped from the weight of a plastic bag filled with tiny bottles of wine, vodka, and whisky. When they'd met in the lobby of the hotel and Frances had whispered that they had an hour to pack their bags, Augusta had shoved her back toward the elevator and said, "Right. Plunder the minibar. And don't spare the liqueurs."

They checked into the St. Tropez and found that their room overlooked the parking lot. They lay on matching twin beds, mini-bottles clustered on the table between them. Together they watched through the filthy window as a woman on a mobility scooter pulled up, answered her phone, and began to negotiate the price of a blow job.

They were too numb to do much but watch. Frances rolled over and stared at her phone, as if it were an oracle leading the way to salvation. She opened her Facebook page and reread the message from Stan. Augusta peered over her shoulder.

"Stanley wants to know when you'll be home," she read, and Frances, scowling, clapped a hand over the screen. Augusta rolled back onto her pillow, sending a cloud of dust motes into the air. "Stanley's the fellow from the awards night? The drunk with the lovely grey quiff? He's not too old for you, is he?"

"No," Frances said. "He's not. He went grey early, that's all." She sat up and hugged her knees, and Augusta thought she looked like a little girl. "It's not like men are beating down my door, Augusta. It's bad enough not to have a job or a home, but then not to have a boyfriend either...It's like a trilogy of failure. At my age."

"Well, yes," said Augusta. "At the decrepit age of thirty-one. We should probably just shove you off on an ice floe."

Frances turned to her and in the light from the window Augusta could see the warning glint of moisture in her eye. "I think I'm in love with him."

Augusta now kept a wad of tissues constantly at hand.

She pulled one out and handed it over. "If you're certain," she said.

"If I'm certain?" Frances wiped her nose. "God, you're just like my mother."

"Then your mother must be a very clever woman with a magnificent bosom." The beep of an incoming message sounded on her phone, but Augusta ignored it. "I'm only worried that you might be confusing love for the man with love for the life he gave you. A job that you adored. When you pine for him, perhaps you're just pining for that horrid newspaper. Though God knows why. You'd have a better life shovelling shit on the river bottom."

Frances flopped back on the bed. "Thank you for your advice, Dr. Phil."

"Truth be told, I never did finish my medical degree."

Her phone beeped again, and with a curse Augusta picked it off the chenille bedspread where it lay between two stains, one ancient and one quite fresh. Another message from Kenneth. Before he'd let her go after lunch he'd made her promise that she would come to dinner at his house. The message contained his address and phone number. He'd signed off with a presumptuous x, as if there might be a kiss in their collective future.

Augusta reached for a tiny bottle of white wine, handed it wordlessly to Frances. She chose a red for herself. They lay in bed watching the woman outside haggle for her services, scything the air for emphasis.

Augusta's phone rang, and she snatched it off the bed and barked, "Stop hounding me, you great knob!" Her mouth opened in a comical O and Frances heard her say, sheepishly: "It's you, darling. Apologies." After she'd hung up, she sat staring at the phone for a moment.

"That was my friend Alma calling from London. My elderly friend Alma. She wanted to know if I'm in some sort of trouble. Apparently she'd been following the convention on a tweetstream." She looked up at Frances. "What the fuck is a tweetstream?"

twenty-seven

Frances had exhausted all the free reading material in the motel room: last week's copy of *LA Weekly*, an issue of *Freedom* magazine with a young Scientologist pop star on the cover, and a pamphlet about Disneyland. She'd even considered the Bible in the drawer by the bed, but its pages were gummed together.

Anything to keep her from the thoughts that chased each other endlessly, fanged mouth to chewed tail. *Useless, useless, useless*, said the fanged mouth, and she heard herself repeat it out loud: "I'm useless."

She clapped a hand over her mouth, but Augusta was in the shower and hadn't heard. Had Augusta ever stood on a threadbare carpet chastising herself out loud? Frances doubted it. Augusta would have drowned the spiteful little voice instead. She longed to see her parents, who remembered what she had once been, and wouldn't despise her failure. She longed to see Stanley, who had recognized her potential. Stanley, who courted catastrophe.

Frances swung her feet off the bed. Empty bottles

formed a cliff face on the bedside table. She could hear Augusta in the shower, occasionally exclaiming in disgust over the quality of the motel shampoo.

She brought the wastepaper basket over and began dropping the bottles in. The sound of them hitting bottom reminded her of something, and after the last bottle fell she wandered over to her suitcase and pulled Augusta's memoir from it. She came back to the bed, stretching out, and turned to a page she'd dog-eared when she'd first read the book.

The Wrecks of Wreckford Hall

Cars are the enemies of drinking. Not only for the reasons you'd imagine—a ton of metal being a serious weapon in the hands of someone who can't even get the keys into the ignition.

No, cars are the great betrayers of drunks. They are not our friends. Think of the number of celebrities you've read about whose shameful addictions finally became public, and it usually involves a vehicle of some kind. Crashing late at night into a café window, driving endless circles in some suburban roundabout, unable to find the proper exit. Paparazzi mysteriously always on hand to snap the poor bastard being led away from his Lotus by the cops.

Or you're betrayed by what's inside your car, because really, it's a little travelling house, isn't it? The wife thinks you've given up drinking until one day she can't use the brakes because a tin of Scrumpy Jack has lodged under the pedal. You must never underestimate the determination of a person who needs to get high. I endured countless AA meetings just to reassure myself that there was someone more abject than me.

A car was my undoing, the first time. Not that I was behind the wheel. If I have a motto, it's this: Why drive when you can be driven? In those first few years on *Canals*, when the producers were filled with joy at Kit Gallagher's hold over the audience, a car was placed at my disposal every morning and every evening to take me to and from the studio.

Joe was my driver — sainted Joe of memory. Each morning at six he'd come collect me. I'd find him leaning against the black sedan, holding a sugary coffee for himself and one for me. For the better part of an hour he'd regale me with the stories of his three ungrateful children, who didn't know how good they 'ad it, and who insisted on speaking an unintelligible mishmash of Cockney and West Indian patois they called "Jafaikan." It was a very long ride.

For this reason I kept a plastic bottle of contact lens fluid in my bag. Although, having reached this point in my story, you will probably have guessed that the bottle was filled not with EZ No-Rub Kleen but with vodka, bought in gallon bottles and painstakingly decanted into the smaller containers nightly. Each morning I pretended on the long drive to Surrey first to place my contact lenses in, and then to fiddle with them, and occasionally even to retrieve them from the floor, while Joe mourned his lot from the front seat. I was quite proud of my little ruse, in the way drunks always are when they think no one has noticed.

One morning I asked Joe to stop the car at the news-agent's so I could buy a pack of Marlboro Lights. It must have been close to Christmas, because the man behind the counter was wearing a red elf's cap, ringed with a circlet of bells. When we first heard the screams, the shopkeeper's head jerked toward the door and set the bells dancing. I grabbed the cigarettes and ran outside, sure that Joe was trapped in a death struggle with some south London hoodie.

But there was only Joe, clawing his way out of the car, one hand frantically pawing at his eyes. His foot caught on the curb, and next thing I knew he was lying on the pavement of Croydon, faced screwed in pain, screaming: "Some fucker's burnt my eyes!"

Two weeks later I arrived with one suitcase—carefully examined for EZ No-Rub Kleen bottles and other suspicious vessels—at Wreckford Hall in Hertfordshire. Kit's absence was hastily written into the show; I believe a lucky scratch card had finally provided her with the means for a much-deserved holiday in Benidorm. Go, the producers said, and we'll pay. Get well. They were tired of me. Joe's vodka blindness was quick to heal, but the potential for a lawsuit hung in the air.

It was not the first time I had shamed myself on the set of *Canals*—there were days, I've been told, when I could barely make myself understood, though in my ears I sounded like Sybil Thorndike speaking into a crystal pitcher. Delusions, my dearest companions. Alma protected me as best she could, writing Kit's lines on a notepad I could carry with me as if I were consulting that day's specials. Even her faith wasn't enough of a safety net, in the end.

It was the first time my failings had harmed a colleague. I was mortified. My employers could no longer afford to look away, and so instead they sent me to the end of the Metropolitan Line. To Wreckford Hall.

It was not my first time in…what shall we call it? In treatment? In trouble? Let's defer to our American cousins: in a rehabilitation facility. Not the first time, and not the last. If there's a thimbleful of wisdom I've scraped together over the years, it's this: No one can order your recovery. You must pay for it yourself, in all ways.

I hadn't lived with anyone, not properly, since I'd left home at seventeen; if you've read this far, you'll know my fear of enclosed spaces, and of proximity of most kinds. Those anxieties, a counsellor would soon tell me, were the walls that shut me off from the world. "The ego's leash," I think he called it.

Like all the patients at Wreckford, I was assigned a roommate. I was quite lucky to draw Margaret, a binge-eating, bulimic mother of three from Kent, who was kind enough to extend her housewifely skills to my half of our nunnish cell. Whether she considered herself equally fortunate is a matter for Margaret's memoir.

Margaret was fat, and had once been jolly, until her family grew tired of the sour tang of vomit in the house and the mood swings that accompanied the fluctuations in her weight. We walked the grounds of Wreckford Hall on our four stumpy legs, Margaret so she could work off some of the Hobnobs she'd snuck into our room (secreted in a box of sanitary pads) and me so I could smoke. Unfortunately, the minor lord who had sold the hall to pay his gambling debts had some years earlier also sold the gardens to a golf club. The grounds were pimpled, at all times, with men swinging clubs and chortling together in tiny clumps. More than once as we walked the lovely, even grass we'd hear screams of "Fore!" Once Margaret took a ball in the stomach, which I thought would make her cry but instead caused her to run screaming at the man who had made the shot, rip the club out of his hand, and begin beating his golf cart with it. Unresolved anger, we were told at that afternoon's group meeting, was the root cause of Margaret's illness.

Well. You think I'm mocking the whole process, that I never took it seriously. It is true: because I hadn't arrived under my own steam, I was as truculent as a twelve-year-old sent to the head teacher's office. The whole experience seemed like primary school in microcosm, only much worse because we couldn't get away and steal our parents' alcohol. The hierarchy was just as impermeable. Those at the top, the coolest kids, were the serious addicts—heroin, cocaine—and anyone who had tried to kill either themselves or a loved one. My own minor celebrity and entirely predictable pill-and-alcohol use placed me in a category just below this. At the bottom rung, just as in primary school, were the food phobics, the undereaters and the overeaters, the bingers and vomiters.

Wreckford, unlike some other more authoritarian (and expensive) facilities, allowed visitors, but in the weeks I was there no one came to visit me. That's not true; Alma visited regularly. I could always tell that she'd eaten a package of mints just before her arrival to mask the scent of her lunchtime gin. A true friend.

"I'm not sure I entirely understand why you're here,"

she whispered, the first time she visited. We sat on a bench underneath a copper beech, the golfers hacking and swinging in the dip below. "There was that incident with the driver—poor man—but he was compensated, and his eyesight has almost entirely returned. Apart from that, though, who have you harmed? In my day, one was nearly always potted before the curtain went up; it helped with one's nerves. I was in *Private Lives* once in Wolverhampton when the fellow playing Elyot pretended to look for an umbrella in the coat rack upstage. But really he was sicking up the pie he'd had at lunch. I covered with the loudest laugh I could manage, and eventually he turned around, said, 'Amanda, darling,' and we were off."

"Times have changed," I said. "Liability. Insurance premiums." Alma just shook her head. "Atonement," I said.

She turned to me, sharply: "There's nothing to forgive. You have made a series of small mistakes, as we all do."

But this was not the belief system operating at Wreckford Hall. There was always somebody who had been harmed, whose forgiveness was just out of reach.

The problem was, I agreed with Alma: I didn't think I owed anyone an explanation. At this early stage of my recovery, I didn't think I belonged there, among the falling-down drunks, the blackout artists, the zombies who put needles in the veins of their feet because all their other veins had collapsed. I'd never put a needle in my body in my life; my fingernails were clean; how could I be a junkie?

You couldn't say that at the meetings, of course. So I developed a convincing line in contrition as my bottom slowly moulded itself into the shape of the folding chair and I ate so many biscuits my trousers wouldn't do up. At our daily group meetings I learned to recite a list of mea culpas—I'd disappointed my friends, my colleagues, myself. It was as easy, as rote, as saying the rosary had once been.

Once a week there was Face to Face Day, which everyone dreaded. With good reason. On this day, we gathered in the central meeting hall, our circle of folding chairs expanded to include family members we'd wronged. Any relative could attend—father, wife, child—to lay out the trail of betrayal and lies and misery the addict had left behind. It was excruciating to watch, a cross between a Quaker meeting and a Maoist show trial, long stretches of silence erupting into desperate, teary incriminations.

Margaret's daughter came every week to accuse her. Neither of the other children or the husband could be bothered, but this girl—a pale, lovely woman of thirty who looked ten years younger—took a two-hour coach ride to Wreckford every week to inform her mother that she had ruined her life, that her own disrupted eating habits meant no man would ever love her.

"I was fishing Black Forest gâteau out of the bin when I should have been out meeting someone nice," she accused her mother, while Margaret sat weeping into a shredded tissue.

I'd try to cheer Margaret up before the weekly session, but whenever I reminded her over breakfast "It's Fuck You Up Day!" she would only smile grimly and return to her grapefruit. She was not a Larkin fan.

But by now you've seen the hole in my narrative, the

emptiness of my bravado. Where were the people I'd fucked up? Who came to accuse me? The answer is: no one. I sat and watched my fellow patients being flagellated and chastised until they were broken and numb, and thought: *Shouldn't that be me? Where are the people I've tormented?* But no one came, and I sat, day after day, alone with my thoughts, and tortured myself.

"It might not have happened precisely that way," Augusta said, reading over her shoulder.

With a yelp of shock, Frances dropped the book. "For God's sake, Augusta. Don't sneak up on people like that. You nearly scared me to death."

"I would hardly call it sneaking, darling. You could hear the crushing of mouse turds in this broadloom from a mile off." Augusta sat on the edge of her bed, drying her hair with a towel, a cigarette perched at the corner of her mouth. She'd draped the other ravelled-edge towel over the room's smoke detector. "I'm merely saying that things may have unfolded slightly differently at Wreckford Hall. Charlie and Kenneth may have shown up once. Or possibly twice. But I believe I had an infection, and couldn't see them. Anyway," she tossed the towel aside and walked, naked, to the open window, "those Face to Face sessions were unspeakably dreary."

Averting her eyes, Frances reached for the book she'd dropped. "You'll probably say I'm horribly provincial, but don't you think your readers might have liked to know the actual events? Otherwise it's just...I don't know. A performance."

Augusta turned away from the window, and Frances noticed, for the first time, the silvery stretch marks that banded her waist; Frances's mother had a matching set.

"Darling," she said. "No one wants the facts of a life. They want the story."

Frances sat up on the bed. Around her were the notes she'd been making for the book outline. *Giving Life the Finger*, she'd written on the top of one page. *A Survivor's Guide to Overcoming Adversity*.

"Fine," she said. "Then tell me a story. Something we can use."

Augusta turned to face her, hands on hips. A shelf of ash broke from her cigarette and drifted to the floor. Frances was reminded of a visit she'd taken once to the British Museum, where a statue of Artemis, liberated from a Greek villa, stood glowering in a forgotten corner.

"Oh, don't worry," Augusta said. "When I'm finished, you shall have your story."

twenty-eight

"Here is what I don't understand about your country," said Augusta, staring over the top of the plastic menu. "You will quite happily drink liquid butter, and yet even a drop of alcohol is considered poison." She flapped the menu at Frances. "Not even a beer on this thing."

They had spent a fitful night at the motel, the sound of traffic and early-morning assignations disturbing their sleep. At one point, Frances had awoken to find the room shaking and bolted from bed, ready to scream "Earthquake!" It was only as the rumbling rose to a rhythmic crescendo that she realized the earthquake had its origins in the bedsprings next door.

At noon, they'd stumbled across the street. Frances was too tired to explain that this pancake house was the cheapest place to fill their stomachs. Listlessly, she pushed her menu away and stared through the window.

Out on the sidewalk, a man sat in a wheelchair, a dirty Starbucks cup in his lap. He'd fixed an American flag to his armrest, and it hung unmoving in the hot morning air.

The dog curled at his feet wore an American flag bandana. Frances had watched for fifteen minutes and only one person had dropped change in his cup.

How had he arrived there? How would he get home? It was not a city built for the disabled. She thought of her father, 300 miles up the coast, and the clifftop paths he could no longer enjoy. She drew in a ragged breath.

"No," said Augusta. "No tears before lunch. I thought we agreed on this one rule."

"I'm not crying," Frances muttered. "It's the stupid sun—oh, shit."

"I did see shit on the menu," Augusta said. "But I generally avoid it at breakfast."

Frances stared into the dimness of the restaurant. "I don't believe it. I know that waiter."

Augusta craned her head. "Madam with the beard?"

Frances slumped as deep into the banquette as she could, pulled her sunglasses over her eyes. "We should get out of here."

"And miss my delightful breakfast of buttery butter fritters with butter sauce? I think not."

"Oh, God," Frances whispered. "He's coming over."

The waiter who approached their table carrying a water jug had dark hair swept low over blue eyes and a trim goatee. A necklace of Chinese characters was tattooed across his throat. He seemed ridiculously enthusiastic, considering the hour and the establishment.

"How are you ladies this morning?" he asked. "I'll start you off with some water." He filled Augusta's glass, and then as he turned to Frances he stopped, mouth comically agape.

"Frances?" he said. "Dude, is that you?"

"Hey Jason," she said, and slid her sunglasses off.

He put a hand on one skinny hip, and shook his head. "This is so random. What are you doing in L.A.? Last I heard, you had a job in London."

Under the table, she clenched her hands together. "Yes, that's right. At a newspaper called the *Advance*."

"I know!" Jason crowed, and the diners at the next table turned to look. "You totally escaped this chicken coop. You're the only one that did. So, you here working on a story?"

Augusta watched as Frances struggled to find something to say. "She's actually got a very important assignment. With me. We are writing a book together." She ignored the look of relief on Frances's face and held out her hand. "Augusta Price."

The boy wiped his hand on his apron and took hers. "Jason Benedetti."

Frances had found her voice. "Jason and I went to journalism school together." She didn't add: And I was a little bit in love with him, because he never went to class and he played Fugazi in his room at full blast, and I used to dream about sliding between his rancid sheets.

"Frances was our star," the young man said to Augusta, and she could see by his pupils that he'd been hitting the bong already that morning. She wondered, briefly, if she could ask to join him. He slapped the table with his pad. "We always knew she was going places."

"Not really," Frances said.

"Absolutely, bro! You had wings."

"That was then." It came out as a bark, and Jason stared

at her, head cocked. She forced a note of brightness into her voice. "So, you stayed in L.A."

"Yeah," he said, "it's not London, but it's holding me together while I get my project on track." He leaned over the table, lowering his voice. "My real thing is this Tumblr I've got going. I've been posting all these hilarious sex ads I find on bulletin boards. You would not believe the shit people are capable of. It's sad, too. It's like our world in a microchip."

"Microcosm," said Frances, before she could stop herself.

"Yeah, well." He straightened up. "I've got a meeting with Fox next week. I'm pretty sure they're going to buy it."

"They're going to buy your Tumblr of sex ads?"

Augusta said, "You may as well be speaking Urdu," but they both ignored her.

"It's where the money is, dude." He made a karate chop motion in the air. "Now what can I get you ladies?"

Once they had ordered, Frances slumped in her seat. "That was brutal."

"Nonsense. That boy seemed to think highly of you."

"Only because he doesn't know what's become of me."

"What's *become* of you? Poor, soiled Victorian maiden." Augusta moistly unpeeled herself from the vinyl banquette. "Let's finish our butter and find some real sustenance, shall we?"

Beside them, a fake boulder emitted the voice of Lionel Richie. Augusta peered at it, swaying, and put her hand on a fibreglass palm tree for support.

"I have never seen anything so beautiful," she said.

It had seemed the most natural thing for Frances to bring them to the least natural place she could think of, a shopping mall in the centre of the city disguised to look like a nostalgic dream of main street. They stood quite drunk on an acrylic patch of lawn and watched a trolley car trundle shoppers past an ice-cream parlour that sold smartphones.

"Man's triumph over that bitch, Nature," Augusta said. "I adore it." Her eyes shone as she took in everything: the security cameras disguised as trees, the burrito joint pretending to be a Mexican ranch house.

"There," said Augusta, pointing at the restaurant. "The X on our map." She staggered toward it, and Frances, with a silent prayer, followed. This would be their third stop since breakfast, each one foggier than the last. Frances had pulled her credit card at every stop. She tried not to picture it, hot with overuse.

A group of women sat with their children, having coffee next to a chlorinated brook. It seemed to Augusta that a magical transformation had happened to motherhood in the past two decades. These women did not appear beaten down or rubbed raw. They all had glistening, honey-coloured hair and legs as long as ladders.

"Hecubah," called one of the mothers to a tiny girl who ran past in a long lace dress. "Hex, get back here!"

"That child looks just like Stevie Nicks," said Augusta. "Before the cocaine, of course."

A half-hour later they were still sitting on the Mexican restaurant's patio, a metal pail heaped with ice cubes and miniature bottles of beer between them. Frances had had one; Augusta, more.

"What is wrong with this country?" Augusta said. "Enormous plates of food and miniature drinks. The universe turned upside-down. Like putting Australia at the top of the world."

"Maybe," said Frances, "we could put that in the new book. 'Upside-down world.'"

"The book?" Augusta pulled a bit of lime pulp from her teeth. Another bit was stuck to her right breast, a tiny, lewd green tongue.

"The guide to overcoming crisis. Which we're supposed to be working on."

"Oh dear God, that book. Books," said Augusta, pulling a face. "Why on earth do people write them? I'll tell you why." She leaned across the table, and Frances caught a bottle just as it went tipping sideways. "To win. So your side of the story can win. Because they last forever, those fuckers. Longer than movies. Longer than music. Much, much longer than love."

Frances opened a second beer. "There are other reasons to write."

"No, darling, it's about your truth clobbering someone else's." Augusta caught the elbow of a passing waitress. "Two margaritas, my love. I think this time we shall have—" she squinted at the menu—"the tub o' fun size."

A ray of setting sun caught Augusta's hair, setting it alight, glistening off the lime pulp stuck to her breast. A little boy at the next table had his eyes fixed to her chest.

Augusta met the child's gaze. "It's not nice to stare at a lady's treasures," she said. "Unless you're invited to do so."

The boy's mother gasped and drew her son close.

A blanket of beer cheer wrapped Frances in its warmth,

and made her reckless. "What I don't understand," she said slowly, "is what you're so worried about. What could Kenneth possibly write about you that you haven't told the world already?"

"What lies, you mean," said Augusta. She reached for the jacket that lay draped over the back of her chair. The sun had set behind a clock tower whose hands were permanently fixed at noon. "It's getting chilly, isn't it? I believe we're sufficiently fortified for the next part of our mission."

She scraped her chair back and stood, unsteadily, while the little boy at the next table covered his mouth, laughing. Augusta formed a gun with the forefingers of her right hand and aimed it at his forehead.

"Unless," Frances said slowly, "unless he's going to write about Charles. And your dysfunctional little family."

But Augusta had already left, stitching a crooked line toward the exit.

twenty-nine

Magic hour, and a pale washed-purple sky made every living thing glow with health. Even Augusta, who otherwise might have looked quite green. Frances kept her companion upright with one hand as they left the mall and swayed together down Third Street.

They barely survived the walk three blocks west: Augusta's spindly heel caught in a grate in the middle of the road as they crossed against the lights. A pest-control truck barrelled down on them, a huge cockroach rising from its front grille like a dragon on the prow of a Viking ship.

"Shit!" screamed Augusta, wrenching her foot free just in time to fling herself out of its path.

The truck roared past, the driver giving them an idle, curious glance. Augusta shook her fist at him and hobbled to the safety of the sidewalk. She'd left the heel of her shoe behind, still trapped in the grate.

From the safe vantage of the sidewalk, they found their bearings. They stood outside a bright-pink shop catering to female roller-derby racers. In its window hung a row of knee socks embroidered with words that must have significance for a younger generation: nerd, bacon, gay. Above them, floodlit against the twilight sky, a billboard warned that the world would end on May 21st: THE BIBLE GUARANTEES IT.

With a stifled burp Augusta pointed to a shopfront with a sandwich board outside, designed to look as if it had been typed on an ancient Underwood. HELL YES BOOKS.

"Time to beard the cat," whispered Augusta, staggering sideways on her uneven shoes.

"The lion," Frances whispered back.

"Shhh," said Augusta as they crept toward the shop. Her finger somehow missed her mouth. "They'll see us."

"Fuck they will," said Frances, emboldened.

Through the window of Hell Yes Books, they watched a handful of customers leafing though manga comics, guides to film-set locations, short-story collections by maverick directors.

Augusta's nose pressed flat against the window as she peered inside: no sign of Charlie. A young woman in cat's-eye glasses sat reading at the till, but there appeared to be no other employee in sight.

"Look," hissed Frances. The sandwich board advertised an event that evening: Sister Mary Martin would read from her bestselling memoir, *Cells and Frames: My Escape into Film*, with a book signing to follow.

"Maybe that's where he is," Augusta slurred. "Supravising the reading."

"Supervising."

"So I said."

Augusta lurched toward the door on her one broken heel, a sheriff from an old Western. Gathering herself, she entered the shop with a regal smile for the girl behind the till. The effect was ruined as she pitched sideways, her shriek mingled with the scream of an animal in pain.

"Watch for the cat," called the clerk, as Frances leapt forward to catch Augusta.

A Persian the size and shape of a footstool scurried under a nearby table. They stood, breathing hard, Frances's arms wrapped around Augusta's midriff. The other customers had turned to stare.

"Reading?" inquired Augusta, pushing the hair from her face with great dignity.

"In the back," said the girl at the counter. "But it's already started."

Head high, Augusta hobbled between bookshelves, pausing only to move Gwyneth Paltrow's cookbook to the very bottom of a stack. At the back of the shop, a heavy curtain had been drawn. Pale light gleamed from around its edges. A low voice was speaking within, the words indistinct. Augusta stopped, one hand at her throat.

"He mustn't know we're here," she whispered.

Frances felt the effect of the afternoon's drinks and those that had come before. She sailed, beer-tossed, on an unfamiliar sea. The room and her stomach heaved in concert. She needed a bathroom, and a bed, possibly with a bucket beside it.

Augusta limped over to the curtain and tugged it aside a fraction. Frances crouched underneath her and shoved her head in the gap just below. A dozen rows of chairs were wedged into the small, dimly lit room, almost every seat taken. Immediately in front of them, between the curtain and the chairs, a table was piled vertiginously high with a mountain of books, each featuring an elderly woman on the front cover, her round face smiling under a cap of bushy grey hair. The same woman stood at the front of the room, dressed in shades of beige, from her sturdy Rockports to the cardigan draped over her shoulders.

Next to her, under a single spotlight, stood a slight young man in a T-shirt that showed Peter Lorre, haunted, staring into a mirror. The young man's toffee-coloured hair stood up in stiff peaks from a pale face and his voice, as he spoke into the microphone, came from a place Frances couldn't name. New England, maybe. Or Canada?

"And I want to thank Sister Mary Martin for kindly overlooking the name of our book shop and coming to join us tonight," he said, to a chuckle from the crowd.

Above her, Augusta said, "He's lost his accent. I don't believe it."

A man two seats away turned to glare at the noise, and, seeing them hiding in the curtains, put his finger to his lips.

"I think this may be a first for us," the young man said. "We've had some unholy guests, but I think this is the first time we've ever had anyone who's actually taken holy orders."

"A fucking nun," said Augusta, incredulous. She put out a hand to the table of books to steady herself, and the tall stack teetered. "He never invited me to read, but he asks a goddamned nun."

The man sitting nearby frowned at her and made an ostentatious show of leaning forward to listen.

Frances, crouching under Augusta, reached out to steady the stack of books with one hand. It felt as if her head would split in two. Surely Charlie would see them at any moment, or he'd hear his mother's slurring from her hiding place?

"Augusta, please," she whispered, not sure what she was pleading for.

Augusta swayed above her and reached down to clamp a steadying hand on Frances's head.

The young man, caught in the spotlight, was too intent on his purpose to notice the distraction.

"It's not every day you find that someone who lives a life of seclusion and contemplation has written a best-selling book, but that's exactly what happened to Sister Mary Martin when she sat down to remember the ways that her favourite movies informed her devotion. It's a book she wrote only for herself, never intending that anyone else would see it. Fortunately for all of us, a friend at a university read it and convinced her to share these remarkable observations with the world. And, as we all know now, that book has touched a resonant chord." He turned to the elderly woman, who gave him a shy smile. "I think it's fair to say this is not something you expected."

She shook her head, fingering the small cross that hung around her neck.

A sound like ripping paper: Frances looked up, horrified, to see Augusta catching the tail end of a burp with her hand. She swayed against the curtain. The man in the audience was furious now.

"Shhhh!" he hissed, and jabbed his finger at the empty seats beside him.

"Augusta," Frances whispered, low and urgent. "Charles is going to see us if you don't keep quiet. We should sit down. Come."

Reaching up, she caught Augusta's hand and tugged. As she tried to rise from a crouch, her shoulder caught the edge of the table. It began to shudder, its feet rattling unsteadily against the wooden floor. *No*, Frances thought, *no no no*. She reached with one hand to steady the books, but as she did she pulled Augusta, already unbalanced, off her one good pin. Augusta gave a little howl as she tumbled, face-first, into the teetering stack of books and surfed a wave of bestselling wisdom all the way to the floor.

thirty

When Charlie was a newborn, Augusta sat for the first few weeks, stared at him, and wondered: *Who do you remind me of?* All he really resembled was an angry baby crocodile, with his open wailing jaws and rubbery thrashing. She picked him up, he cried; she put him down, he cried louder.

Every day she wished for her mother, her ineffectual, hand-wringing mother, but her mother had followed her father to the grave after only eight months. Eight months' peace the woman got, after two and a half decades of torment. A tumour had appeared in her mother's abdomen not long after her father died, one toxic guest moving in to replace another.

So Augusta patted and prodded Charlie, and tried slipping her battered nipple into his frantic mouth, but nothing calmed him. She felt as if she were trying to knit a sweater while wearing oven mitts. No one she knew was any help. Who did she know? Notting Hill coke dealers and cross-dressing performance artists; selfish bastard actors who were babies themselves; and women like Alma who'd had terminations all through their lives and now couldn't bear to look at babies because babies were the road not taken. Soon she realized who her friends were—really, who her friends were not. She had no one.

She had Ken. The last person she imagined would come to her aid, a tough Salford lad from a family where only women looked after babies. But he arrived at her flat one day, a little more than a week after Charlie was born. The longest ten days of Augusta's life. Each day had a hundred hours in it, and in each of those hundred hours she'd been awake holding an egg in both hands. Or so it seemed.

When he arrived, she was too tired to cry. She'd taken the final Darvon the doctor had given her to dull the pain of her stitches, a supply that was supposed to last the month. Luscious pink pills, fat as raspberries, why did they make them so enticing if they didn't want you to take them all at once? She opened the door to find Kenneth in a pirate shirt and knee-high suede boots, his arrival heralded by a cloud of scented hairspray: Midnight Oleander. He'd been given what he regarded as a promotion at the BBC, from rewriting news to producing segments on up-and-coming pop bands. Augusta thought it wasn't much of a job for a grown man, and told him so.

His new position seemed to require fancy dress. She tugged on his sleeve as he came in. "You off to audition for *Bluebeard's World*, Ken?" She was quite proud of herself for mustering the energy.

"Oh, ha," he said. "I hear they're looking for wenches. But you'll want to wipe the sick off yourself first."

Charlie had thrown up on her that morning and a crust marked the sleeve of her shapeless tunic. Ken leaned down and kissed her on the cheek, and she felt him inhale greedily. Even when she was rancid, he couldn't get enough.

"Give us the baby, Augusta."

He took the squawling, starving crocodile from her arms and held him up to the light, as if he were a diamond and this would reveal his facets. Charlie's face was covered in an angry scurf of baby eczema. His umbilical cord had not yet fallen off and hung from his belly like a tiny, desiccated sausage-end. Ken looked up at him and an enormous smile broke across his face.

"Bless," he said.

To Augusta's astonishment, the baby quieted, perhaps out of terror, for he was now seven feet in the air and all that stood between him and the hard floor was a wild-haired pirate.

Kenneth headed for the sofa, the baby tucked under his arm. He sat, carefully placing two hands behind Charlie's head, and looked at him closely.

Finally, he tore his gaze away from the baby, and his eyes caught the light in the gloom of the flat. "Is he mine, Augusta?"

"Absolutely, he's yours," she said, reaching for her cigarettes. "Just give me a minute to pack his things."

"Because he looks like me," Kenneth said, peering down at the baby's mouth. "Born with a tooth, just like me. My mother used to say I nearly sawed her in half."

She flopped back in her chair, happy to have her arms to herself for just a moment. Was he Ken's? Without much heart in it, she'd tried to do the math but that month, the crucial month, was a blur. The *ayahuasca* had punched a week out of it, possibly two. For a moment, she was glad her parents were dead. Her father would have never spoken to her again, except to remind her of the shame she'd brought on the family. She would have a better chance of identifying next year's Grand National winner than her baby's father. Would it be so bad if it were Ken?

Over the next decade the question rarely came up; they were both afraid of the answer. Instead, they settled into a routine that suited them. Kenneth became a permanent fixture in her life, a father to Charlie, doggedly ignoring her taunts when she tried to drive him away. For months they would be at opposite poles, their only connection the boy, and then they would hurtle back together in passion, two magnets with no will of their own. He was a good parent, far better than she was, and no other candidate had ever come forward.

At first, he'd ignored her waywardness and its effect on the boy. It was easy enough when Charlie was a child, with a child's fuzzy grasp of the world.

Then one afternoon Kenneth had walked into the kitchen where Charlie, aged eight, was carefully straightening lines of laundry detergent on the counter in front of a school friend. They each had a drinking straw in their hands. Charlie's friend was just leaning forward to snort when Ken, with a bellow, launched himself across the kitchen.

"What?" said Charlie, angry and in tears, after the friend had been sent home. "It's just fun. I've seen loads of grown-ups do it. They do it and they laugh."

By the next month, Ken had found the school in Sussex, progressive and welcoming to unorthodox parents. Augusta feigned sadness—rather well, she thought—when she said goodbye to Charlie at the school gates.

"You go in with him and get him settled," she said to Ken. "I don't want to cry."

More than fifteen years later, she sat with the young man who was now a stranger and tried to keep the tears back. The blanket of tequila had slipped away, and she felt as naked and miserable as she ever had. How in God's name did people cope with these emotions all the time?

Charles sat staring out the window at the traffic that streamed past in the night. He hadn't said much on the way to the café, smiling tightly at her babbled apologies, catching her arm once as she pitched sideways on her broken heel. Frances had skulked back to the motel, her face a crimson beacon of shame.

"Do you need a few more minutes?" Augusta looked up, startled, at the waitress. She had fine, elfin features under a severe dark bob, and a smile aimed at one of the people at the table. Charles shook his head, and ordered coffee and two slices of lemon meringue pie. The menu held no welcome for the alcohol-starved; Augusta had already checked. With a grimace, she ordered a coffee. The waitress gathered their menus, her dark eyes on the boy. He didn't notice, or pretended not to.

Her son sat across the Formica table, silently shredding a paper napkin. Had he always been so beautiful, or had the alchemy of the sun changed him in some profound way? Most men grew coarser when they left their teens behind, but Charlie—Charles, he had already reminded her once—was refined, his features more sculpted, golden skin drawn across high cheekbones. His freckles had almost faded. Whose freckles, exactly? She should tell him how handsome he was.

"When did you lose your accent, then?"

He looked up at her, eyes narrowed. Kenneth's eyes? Possibly.

"That's what you want to know? We haven't talked in how long?"

"Seven years."

"Six and a half, actually."

"Well," said Augusta, "it seems longer."

The silence stretched between them. Augusta was framing apologies a thousand different ways when the waitress returned with their coffee. She poured one sugar into her cup, a second, a third. The boy took his black.

Caffeine and tequila, the poor woman's speedball. When she laughed under her breath, her son scowled.

"I'm glad you think it's funny," he said. "Making a spectacle of yourself like that."

This was something she had always found both endearing and mystifying, his deep seriousness. There was a formality to the way he spoke, even when he was a child, that charmed adults.

She said, "Do you know the joke about the man who went to a party and drank half the liquor?" He shook his head, fingers working steadily at the napkin. "Well, he also took half the drugs and tried to shag half the women." She paused. "He made a complete monocle of himself."

The boy grunted, but didn't look up at her.

"Oh, come on Charli—Charles. I saw that smile. A mother can always tell."

"Really?" he said, quick as a flash. "Then how would you know?"

She took a deep breath, and bit back a retort. He was

entitled to at least one cheap shot. The waitress arrived to break the silence, sliding two plates onto the table.

"I remembered that you like lemon pie," the boy said. "Or at least you used to." He handed her a fork, handle first. "There was that time I went to Morrison's to get one for your birthday, and the manager wanted to call the police because he thought I was too young to be out on my own."

She had no idea what he was talking about. Which birthday? A day so important to him it had lodged in his memory for years, and she had no recollection.

"I've felt guilty from that day to this," she said. "And I still adore lemon pie." Half-heartedly, she poked the meringue. "I'm sorry, Charles."

He had stopped in mid-bite, and she realized how ambiguous that statement was, and how woefully inadequate.

"For this evening, I mean. Embarrassing you was not part of my plan."

The boy looked at her as if she'd promised an elaborate trick and instead had produced a dead rabbit. After a moment he said, "I apologize as well, Augusta. It was a cruel thing I just said."

He bent toward his plate, and she knew, in a sudden rush, that she'd only have this time with him. This short evening, already half-ruined. The paralyzing weight of seven years' silence crushed her. Building a bridge toward him, that's what she should be doing. But she couldn't let go of the furious impulse that had driven her here, the gnawing worry that hollowed her.

She reached into her purse for her lipstick and compact. "Are you seeing anyone, Charles? God knows loads of girls must fancy you."

"Mmm." He shook his head. "Too busy."

"Even though you've got a professional matchmaker right by your side?" She tried to keep her voice casual. "I'm sure Kenneth could help."

"I'm sure he'd like to."

The compact opened with a snap. She kept her eyes on him above the mirror.

"I hear Ken's quite busy these days. The radio show. His new book."

"Busier than ever, I should think."

"It's fascinating to me," said Augusta, rolling bright crimson over her bottom lip. "One minute he's a journalist in England, the next minute he's here and he's an expert on romance. Which is a bit of a joke, of course."

"Do you think so?" the boy said, his face blank.

"Darling, I know so. Having been on the receiving end, so to speak." Augusta pressed her lips together. "Unless of course the book he's writing isn't about romance at all. Maybe it's about his own life. Lessons he's learned. People he's known. Lies he now believes."

Charles shrugged.

"Oh, Christ's sweaty bollocks, Charlie! Charles." His obstinacy was a goad. "Because he's going to write what he thinks he knows, isn't he, no matter how wrong—"

"As if," the boy said, suddenly fierce. "As if he'd do that. That's your territory."

She tried to think of something wounding to say.

Charles lifted his shoulders. "Why do you think he'd even write about you?"

She stared at him.

"I mean, you didn't write about him, did you? In your

book." He sat up straighter, and his wet palms squeaked against the vinyl. "Or me."

"I was trying to protect you," she said, stricken.

"The time to protect me was when I was sixteen, and you made me choose between the two of you."

The deadly calm of his voice pinned her back against the booth. She was immobile, but her thoughts raced: *What is he talking about? Made him choose between us?* She fished blindly for a memory but there was only darkness.

Finally she managed to whisper, "I never."

He pressed on, as if he hadn't heard her. "You told me if I chose to live with Ken, I'd be betraying you and you didn't want to see me again. We were at your flat in King's Cross. I'd been staying with you since school ended, and there was a row…" He shrugged. "I don't even remember what it was about now, but you told me I had to choose between the two of you. I said I wouldn't, so you handed me a bin liner and told me to put my clothes in it." Charles's eyes never left hers. "Then you gave me cab fare to Ken's. I must have rang you ten times the next week, Augusta, and no word."

She sat staring at him, his words whirling in her head. "I don't remember."

"That doesn't surprise me," her son said. His voice was flat and cold; he might have been telling her about an operation he'd had long ago.

She couldn't speak; the angry rush of words that had been there a moment ago lay dry in her mouth. She would never have banished him. Such a thing was unimaginable.

The waitress came to the table, nervously dropping the bill into the hostile silence. Charles reached for it.

"Do you know what it was like, reading your book? It was like looking at old photos and I'd been removed from every one. Like looking at your own family pictures, and wondering who the hell those people are."

thirty-one

There was no reason for Stanley to answer his phone. Now that he'd been sacked, he was most likely sitting at the pub watching Queens Park Rangers lose, his phone face-down in a pool of beer on the bar. He might even be happier that way.

He might be too embarrassed to speak to me, Frances thought, leaning into the motel mirror, its surface dotted and dashed with human effluent. She put on another coat of mascara. *He doesn't want a reminder of our mutual failure society.*

Augusta's head poked through the bathroom door. She had, with the diligence of a master spackler, repaired the damage to her hangover-ravaged face. She had lain in bed most of the day, nursing head and heart after last night's debacle at the bookstore. But as the light had leached from their motel room, she'd risen from the coffin of threadbare sheets and begun to prepare for the night.

"My God," said Frances. "You look like a picture."

"An X-rated picture, I hope." She ducked in front of

Frances to check herself in the mirror and lifted her breasts so they sat higher in the red halter-necked dress. "This frock had better serve its purpose. It's my nuclear option."

Frances started to ask why she was dressed for battle, but Augusta held up a finger. "All will be revealed in good time, darling. What I can tell you is that you should be prepared for action. You might want to have your bag packed."

And then she was gone, stopping at the bedside table to scoop her cigarettes and a small bottle of pills into her bag. Frances watched her shut the door, feeling a curious emptiness in the air.

Frances looked at the time on her phone. It was almost the end of the drinking night in London. It was too late to call. She called anyway. Hitting the Skype button with one shaking finger, she waited for the transatlantic beeping to subside. Stanley answered on the first ring, and she thought: *Desperate for a call from anyone, or just from me?*

"Hello, wanderer," he said, and she almost burst into tears. The tiny screen was kind to a man in crisis: it blurred the shadows under his eyes and the lines on his brow. Frances hoped the screen lied for her as well.

"So," he said. "How's the madwoman? Not you, the other one."

Frances curled herself at the top of the bed. "She just left. I think she's heading for a fistfight with an old flame. And the panel she came out here to do was a complete disaster, because she insulted the other guests. And she nearly got arrested by the airport police."

"A typical day at the office, then." He cupped his cheek

in his hand, as if they were back at the pub, separated by a table and not an ocean.

It was a relief to be able to talk to someone about the precipitous spiral her life now described. "She's like a baby," Frances said. "A big, drunken baby who needs constant attention, and always wants an audience. It's making me feel weirdly maternal. She just does what she wants and damn the consequences. I've never met anyone like her."

"Well, there was Aleister Crowley," said Stanley. "'Do what thou wilt shall be the whole of the law.'"

"She's not actually a dark wizard," Frances said. "Though it might explain why I keep doing what she says." She stretched out on the bed, propping the phone next to her. "It's very odd, being with her. She's screwed up so many times and she doesn't seem to care. I can't imagine what it's like not to worry about falling down, and down…" Her voice trailed off.

"Frances." His voice was gentle. "Everyone's terrified of that."

They sat staring at each other for a moment until Frances sat up suddenly. She turned the camera to face the rocky shoreline of empty bottles on the sidetable. "Oh, and she's turning me into an alcoholic."

"That's supposed to be my job," he said, "if you'd just come home."

Frances sucked in a deep breath. Even sitting down, her legs felt weak. She wanted to reach through the phone and touch his unshaven cheek.

She said, unsteadily, "I'm not sure where home is anymore, Stanley."

From his kitchen in Clapham he scowled at her. "Don't

be so wet, Frances. You've had one tiny fall at a fence. You'll pick yourself back up." He leaned closer to the screen and lowered his voice: "Let's hear more about you. What you've been doing. What you're wearing."

"You can see what I'm wearing."

"I know. Horribly pervy question. Sorry."

She aimed for a sultry voice: "Why, what are you wearing?"

"The usual," he said. "Red thong under my cardinal's robes."

"Ah," said Frances. "That explains why they fired you."

As soon as the words were out, she wished she could pull them back. He forced a laugh, and the compressed sound of it made her feel sick.

"Now I'm the one who's sorry."

"We could apologize until the end of time, Frances. It's my fault we're both out of jobs."

She blurted, "It's only because of you that I ever had a job in the first place. But I've been thinking, it might be a good thing…" Her eye was caught by a dark shape on the table in front of him: a pack of cigarettes. "You're still smoking, Stanley."

"It's a good thing I'm still smoking? Premature death will mean a shorter stay in the poorhouse, it's true." He smiled at her, the funny sideways smile she'd been longing to see.

"No, you idiot. I meant it's a good thing we're not working together anymore. If you're not at the paper anymore, and I'm not…" She paused, willing him to understand. To step into the breach.

He leaned closer to his screen and said softly, "You're not my slave anymore, is that it? I'd be happy to wear the slave toga for a bit, if you'd like."

She brought one finger up to the screen, and he did the same, so that their fingers touched. "You are a tonic, Frances," he said. "And I wish you weren't a bloody continent away. You could come sit in my kitchen and help me stick pins in my oligarch doll."

A sudden sound from outside made her look toward the window: the whirring of gears, a muted curse. The local call girl must be heading to work.

She turned back to the phone, suddenly giddy. It was as if the miasma of the past few days had lifted and burst, leaving something bright behind. "You've never been to Los Angeles, have you?"

"I've never been further west than Swansea, and I regretted even that."

"Then I'm going to show you around."

For the next ten minutes she gave Stanley a tour of her world, holding the phone in front of her like a candle. She showed him the unfilled pool, the cut-price liquor store across the street, the tracksuit-clad prostitute gliding off to work on her mobility scooter.

"It really is a city of dreams," he said once she'd brought him back inside.

"Astonishing that anyone ever leaves," she said. Gathering her courage, she blurted: "You look wonderful, Stanley. You look ten years younger. Leaving that place has saved your life."

"I'm just wearing a lot of makeup," he said, but she could swear he was pleased. "To be honest, things aren't entirely pear-shaped. I do have something exciting happening."

She felt her heart tumble down her ribcage. He was going to tell her he'd fallen in love. A woman had saved him from despair.

"It's actually a marvellous professional opportunity for me. And I was thinking, it could be great for you, too, if you wanted to come on board." His face was suddenly serious. "Frances, how do you feel about cats?"

thirty-two

At some point after she'd left him, Ken had learned to cook. For supper there was filet in Madeira sauce, braised fennel, funny little potatoes shaped like gnarled fingers with buttery flesh inside. Ken had eaten everything on his plate, and with shocking presumption reached over to spear a wedge of steak on hers. As if they regularly ate from the same plate. Augusta wanted to be furious about this, but the Ativan and the wine were preventing her from locating her anger.

In spite of the chilly evening, they sat in his garden— or "backyard," as he laughingly called it in a flat Valley accent. His jacket lay draped across her shoulders. She'd failed to wear many of her own clothes. But how rewarding was the look in his eyes when she'd shown up at his door in the red dress, her arms and chest covered in gooseflesh? It had thrown her into the past to see his comic-book expression, eyes out on springs, tongue practically unrolling like a carpet at her feet.

All around them was jungle, Kenneth's garden a riot of

plants and shrubs she didn't recognize. Before dinner he'd pointed them out to her: winter hazel, jasmine, honey-suckle, each, he said, giving off scent at different times of the year. Charles had chosen the plants, and tended them with maternal devotion.

"You and I between us," Kenneth said, "we couldn't keep mould alive."

Augusta pulled herself upright, a posture she'd perfected when playing a headmistress.

"I gave that child life," she said with asperity. "Although he seems to have forgotten it. He's still furious with me for some unfathomable reason."

Kenneth stared at her in disbelief. "Are you are joking me?"

"I have no idea what you mean."

"You know perfectly well why he's angry. You tossed him out on his ear when he was sixteen. You told him to choose between us, and when he wouldn't choose you, you put his things in a bag and told him to leave." He reached over and took the last potato from her plate. "He was just about to start his A-levels."

"If that had actually happened," she said stiffly, "I would remember it."

A ladybug was crawling along the edge of the table; he took it on the edge of his finger and placed it on the grass. "I would love to see a map of your memory sometime," he said. "I imagine it would be very useful. The rooms you choose to ignore."

Her fingers slid along the teak handle of the steak knife, its blade greasy with dried blood. She should have stabbed him when she had the chance. Her eyes closed.

From a dark, submerged pool, an image floated to the surface: Charlie in the doorway of her flat, eyes narrow with rage, cheeks wet with tears. The image wavered and dissolved. No, that couldn't be a memory. Ken had planted the thought there.

When she came back to the present, to the little garden, he was talking. He was *still* talking.

"The thing no one wants to acknowledge about relationships is that they contain hundreds of truths. When I'm on the radio, people don't call me for advice; they call because they want me to take their side. But I always say—" he paused for effect, and his voice deepened as if he were speaking into an invisible microphone: "Love doesn't have sides; love is like a ball."

"Or an egg," she said slowly.

"What?"

"The Heart Is an Egg," Augusta repeated. "It Can Be Broken, But Never Beaten." Was it a trick of the light, or had he grown paler? "Your book, Kenneth. Why don't we talk about that?"

Augusta had forgotten how hard it was to get such a big bastard drunk. Once, she had relied on his flinty constitution. Ken could pour any amount of alcohol down his gob and still be standing at the end of the night, ready to defend her ragged honour, drive her home, carry her upstairs, and pitch her into bed.

A forest of bottles sprouted from the coffee table in front of them: port, Armagnac, brandy, Jägermeister. Every time she filled Kenneth's glass, she found a way to dispose of her own. A ficus sat on the floor beside the sofa, its soil soupy with digestifs.

"The boy says there's no one in your life." She tucked her legs under her on the sofa, letting the red dress fall away from her thighs. Let him deal with that.

"He's in my life."

"Really, Ken. It can't look very good for Mr. Romance to not have a girlfriend. Like a chef standing in the middle of an empty restaurant."

He smiled faintly, head back against the pillows, an empty port glass balanced on the arm of the sofa.

"Worried about my love life, are you?"

He turned his head to look at her and his eyes immediately were drawn to her legs. *Like a fucking compass needle*, she thought. *Unbelievable.*

"Augusta," he said hoarsely, and inched toward her.

It was too soon; he was still coherent. Her heart was racing with the electric thrill of the caffeine pills she'd taken in the loo after dinner. "For the temporary relief of exhaustion," it said on the box she'd picked up at the Boots in Heathrow. "Maximum four tablets per day." She'd poured eight in her mouth and washed them down with water from her cupped hand. It was tragic to let go of the Ativan's silken buzz, but she needed her wits to be sharp. And his to be dull.

She waved the bottle of Jägermeister at him.

"Oh, go on then," he said.

When she handed him the glass, she let her fingers brush against his ever so gently. As she put the bottle down on the floor, she felt dizzy, nearly swooned. What if she'd given herself angina with those pills? What was angina, anyway?

It had something to do with hearts. She hadn't felt hers tripping like this in years.

"Are you all right?" Ken put a hand on her shoulder to steady her.

Any excuse to touch me, she thought. It was the caffeine pills' fault that she felt a crackling on the bare skin under his hand.

Shrugging him off, she got to her feet, knees unsteady. The sitting room gave nothing away—nothing of his past, nothing of the transformation he'd made of his life. Only the L.S. Lowry prints on the wall hinted at the grim city he couldn't quite leave behind, and a series of framed photographs of Charlie, charting his journey from childhood, indicated that there was a human being he loved.

One entire wall was covered with books. She felt his eyes on her back as she looked at the titles, heard the dull scrape of the bottle as he lifted it from the table. A few novels, but mostly history and philosophy and biography, one entire shelf dedicated to books about famous couples in history.

Her fingers slid along the spines, stopped at one slim volume. She leaned closer to read the title and pulled it free, shaking her head. The book fell open in her hands, and she read: "There are jobs that an Englishman just doesn't take."

"Ah," he said from the sofa. "*The Loved One*. I sometimes wished I'd followed that advice."

"It's my copy. I recognize the HP stains." She looked at him through her lashes. "You saved it, you sentimental fool."

She saw him swallow. One big hand caressed the empty sofa seat. "Augusta," he said. "Why don't you come sit down?" She felt the pull in her gut, the treacherous tug of desire. Turning back to the bookshelf, she put Waugh's novel away. She'd come here for a reason, and she mustn't lose sight of it. Her fingers resumed their travels across the shelf, and she felt a welcome flicker of violence.

"Ken," she said slowly, "where the fuck is my book?"

"No one reads books anymore, Augusta, so it hardly matters."

She joined him on the sofa again, sitting rigid with indignation. The back of his hand rested against her thigh— accidentally, perhaps, but neither of them moved.

"Is that so, darling? Then why are you writing one?"

"I've asked my publisher the same question. She's completely mad, lives in a yurt in Santa Cruz. But she seems to think there's a tiny niche in the self-help market that I can squeeze myself into." He still sounded sober. "How did you know about it, anyway? Did Charles mention it?"

She snorted. "That child. It's like talking to a statue." Augusta picked up the bottle and filled Kenneth's glass, hesitated, filled her own. "He's so self-contained. Nothing like me. Nothing at all." She felt drained of all energy. "I've no idea where it comes from."

"Nor do I," he said quietly. "He's a mystery to me."

As nonchalantly as she could, she said: "He did mention that you might be planning to spill some secrets."

To her annoyance, he burst out laughing. "He did no such thing, Augusta!" Kenneth said when he could finally speak. "I'd have thought you'd become a better liar, with all the practice you've had."

Her fists clenched and for a minute she considered sinking one of them into his smug face. She drew a deep breath and tried to remember what Alma had advised: Act strategically. Only one of you will be thinking with your brain.

She wriggled closer to him on the sofa and he looked at her, surprised. His fingers played with the hem of her dress. Tugging it down, not up, the canny bastard. *I'm only feeling this way because it's been so long*, she thought. *Because it's been so long since I had sex with somebody other than myself. Maybe it wouldn't be so bad…a quick shag, steal his computer, and go.*

She handed him his glass, touched it to hers, and they both threw back their drinks in one go.

"I guess you haven't forgiven me," she said.

He gazed at her coolly. No, definitely not drunk enough. "You'd like to think that, wouldn't you?"

"Think what?"

"That I sit here, night after night, licking old wounds. That I've got pictures of you in a box and I take them out at night and cry myself to sleep."

"Don't be such a knob. My ego's not quite so huge as you imagine. Although"—she reached for her cigarettes, not bothering to ask if she might smoke inside—"I think it's fair to say you probably do have a picture of me somewhere with darts stuck in it."

He shook his head. "You're unbelievable. We have better things to do, Charles and I. There are other things that occupy us besides"—he curled his lip—"memories of you." Stretching, he stood up. "I'll be back in a minute. Try not to cause too much damage." He stalked off toward the kitchen.

"Bring back another bottle," she called after him.

Her hands shook as she put her cigarettes down and rummaged through her bag. Caffeine or nerves? Or something else? Quickly, she texted Frances: **Be outside in 20 min. Lights off.** She added Kenneth's address and phone number and hit send.

She rooted around for another few seconds until her hands closed around a tiny plastic bottle, its ridged lid rough under her fingers. Lorazepam, 2 mg, the label said. Take one as needed. Before she could reconsider, she put her palm against the lid and twisted.

Nothing. She could hear Ken in the kitchen now, the fridge door opening, the clink of bottle on bottle. Cursing, she wiped her palm on her dress and tried again to open the lid. Nothing. It remained firmly attached to the bottle. Fucking child-proof lids. They couldn't possibly save enough children's lives to compensate for the annoyance they caused. The tap in the kitchen was turned on, then off; she heard a cupboard slam shut. Taking a deep breath, she placed her palm against the lid and twisted firmly. This time, it gave.

Four white ovals skittered onto the table. Quickly, she scraped two back into the bottle. She could hear Ken's footsteps coming down the hallway. She crushed two tiny pills with the end of her lighter, grabbed his empty glass, and held it to the edge of the table: she used her cigarette pack to sweep the small pile of white powder into his glass.

When he came into the room, she was pouring them both drinks. He stopped in the doorway, leaning heavily against the frame. He gazed out the window behind her and said, "What I don't understand, Augusta, is why you think I'd give you away now."

She swirled his glass gently, held it toward him but he didn't move. "I'm not sure —"

"That door's been closed for years." His eyes—somewhat less focused, she was pleased to see—slid to hers. "You know nothing about me at all." He reached for the drink, and upended it in one fierce motion. Wiping his hand across his mouth, he sat heavily next to her. "I'm not sure why that surprises me."

It took all her control not to snarl: Why do you think you know anything about me? Instead, she turned to him and tilted her head, an enticement that always worked beautifully on the small screen.

"You know what surprises me? That I agreed to come here tonight." She put her mouth close to his ear, whispered: "But I'm glad I did."

Finally, his eyes began to glaze. He blinked at her slowly, as if he were trying to memorize every inch. As if he were already planning to never see her again.

"'S more than idle flattery," Ken mumbled. "You do look spectacular. Which is astonishing, considering what you've done to yourself."

"Considering what you've done to me."

"Me? I haven't done anything." He inched closer to her on the sofa, his knee knocking hers. "Not yet."

Augusta held her breath. It would be easy enough at this point to delay until he passed out, to make some excuse and leave the room. But parts of her—particularly certain parts—wanted this. So she closed her eyes.

She felt his mouth against hers, not entirely gentle. Then she was falling, and she was in two places at once, here and there, present and past. She wasn't ancient and nearly expired;

she was young and furled with potential. They both were. If she opened her eyes, that's the man she'd see. The first Ken, not the one she'd ruined. They fell back onto the couch, her arms around his neck. For an uncountable time, every other thought was chased from her head. She felt his hands slide down her sides, up to her breasts, slow and warm.

She had no idea how much time passed, only that she was in danger of forgetting herself. She shifted under him. "I'm sorry," she murmured against his mouth.

"What?" He broke away from her, shook his head. He seemed to be having trouble focusing his gaze. "What did you say?"

"Nothing."

She tangled her hands into his hair and pulled him down. He landed on her with a thud, knocking the air from her lungs. He *was* a great lump. What if he passed out on her, and she slowly suffocated to death underneath him? It would serve her right. Panic gripped her and she wedged her forearms under his shoulders. He seemed to have fallen asleep. Now she knew what people meant by the weight of the world.

"Kenneth," she hissed. "Ken, get off me for a minute."

"Mmmm," he muttered.

She wriggled sideways until she'd worked her legs out from under his. With one great heave she shoved his shoulders and dragged herself from under him. She tumbled to the floor, panting, and collected her breath.

"Gusta?" he mumbled into the pillow.

She leaned over, pushed the hair away from his ear, and whispered: "Don't worry, love. I'll be right back. Just need to fix myself up."

He let out a noise that was either sigh or snore. She slid one hand under his cheek and turned his face away from the pillow so that he could breathe. When Charlie was little he'd slept the same way, face buried in the pillow and arms outstretched, as if he were floating in water. Every night she'd tried to nudge his face to the side, but invariably he'd woken up screaming. After a few nights she let him be and hoped that nature was wise enough to wake him before he stopped breathing.

She picked up one of Ken's hands and dropped it; it fell to the sofa with a satisfying thud. Knees creaking, she got to her feet, trailing one hand through his hair. Maybe they should have had one last shag. It might have done both of them good. She stepped over a river of brandy trickling from the neck of an upended bottle. Too late now. Once he realized she'd drugged him and stolen his life's work, it was unlikely he'd want to sleep with her again.

In her handbag she had a list of instructions for disconnecting the computer that she'd taken down from Alma over the phone. She crept out into the hallway and pulled it free: *SAve ffilesto thumb mute fxn BACKED UP IN CLoud??* It might as well be in Sanskrit. As quietly as she could, she began to climb the stairs.

As she reached the top she heard a muffled groan from the living room and stopped, her heart galloping. What if she had done permanent damage? She was used to mixing poisons, but that didn't mean everyone was.

When it was quiet again, she moved through the upstairs hall. The doorway to his bedroom was open, and Augusta saw he'd put a vase of tiger lilies on the dresser. Her favourite flowers. She fought down an unwelcome pang of regret.

238

She was turning back into the hall when a loud bang came from downstairs, and she jumped. It sounded as if two heavy knees had hit the floor. Buggery fuck. She tiptoed out of the bedroom.

To her right, the door to his office was closed. Holding her breath, she reached for the knob. Unlocked, thank God. She could see his laptop on the desk, blinking in the darkness. She flicked on the lights and consulted Alma's crumpled instructions. What in God's name was a wrLESS rotter? There was a rat's nest of cables attached to the computer, each one serving some unknown purpose. In despair, she picked one of the wires up. What if she just snipped it with her manicure scissors?

From the living room downstairs came an unearthly noise, like a bear awakening in its winter cave. *Arroooooogghhh*. Quickly, she began yanking the cords from the computer. One refused to budge and she clawed at it, hands shaking. Finally she realized she needed to pinch the plastic clip at its end, and it slid from the computer. Her prize was free.

Scooping the laptop up in one hand, she turned to head for the stairs. What if this wasn't the only copy of his book? What if he had it on a disc or something? No, that wouldn't be Ken. It was not like him to take two steps when one would do.

There was a crash from the living room, the sound of a bottle falling to the floor. She crouched at the top of the stairs, the computer nearly slipping from her damp grasp. As quietly as possible she began to creep down the stairs, crouched below the level of the banister. One of her knees popped, loud as a firecracker. Over the top of the banister she could just see into the living room, where a beastlike shape swayed against the light.

Fuck. She slid one foot cautiously down to the next step and as she did her toe caught in the hem of the red dress and she slid down the last few steps like an out-of-control bobsledder. The laptop came loose from her grip and skittered down the steps, landing with a clatter on the tiles of the front hallway.

Lying on the floor, her skirt hiked up to reveal knickers that said Friday (it was Wednesday), she waited for the axe to fall. Ken lumbered into view in the sitting room doorway. He swayed like a giant fir tree and she could see, even in the dim light, that his half-closed eyes were confused.

"Gusta?" he muttered, and took a step toward her. As he did, his foot tripped over the empty brandy bottle, the last of its brave fellows. He didn't make a sound as he lurched forward, arms flailing, though his head made a terrific crack when it hit the edge of the stairs.

Now you've done it, Augusta thought. *Now you've done it, now you've done it, now you've killed a man.* Terrified, she crawled over to where he lay. Was he already dead? Holding her breath, she leaned toward him and pressed her ear to his mouth. Oh God, he wasn't breathing. She leaned in closer.

"Arrrggggh," he groaned, and she leapt back.

An exquisite relief flooded her, and not just because she wouldn't have to spend her life in a maximum-security women's jail. He rasped again, eyes still closed, and she leaned closer. His mouth worked.

"You…evil…cow."

Look who's talking, she thought, suddenly indignant.

She was on her feet again, one hand feeling for the

laptop. Kenneth was lying still, but she could see his back rising and falling regularly. Gingerly she stepped over him and past the brandy bottle, past the Jägermeister bottle, past the empty bottles of wine. The pillow sat crushed on the edge of the sofa and she picked it up, tiptoed back in the hallway, and in one quick motion tucked it under his head. He made a sad noise, but that might have just been the sound of her guilt.

thirty-three

"You see, I'd just had surgery when I changed the password," Augusta said. She leaned over the service counter with an expression she hoped suggested vulnerability. "Brain surgery, actually. It was quite traumatic. Whole swaths of my past gone. Sometimes I can barely remember the name of my sister here."

"Daughter," said Frances.

The clerk looked at them impassively. He was a handsome boy with a fall of dark hair brushing his shoulders, his looks marred only by the single brow that ran, uninterrupted, above his eyes. Those eyes said: *I am merely serving time at CyberKrunch. I am destined for greater things. I will humour your little charade.*

"Have you tried your own name?" he said in a monotone.

"Of course I have, darling. All combinations. Augusta, augustaprice, dieaugustadie…" He raised an eyebrow and Augusta said, hastily, "Not that there's any reason that should be the password."

Frances wondered if he could smell the pomegranate liqueur on Augusta's breath; it had been the cheapest alcohol on sale in the all-night Rite Aid, their first stop after pulling into the town of Camarillo at 6 a.m. For three hours they'd sat in the parking lot waiting for the computer store to open, Augusta with the plastic gallon jug of blood-red liquid on her lap. Every question Frances asked was met with a grunt, or silence. Silent Augusta was strangely more disconcerting than the one who swore like a stevedore.

"Children?" said the clerk, running his finger over the keyboard.

"I wouldn't call us children," said Augusta, pulling herself up to her full, inconsequential height, "just because we can't remember this one simple thing."

"The names of your children," he said tonelessly. "Your daughter, for example."

"No," said Augusta. "I wouldn't name anything after her. But…" Her eyes brightened. "Try Charlie."

"It has to be an alphanumeric," the clerk said. "Letters plus numbers. What's his birthdate?"

"1989."

The clerk tapped on the keyboard. "Nope."

"Fuckety Christ," said Augusta, not quite under her breath.

The clerk looked up with new respect.

Frances stirred beside her. "Try Charles instead," she said.

The clerk returned to the keyboard. "Bingo," he said. "You're in."

Augusta's shoulders sagged. "Do one more thing for me, would you, love? I need to print off a file. I can't remember what I called it, but it will be quite a big file." She beckoned the clerk with a finger; its peeling crimson nail had broken, leaving a point like an arrowhead. "It might smell quite strongly of malice."

"I'm not going an inch farther with you, Augusta, until you tell me what's going on. And since you don't drive, and I doubt you want to be stuck in the parking lot of Camarillo Premium Outlets for the rest of your life, I suggest you talk."

Augusta was madly flipping through the printout the clerk had given her, searching, mumbling to herself, licking her finger, taking a swig from the liqueur bottle, returning to the pages. At Frances's words, she looked up.

"I should think it's quite clear what this is. The holy grail. The end of the trail. The grail returned to earth now."

She's even more pissed than usual, Frances thought. The interior of the car reeked of fermented pomegranates. A sticky ring on the floor mat indicated where the bottle had sat between Augusta's feet while she slept, snoring, on the drive north.

They'd checked out of the motel in the middle of the night. Augusta had flung her clothes into her suitcase, and then, when Frances failed to move quickly enough, began shoving Frances's clothes in as well.

"We must move, darling. Chop chop. He knows where we're hiding." Frances had tried to ask what had happened, but Augusta merely said, "All in good time. The story will unfold for your delight. But now let's be on our way. I've faced my demons, and now we must face yours."

They're not demons, Frances thought. *They're my parents, and they love me. They still love me, because they have to.* There was nowhere else to go, so Frances gave in to the pull she'd felt in her gut since they'd arrived. They'd begun to drive north, to the only sanctuary Frances could name. The house she had grown up in, and had left, full of hope.

Frances watched as Augusta skimmed the manuscript, racing a finger down each page before flipping it. They were parked between a pickup truck and a camper van, in a rented car that smelled like a French brothel. Camarillo Premium Outlets was their purgatory.

"I presume this is the lost masterpiece," Frances said. "Deller's book. The publisher's not going to be happy that you've seen it before she has." Augusta ignored her. "Did you sleep with your ex so he'd let you see a copy?"

"Not exactly," said Augusta. "He passed out before things reached such a dire pass. In a manner of speaking."

It was stifling in the car, and Frances rolled down the window to exchange pomegranate fumes for the gasoline-scented air of the parking lot. Still she couldn't breathe.

"What exactly do you mean, in a manner of speaking?"

Augusta was oblivious, turning each page, scanning, cursing, flipping to the next.

"Mr. Romance," she spat. "What cobblers. And do you know," she looked over at Frances, eyes wide with disbelief, "*that* appears to be what this bullshit is actually about." She shook the sheaf of papers. "It's about love. In the abstract. It's nothing to do with what happened. Nothing to do with *me*."

She reached between her legs for the bottle. A tiny drop

of red liquid fell on the page, coursing down the margin. A paralyzing thought gripped Frances. *I'm a fugitive*, she thought. *An unemployed, penniless fugitive. I am going to spend the next five years in an orange jumpsuit sharing a jail cell with a woman named Storm.*

"So Kenneth Deller has probably already called the police."

Augusta shrugged. "If he's got a phone beside his hospital bed."

Frances lurched from the car, crouched in the shadow of the camper van. She was going to vomit. Her head swam with the fumes, with exhaustion, with her father's voice: "When you start something, Frances, always try to picture how it ends, and then see it through. That's your strength, a level head."

She crawled back into the driver's seat. "Did you harm him, Augusta?"

Augusta snorted.

"Is there somebody we should call? The police? An ambulance?"

"I already did that, darling, hours ago. I called 999."

"That is the wrong number!" Frances yelled. "In America the emergency number is 911! Fuck!"

"Well, yes," said Augusta, looking at her as if she'd lost her mind. "I soon figured that out." She shook her head. "Language, my dear."

thirty-four

Frances had no idea how long they'd been parked by the side of the road, staring at her childhood home. On the right, the boardwalk stretched along the clifftops, echoing with the occasional hollow thump of a jogger passing by in the dusk. Frances could hear the ocean crashing against the rocks at the bottom of the cliffs. The white noise of her childhood.

Across the road, she watched her mother pass in front of the wide bay windows, carrying the good candlesticks into the dining room. Her mother had hesitated for only a second when Frances phoned from the parking lot in Camarillo to say that she was on her way with a friend.

Frances had kept her voice brusque, daring her mother to protest at the short notice. But she hadn't. Instead, with the grace that Frances resented and envied, she said, "I'll go to the market and get two more chops. It won't take a minute." There was a brief silence, the sound of bitten-back tears on either end of the line, and then: "Your father will be so pleased."

No, he won't, Frances thought. *I have no offerings that will please him.* She sat in the car, watching her mother draw the curtains. The house was almost as she remembered: three storeys cross-hatched with Tudor beams, an incongruous Victorian tower jutting from the seafront edge; Frances had hijacked that tower for her own at the age of six, in the grip of princess mania. And yet it was unfamilar, disfigured like an old friend after an accident: two hydrangeas that had once flanked the porch were gone, and in their place was a wooden wheelchair ramp, its pine planks still yellow-fresh and unmarked by salt air.

Augusta slept against the car window, a patch of fog blossoming near her open mouth. What if she had indeed killed Deller? *We're fugitives*, Frances thought. *We're fugitives and we don't even have a hostess gift.*

Gently she prodded Augusta's shoulder, and Augusta shuddered to life. She jerked away from the window, eyes widening at the sight of the ocean: "Are we in Dover?" she whispered. "I'm not allowed in Dover."

"Wrong side of the world," Frances said. "We're in Cambria. My hometown. And that is my house." She paused. "At least, it's my parents' house."

Augusta leaned across her to peer out the window. She had to fold herself over the purloined computer, which stuck out the top of her handbag. Augusta's phone beeped, but she ignored it.

"Very nice. A bit Anne Boleyn for my taste, but handsome." She took a mint from her purse and offered one to Frances. Her phone beeped again and Frances, exasperated, reached for the purse. Augusta slapped her hand away.

"For God's sake, Augusta," said Frances, stung. "I wasn't

going to touch your precious computer. I just wanted to help you check your messages."

Slowly, not taking her eyes from Frances's, Augusta reached into her handbag and retrieved the phone.

"Evil things," she said, handing it to Frances. "They're supposed to connect us, which is utter rubbish. We've never been further apart. Idiots chase you down the street taking pictures so they can wank over them later—"

"Mmm," said Frances, not listening. "Who's David?"

"David?" Augusta sat up suddenly. She ran a finger over her eyebrows, as if a camera might appear at any moment on this rocky stretch of coast. "David is my agent. What does he say?"

Frances scanned the phone. "He's left about eight text messages and emails, and they're increasingly hysterical. Something about a show called *Circle of Lies*?"

Augusta fell back against the seat, oblivious to Frances's curious stare. She'd always believed that fortune would smile on her once again. *Circle of Lies*. The betrayed Q.C.'s wife. The part she'd fought for and lost. Finally, the producers had come to their senses. They knew the strengths that she—and only she—could bring to the role.

Augusta tried to remember the script, but she'd read it so long ago. A jammy, complex part. She could see it now: the wife would be hurt, but not bitter; afraid, but stalwart. Augusta practiced noble resignation in the car window for a moment, not noticing that Frances had gone white. The girl was staring at a new message on Augusta's phone, which said simply: **I WILL FIND YOU. YOU WILL PAY.**

Augusta was too lost in her daydream to see Frances frantically stabbing the delete key. After a moment, she turned and said, "Let's meet your parents, shall we? I imagine they keep an excellent cellar."

They walked across Moonstone Drive and up the long, sloping driveway to the door. Augusta's heel caught between the planks in the ramp and Frances bent to free her. "It's new, this ramp," she said in a rush. "My father's been in a wheelchair for only a little while. He hates it."

"Of course he does," said Augusta, fixing her lipstick in the door's pebbled glass. "He must think his life is over."

"I wouldn't put it quite that way—" Frances began, but before she could answer the door opened.

Augusta felt an odd jolt of recognition: the woman in the door was Frances in twenty years, Frances with the edges neatly stitched. She had the same dark hair and hazel eyes, but the older woman's hair was glossy and richly highlighted, her eyes subtly outlined in brown pencil.

Frances stood on the porch, unsure, until her mother stepped forward and wrapped her in two slender brown arms.

"Oh, sweetheart," she whispered. "I'm so glad you're home."

So that's how it's done, Augusta thought.

Frances stood in her mother's arms for a minute until Augusta coughed.

"Oh," said Frances, breaking away and brushing at her eyes. "Mom, this is my...my friend, Augusta. Augusta, this is my mother, Jean Bleeker."

Jean extended a hand, the tiny gold charms on her bracelet swinging. There was nothing in her face but welcome, and Augusta marvelled once again at the American capacity to accept with a smile whatever astonishing shit life threw at them.

"I'm delighted to meet a friend of Frances's," she said, and beckoned them in.

The marble-floored entrance foyer was nearly as large as Augusta's London flat, and smelled of something alien and citrus, which after a moment she realized must be furniture polish. As Jean led them through the hallway, Augusta noticed a sawhorse leaning against a wall; the archway to a vast, pale sitting room was ragged on one side, the raw edge of drywall exposed. Jean caught her eye: "We're widening the doorways," she said.

Frances had regained her composure: "Where is Daddy?" she asked.

"He'll be down shortly," her mother said. "He needs to nap quite a bit these days."

Jean reached out to touch her daughter's hair, but Frances broke away and walked across to the bay window that looked over the ocean. Jean stared after her for a minute, and then turned to Augusta: "Well, let's make you at home. Shall I take your bag?"

Augusta clutched the purse with a convulsive jerk, setting her rocking back. One of her heels clacked loudly in the silence, and she didn't dare look down to see if she'd cracked a marble tile.

"Thank you, no," she said, feeling the laptop cool and hard against her chest. "I won't bother you with my baggage."

She reached for a smile, but the distance was too great. Jean Bleeker hadn't noticed; she was staring, once more, at her daughter.

thirty-five

How much longer would this spectacle continue? Frances watched, appalled, as Augusta draped herself over Len Bleeker. One hand lay on her father's shrunken forearm, the other around the back of his wheelchair. Augusta had practically taken her breasts out for weighing. They tumbled from her peasant top, twin moons reflected in the silver Georg Jensen candlesticks.

Frances had expected her father to look older, but she hadn't expected him to be so diminished. Len Bleeker had always had a giant head, an Easter Island statue of a head, with a slab of a nose and wiry eyebrows overhanging dark eyes. "This head has never found a hat its equal," he used to say. But now this vast promontory sat on the spindly shoulders of a child, a boy with rickets. He looked like a bobble-headed doll sitting on a car dashboard.

The cruelty of the thought shocked Frances and she reached for her wineglass. Third glass of the night. Her parents did indeed keep an excellent cellar, which had sat untouched since the onset of her father's illness.

"What a magnificent vintage," Augusta had purred. "I feel I'm at the Savoy."

Three bottles sat on the table, and Frances watched as Augusta topped their glasses with a 2001 Dominus. It didn't seem to bother Jean that this stranger had usurped her hostess's role, and possibly her husband, too. Frances's mother held a hand over her wine glass, shaking her head as Augusta moved to fill it.

Len raised his wine to his lips, hand trembling, and Frances felt her temples pulse. He wasn't supposed to drink. Why wouldn't her mother say something? But Jean sat back, a small smile on her face, and listened to her husband reminisce about life in the old country. Frances took another gulp.

Len had spent a half-hour telling Augusta about his childhood in Coventry, playing in the ruins of the cathedral, wrenching his ankle on the edge of a bomb crater. The combination of poverty and postwar rationing meant that he was always hungry. When he arrived in Los Angeles in 1964, he'd stood in the bread aisle at the supermarket, paralyzed by choice.

"I've always missed certain things about home, though," he said. "Telly, for one. Television's useless in this country. Everybody's so bloody cheerful all the time. In England you knew you'd at least get a proper laugh." He mentioned a name that Frances didn't recognize, and Augusta, smiling, leaned over to whisper something in his ear.

"A nonce, you say?" Len Bleeker's mouth fell open in shock and delight. "But he was married to that girl from the horror films, with the lovely—" He raised shaky hands and cupped a pair of breasts.

"Who was born a bloke," Augusta said.

"No," Len breathed.

He placed a hand on Augusta's; it was twice the size of hers. His wheelchair nestled inside a specially designed panel which slid from underneath the teak dining table and allowed him to sit at its head, as he always had.

Frances lurched to her feet. She couldn't watch any more.

"Mom," she said, "I'll get the dessert."

Her foot caught in the bottom rung of her chair and she nearly tripped. Augusta had eyes only for Len; they were talking about the best pubs in Coventry.

In the kitchen, Frances went to the sink to splash cold water on her face. She had to bend nearly double; the appliances and counters had been lowered to accommodate the wheelchair. As the water hit her, Frances remembered how furious Len had been when a county bylaw forced him to make his appliance stores wheelchair accessible. He'd grumbled about political correctness gone mad, and had considered challenging the bylaw in court. Finally, grudgingly, he oversaw the refit of his six stores, the entrances widened and elevators installed.

Frances pressed a tea towel to her face. If only she could have come back here boasting of a single triumph, no matter how small. If she could have given her father a tiny bit of light. Instead, nothing. She was a giant among the pint-sized appliances, but felt as small and helpless as a child.

She didn't hear her mother come in. A cool hand slid across her shoulders and she stiffened.

"I can't believe you haven't said anything," Frances said.

"About what, sweetheart?" Her mother bent to open

the refrigerator and took out a bowl. Raspberry fool, her father's favourite.

"About Augusta, fawning over Daddy." The words sounded slurred to her own ears. The water hadn't sobered her at all.

"Oh, Frances," her mother sighed, straightening. "Do you know how long it's been since anyone flirted with your father?"

She turned away, sliding the bowl onto the counter beside a stack of dessert plates. In the hall, a phone rang: Augusta's phone. Frances felt her shoulders clench, waiting for Augusta to answer it, but there were no footsteps. The shrill sound stopped, but after a few seconds it began to ring again.

Jean turned to her daughter. "You might want to get that, darling. It might be important."

Frances stalked into the hall, seething. Did Augusta know nothing about roaming charges? Of course she didn't. She was not the sort of person who shopped around for the best monthly plan. She fished the phone out of Augusta's purse and barked, with more force than was strictly necessary, "Yes?"

A moment's hesitation on the other line, and then an Englishman's voice: "I'm sorry, I must have the wrong number. I'm trying to reach Augusta Price."

Frances bit back annoyance. The English were always sorry, or at least they pretended to be. "You have the right number. This is her friend."

"Oh." Now the man on the other end sounded even more confused. "I'm sorry. I didn't...I didn't know—"

"That she had a friend? Yes, well, the situation is

extremely fluid." Frances was pleased; it was something Augusta might have said. "One moment, I'll find her."

"If you could please tell her it's David, her agent."

Clapping a hand over the phone, Frances walked down the hall to the dining room. Where there was no one. For a moment she stood, confused. Augusta was gone; her father, in his wheelchair, was gone. A profound sense of dislocation ran through her: the Englishman's voice on the phone pulled her back to London, but she was here in California, her home.

She spun around, suddenly terrified. What if Augusta had run off with her dad? Wheeled off, more like. Hysterical laughter bubbled to her lips, and she heard a tinny voice on the telephone: "Hello? Augusta?"

From out in the driveway came a shriek, spine-piercing in the still night. Frances nearly dropped the phone as she ran to the front door and yanked it open. Across the road, past the cliff's edge, she could hear the sound of the surf. Moonlight picked out little peaks far out to sea. But there was silence from the front yard. Frances stepped out onto the porch and felt her stomach lurch.

There, at the top of the sloping driveway, next to the wheelchair-adapted Escalade, Augusta held onto Len's wheelchair with the tips of her fingers.

"Do it," her father said. His whisper carried on the night air.

Before Frances could rush down the stairs, Augusta had let go, the wheelchair picking up speed as it careered down the grade toward Moonstone Drive and the cliff beyond. Len squealed, hands clutching the armrests. He had a few seconds' head start before Augusta began thumping down the slope after him.

Catch him, Frances thought, *catch him*, while another part of her brain noted: *She's moving fast for a drunk in heels.* It looked as if Augusta *would* catch him, the distance between her outstretched hand and Len's chair narrowing, until she stumbled and nearly fell. Frances let out a froggy croak of fear. Augusta righted herself and plunged on. At the last moment, just as Len touched the edge of the road, she reached out to snatch a handle, yanking the chair in a wild, spinning arc.

Panting, she pulled Len's chair to a stop and turned to Frances with a triumphant smile. She swept the hair off her forehead and said, "I used to do that with Charlie's pushchair."

Frances felt the sag begin in her knees and she slumped against the doorframe. From the phone in her hand she could hear David's voice: "Augusta? What is that noise? Has there been an accident?"

Len Bleeker took a deep breath. There was a vivid pink flush on his cheeks. He slowly turned his wheelchair at the foot of the drive and beamed up at his daughter.

"Frances," he said. "I like your friend."

thirty-six

Her fingers traced the words she'd carved into the bench twenty years before. The summer Frances turned eleven, she read the Brontë sisters and cursed the fate that placed her in a tiny town on California's coast, and not on Yorkshire's moors, where she belonged. The words were still there: *Frances Suzanne Bleeker, here 2day gone 2moro.*

And back the day after that. She straightened up, trying to spot sea lions' heads in the water below. But the sea was black, and the moon had ducked behind clouds. Len and Jean Bleeker were tucked up in bed, Len vivid and preening from his adventure. He'd cackled with pride even as they placed him on the stairlift. Frances wasn't sure whether to report Augusta to the police or give her a medal.

She heard the gravel crunch on the path behind her, smelled the Benson & Hedges and Arpège.

"Darling," said Augusta as she sat down heavily. "It's time to pack the sled and say mush."

"We'll be gone soon," said Frances. "Only three more days before we fly back."

"You don't understand," said Augusta. "We must leave sooner than that." She placed a hand on Frances's knee. "David has secured a reading for me. It seems the actress who had stolen my role has become unavailable. Something about a surgery gone terribly wrong."

"Oh, yes. You mentioned this. A miniseries, isn't it? *Circle of Deceit*."

"*Circle of Lies*, darling. A subtle but crucial distinction. And this role will return me to my proper place. A bit of press, perhaps even some attention during awards season…" Her face fell ever so slightly. "Of course, it's been a while since I read for a producer. Or had to memorize lines. I'm not entirely sure I'd know what to do in an audition any longer."

Frances felt an odd rush of tenderness. "But you want to do this?"

"Of course I do. I must work, darling. Work is what remains, after everything else has gone. *Arbeit macht frei*, if I may quote the Nazis without reproach. Work is what we leave in the world. Even if it's rubbish, which is usually the case."

Frances hugged herself. If they went back to London, and Augusta returned to work, she could finish the outline of the book. It would be the path back to self-respect, for both of them. She looked out over the dark ocean, toward home. "That book advance isn't coming, is it, Augusta? The publisher's not sending any money."

Augusta shifted on the bench beside her. "I'm afraid not, darling. At least not in time to help us."

It was comforting to hear the truth spoken for once. "I'll change our tickets," Frances said. "We'll go home early."

Augusta clutched her hand, and Frances realized for the first time how small it was, a child's hand. When Augusta spoke, her voice caught: "Thank you, Frances. You've been so good to me. Almost like a — well, not like a paid servant, anyway."

Unpaid servant, Frances thought. "Two things, though. When we get back to London we must begin seriously on the book."

"Absolutely." Augusta made the sign of the cross over the right side of her chest. "Virgin's honour."

"And I want you to give Kenneth Deller his computer back."

Augusta sucked in her breath, jerked her hand back.

Frances said, "It's not like you're mentioned in his book, anyway."

"Thank you for reminding me. I am quite aware of that absence." Augusta reached into her pocket, drew out a crumpled pack of cigarettes and a lighter. A small burst of flame lit her face, lengthened the bruised shadows under her eyes. "My son and his father seem to have forgotten that I was once a rather important part of their lives."

"I'm sorry, Augusta. Being ignored is worse than anything." Frances wrapped her arms around herself. "Believe me, I know."

It was a long time before Augusta spoke. "Eventually everything comes back to bite you in the arse," she said. "Even the things that used to kiss it."

* * *

Out on the driveway, Augusta crouched by Len Bleeker's wheelchair. Jean and Frances watched them through the window in the hall.

"That's another thing," Jean said. "No one ever bends down to your father's level anymore. He spent his whole life looking down on people, now he has to look up."

"She just wants him to look down her top," Frances said.

"Fine by me," Jean said. "He's tired of looking at mine."

Frances's mother went to the side table in the foyer and opened a drawer. She took out a thick wedge of cash, neatly gathered with a mother-of-pearl clip, and held it out to her daughter.

"No, Mom."

"Yes, Frances." Her mother took her hand and pressed the money into it. She didn't let go. "I don't want you feeling badly about this. Everyone needs help from time to time. When you finish helping Augusta with her book, you can pay us back, if you'd like."

The bills in her hand were worn and soft, a pleasing thickness, comforting as a duvet. Frances wondered how long her mother had stashed them in the drawer, waiting for an emergency like this. The fact that her parents knew, in advance, that she'd need rescuing was more than she could bear. She pressed the money back into her mother's hands.

"I can't."

Her mother drew a sharp, exasperated breath. "Of course you can, sweetheart—"

"Mom." Frances felt her teeth come together, hard. "It's not about the money. It's about me picking myself up—"

"And we can't help you?"

"—on my own," Frances finished. "I would just like to feel, for one day, that I was capable of fixing my own fuck-ups."

Her mother pursed her lips at the profanity, and Frances thought how easy it would be to run up to her room, to hide here in a house gleaming with lemon polish, unsullied by doubt.

"Oh, Mom," she whispered. "I'd wanted to come back with more than this. A bit more to show for myself."

Jean shook her head and placed the money on top of the side table. She cupped her daughter's face, and there was something in her eyes Frances did not want to see. "I dropped out of college to marry your father," she said. "I've looked after him ever since. Every day I worry that my life's been a waste." She slid her hands around Frances's waist and gripped tightly. "At least you've had adventures."

There was a choking tightness in Frances's throat. "You know what you can give me, though? Some Kleenex for my purse. I have a friend who hates the sight of tears."

thirty-seven

Augusta's eyes were closed when they pulled into a Chevron station on the outskirts of Ventura. She did not hear Frances get out of the car and close the door as gently as possible. She woke only when Frances returned, slamming the door and throwing herself into the driver's seat. The girl slapped the steering wheel with open palms.

"They took my goddamn credit card."

Augusta struggled to remember where she was. The air smelled of petrol and chewing gum. A bright light bathed the car, but beyond the pool of light was nothing but darkness and the sound of motorway traffic.

"Oh, no," she said. "Was it a stick-up?"

Frances turned to look at her, and Augusta was pleased to see that she had not, as of yet, started crying.

"They confiscated my card, Augusta." Her hand flapped at the little shop, glowing in the dark. "The girl took it... she saw some message on the display, and she snatched it right back out of my hands. Like I was a criminal." Augusta saw an ominous glint in the corner of Frances's eye. "She couldn't have been more than eighteen, and here she is taking away my credit card."

Augusta considered the gravity of this disaster. She said, "Did you at least get my cigarettes?"

A pack of Benson & Hedges landed in her lap.

"I think the kid felt sorry for me," Frances said. "Which is terrific. A girl wearing braces who works in a Ventura gas station feels sorry for me." She turned to Augusta. "You're sure you didn't bring a credit card?"

"No, darling, I told you. My credit cards are in a safe-deposit box in Zurich along with my diamonds and bullion." Augusta rolled down the window and threw the cigarette wrapping out. "We can do without at this stage, surely? We're flying home tomorrow evening. We can sleep in the car if need be. There is always the business lounge at the airport if we need sustenance. I shall tutor you in the dark arts."

Frances was silent, her gaze lost in the distance.

"Frances?"

"There's a fee for changing our flights home," she said. "$150 each. We have to pay at the airport before they'll let us on the flight. I was going to charge it."

Augusta undid her seat belt, which suddenly felt constricting. Her dream in reach, now floating away.

"I have to get home," she said. "I need to get that script from David for the audition."

"Yes," said Frances absently. She was silent for a moment. "There is something we could do."

"Return to that lovely motel in Hollywood and offer to perform sex acts on the local citizenry? I nominate you, darling. Your joints are much more flexible."

Frances's eyes were cool in the dim light of the car. "We could return the computer to Deller. I'll bet he'd happily lend us a few hundred bucks if we gave it back."

Augusta shrank back in her seat. She pulled the laptop close to her chest. "I much prefer my plan."

thirty-eight

"There!" Augusta shouted. "Pull over, for God's sake."

"Augusta," said Frances, knuckles pale on the wheel, "there are six lanes of traffic preventing me from pulling over. You cannot bend the freeway to your will."

But of course she could. A mile later Frances found an exit, circled, and took the first northbound ramp. They drove back up the Ventura Freeway. After a few minutes, Augusta gestured frantically at the neon sign and they pulled into a parking lot filled almost entirely with pickup trucks.

"The Lonely Heifer," said Augusta, as she stepped out of the car. "One lonely heifer calling to another. Kismet, don't you think?"

Frances looked at the bar in front of them. A honky-tonk, her mother would have called it. A pair of ox horns hung over the front door, and a sign in the window showed the cartoon of an angry bull's face next to the words, TAKE THE BULL BY THE HORNS. BEAT JERRY AND WIN BIG! Their rental car sat dwarfed between two Dodge Rams.

One of them had a bumper sticker, its message nearly obscured by mud: DRIVER ONLY CARRIES $20 WORTH OF AMMUNITION.

"Nice place," said Frances.

Augusta was already dragging her toward the door. "We need to regroup, darling. A winning strategy is always aided by a few drinks. So said Churchill."

"There's the small matter of us having zero money."

Augusta regarded her with pity. "Have I taught you nothing in all this time?"

"I'm driving, Augusta."

"No, you're whinging." Augusta pushed her back an arm's length and stared at her in the parking lot's halogen glow. "Trust me, self-pity does nothing for your complexion."

Frances was working on a retort when Augusta pulled her through the doors. It was dark inside, the gloom cut by the light of a dozen neon beer signs. Faith Hill was singing that love was merely an illusion. A line of men stood at the bar, watching a car race on a giant television. Almost as one, they turned when the door opened.

The fellow nearest the door was a giant in pressed jeans, his head a granite slab under a greying crew cut. He saw Augusta and the rock of his face split in a wide smile.

Augusta whispered, "My God, you grow them large in this country. That one's the size of a fridge. No, he's the size of the box the fridge came in."

She tossed her hair back as if the stage manager had just called her entrance, and strode to the bar.

"Fine! I'm going to the ladies,'" Frances called after her. She spoke to empty air.

Sighing, she headed for a sign on the wall that said HEIFERS. She passed an empty dance floor, and a corral next to it where a mechanical bull sat, still and riderless, under a spotlight. A cluster of foam mattresses were piled under the bull, their covers worn with hard use. On the wooden fence separating the bull from the bar was another sign: CAN YOU BEAT JERRY? WIN $200. NO BULL!

There was a chair in the restroom and Frances collapsed into it. The latest indignity was too much to bear. To be without a credit card—to have it repossessed, as if she were a criminal—it felt as though the ground had given way beneath her. Why had she never appreciated the sweet, sweet sound of the cash-dispensing machine when she'd had a chance? The click of the money-gate opening, the swish of bills sliding through. A quotidian act of magic, taken for granted.

Every day with Augusta had felt like the end of the road, and yet there always seemed to be more road taking them into the unknown. Frances looked at herself in the mirror. She was tired of being a thing at the end of a string, jerked and pulled this way and that. She could take control of this one moment. The journey back to self-respect could begin with one small step. For Augusta's sake, and her own, there was only one thing she could do.

With shaking hands, Frances reached into her purse and pulled out her phone. She scrolled to her sent messages, and found the address and phone number Augusta had sent from Mr. Romance's house. She typed a message quickly and, before she could think twice, hit Send.

Mr Deller u can find us Lonely Heifer, Ventura Frway. We have whats yours

At the bar, she found Augusta cementing her friendship with the giant. Ross—Frances thought he was called Ross, but it might have been Hoss, or even Boss—was a divorced building contractor. He was also missing a finger on his left hand.

Augusta appeared to be enjoying Ross's courtliness, and not paying for her drinks. She did not even seem to mind the beefy four-pronged hand at the small of her back, or that he was inhaling her cloud of hair.

A trio of drinks appeared on the bar in front of them. Ross cupped the tequila glass, brought it to his mouth, and slammed it empty on the bar.

"Now you," he said to Augusta. "If you think you can take it."

She raised an eyebrow at him. "Do I look like a woman who's having her first shooter?" She raised her drink to him. "Up your auntie." And with one smooth motion she tipped it into her mouth and slid the glass across the bar for a refill.

The big man clapped Augusta on the shoulder and nearly sent her flying. Kenny Chesney was singing about wanting to quit women and whisky, and Augusta raised her voice over the music: "What terrible accident befell your hand?"

Ross leaned closer, slid a hand down Augusta's back: "What's that, honey?"

"You appear to be short a digit," Augusta yelled.

"Oh," he said, taking a long pull from his beer. "Wedding ring. Didn't notice it was caught in the gate of my truck. Slammed it shut. Goodbye finger."

"Did you hear that?" Augusta said to Frances, sliding a

shooter toward her. "Marriage is hazardous to the health. As I have always said. But no one listens."

In the light of the Miller High Life signs on the wall, Augusta was savage and beautiful. She glowed with the success of her nine-fingered conquest. The men in the bar, even the young ones, watched her over the tops of their beer. Frances, on the other hand, felt green and queasy, and not because of the tequilas that Ross and his friends kept buying. She had done a very bad thing.

Or perhaps it was a very good thing, but it was too soon to tell. They were in the eye of the storm, the period before chaos descended, and only Frances saw it coming. Augusta was oblivious, and fond of their new friends.

Frances spun her stool away and nearly slid off. Too much tequila, too many nerves. In the mechanical bull's enclosure, one of the bar staff was checking the saddle, pulling on the cinch that kept it in place. The saddle's horn was shiny with use, its stirrups scuffed and peeling.

"You gonna give old Jerry a try?"

Frances spun back around to face the bar. "I beg your pardon?"

The bartender had a wide, friendly face, square teeth set in a square jaw. An American face. "Contest starts in twenty minutes. Every Friday night, all these boys try to beat Jerry. Stay on his back two minutes, win two hundred bucks."

"I could use two hundred bucks."

The bartender laughed. "Get in line, sweetheart." He poured a tequila; the shot glass was dwarfed in his wide brown hands. Sliding it across the bar, he said, "This is on Ross's tab."

Frances stared at it. One more drink and she'd be under the table, but she wanted to be oblivious for what was to come. She whispered, "I've done a very bad thing."

The bartender looked at her for a minute, and the concern in his eyes might have been professional, or it might not. "You and me and everyone in this place."

The bartender moved on to serve another customer. Augusta loudly regaled Ross and his friends with a story about a famous action star whose wig had fallen off mid-coitus. How long did it take to drive from Los Angeles to Ventura? There was still time to make a confession and escape. Closing her eyes, Frances poured the drink down her throat. It was vile, and wonderful.

thirty-nine

The bearded man whipsawed off the back of Jerry the bull, sailed through the air and landed with a thud that shook the entire bar.

"Dear God," said Augusta, thrilled. "That was like watching the Leaning Tower of Pisa fall."

Ross hooted. "Tower of Pizza, more like."

Frances slid from her stool and stumbled over to the fence surrounding Jerry's corral. The bearded man lay on his back on a battered foam mattress, unmoving. She leaned closer: the white lettering on his T-shirt ("Free Moustache Rides") was definitely quivering; a slight movement, but movement nonetheless.

She turned back to the bar and shouted, "He's alive!"

"'Course he's alive," said the bartender, whose name, she had learned, was Kyle. "That boy comes in here and falls off every week, regular as clockwork. He's got Kentucky-fried brains." Behind her, the fallen contestant groaned and rolled to his side.

Frances made her way carefully back to the bar. It had

been ninety minutes since she'd sent the text, plenty of time to get from West L.A. to Ventura. Perhaps he wasn't coming. Perhaps he couldn't care less.

"Augusta," she said, as she slipped back onto her stool. "I should tell you something."

Ross had his face buried in Augusta's neck but she shrugged him off.

"Are you all right, darling?" She leaned in closer to peer at Frances. "Are you going to be sick? Shall I take you outside?"

There was worry in her voice, and Frances felt a pang of remorse at the betrayal she had just set in motion. "No, I'm fine. It's just—"

"That's good," said Augusta. "Because I want you to see me squeeze the life out of that bull."

Frances shook her head to clear the tequila from her ears. "I thought I just heard you say—"

"That I'm going to ride the bull. Yes." Augusta tipped a shot of tequila into her mouth and squeezed a lime in after. She seemed at once incredibly drunk and remarkably sober, an ancient sea captain who no longer feels the force of the waves.

This was more chaos than Frances was prepared to handle. "Augusta," she said, "that's insane."

But Augusta was already standing. "You worry too much," she said. "I once played a witch on an episode of *Hammer House of Horror*, and I was required to ride a horse." She paused. "Though it might have been a donkey."

"That thing," Frances pointed at the bull, now riderless. "That thing will kill you."

273

"Ridiculous. Do we or do we not need two hundred dollars?"

Frances felt defeat settle on her. "We do."

"Well, then. You're just worried I'll end up crippled and you'll have to change my catheter. Which may be a valid fear." She brushed the hair from Frances's forehead, a disturbingly maternal gesture. "If I break my neck, I bequeath you everything I don't own."

Ross, swaying, turned to the bar: "This little English girl's gonna ride Jerry! Show you ladies how it's done." A chorus of jeers greeted this announcement.

It seemed imperative to Frances that she stop this madness. There must be a brake somewhere. Hysteria would only act as a goad. So she counted slowly to ten, though she missed seven and had to go back.

She took Augusta's arm, careful not to seem desperate, and said, "Look, I understand that you think we need the cash. But we don't. I can call my parents in the morning, they'll transfer the money to my account. We're fine."

Augusta put her hand on Frances's and squeezed. The beam from the fly-speckled light above had shrunk the bar so it was just the two of them, a pair of actors oblivious to their audience. Augusta held the girl's eyes.

"Is that what you want, to ask your mother for help? I believe you turned her down once already. I don't want you to sell your independence for me." Frances didn't know what to say. Slowly, Augusta peeled the girl's hand from her shoulder. "You've done so much already, Frances. Don't think I don't know. Let me do this. For us."

Augusta slid off her stool, suddenly the clearest head in the room. She blazed with purpose, and her light fell across

Frances's clouded brain, illuminating something that had always been there. *She's happy because she's going to perform*, Frances thought. *Even if she dies, it'll be fine because she's dying on stage.*

She reached for Augusta's arm but her hand flailed at empty air. Augusta had dropped her purse on the floor, the computer landing with a crack that echoed above the sound system's steel guitars. She strode toward the bull as if she were making an entrance on opening night.

"Even if you win it's not enough money," Frances yelled. The words formed a slurry cake in her mouth.

Augusta ignored her. She had reached the fence. The hooting in the bar reached a deafening pitch, and Ross was howling like a coyote. An assistant opened the gate and Augusta strode toward the mechanical bull, her hair a torch under the overhead light.

Frances wished she could remember the words to Hail Mary, which her friend Katie had taught her in ninth grade, when it appeared Katie might be pregnant and destined for an overseas convent school. In the corral, Augusta kicked off her heels and held one bare foot out to the bull wrangler.

"Ready for mounting."

"You are bloody well not!"

The voice cut through the babble, drowning out Luke Bryan on the jukebox. Frances knew exactly who it was before she turned to the door and saw the tall man she'd met at Fantasmagoria™. She recognized his dark suit and broken nose, if not the lurid purple bruise on his temple. His mouth was set in a hard, bitter line. In Deller's shadow stood Charles, the boy from the bookstore. Augusta's son. Frances felt her stomach lurch. She hadn't expected the boy.

Augusta was immobile under the harsh lights, one hand on the saddle, her mouth a black cave of surprise. In a second, though, she made her decision: stepping hard on the assistant's cupped hands, she swung herself into the saddle.

Kenneth moved quickly across the bar, shoving people out of the way with both hands.

"Get down," he barked.

"Piss off," Augusta responded, and flung a thumb up at the assistant. He moved over to the controls, and the bull began a slow gyration, gently tipping forward and back.

"Augusta," Ken called. "You're no good to me dead." He plunged toward the corral, but Ross pulled him up short.

"Hey," said the contractor, "I don't know where you come from, but this is a free country. Let the lady ride."

Frances heard an echoing murmur: "Let 'er ride." Ken removed Ross's hands and shoved him away, roughly. Ross shoved back. Charles suddenly bobbed up between them, a puppy between two mastiffs.

"Get out of my way," Kenneth snarled.

Ross leaned in, pumped with the courage of Sauza Gold: "Who the hell are you, the king of England?"

Kenneth grabbed a handful of Ross's shirt: "We don't have a king, you imbecile."

Suddenly a shriek sliced through the bar. Charles whirled away from the two men and ran toward the corral. *I don't want to look*, Frances thought, *I don't want to look*. But she did.

Augusta's hair whipped behind her as her head snapped up and down, side to side. Jerry heaved and bucked, but she stayed on. Improbably, against the odds, she was beating the bull.

At the side of the ring, the assistant grimaced. He pulled a lever toward him and suddenly the bull's movements became frenzied. It whipped this way and that, pitching and rearing like a boat caught in a hurricane swell. Augusta's face was white with concentration. The bull gave one diabolical twist and Frances heard, from beside her, a strangled shout: "Mum!"

Augusta must have heard it too because she looked up and in that moment when her attention strayed her hand slipped from the saddle. They watched as she arced gracefully through the air and plummeted toward the earth.

The ambulance doors shut. It turned out of the parking lot onto the freeway, lights flashing. "I'll meet you at the hospital, Frances," Kenneth said. "Charles, are you coming?"

The boy stood next to Frances, shivering in the night air. He wore only a T-shirt and Frances wondered, absurdly, if anyone had ever told him to put on a sweater when he went outside. Charles shook his head. Ken seemed to want to say something, but he merely nodded and gripped the young man's shoulder.

"2002," said the boy, his eyes on the ambulance as it disappeared into traffic.

They both turned to look at him. "Easter, 2002."

"Dear God, yes." Kenneth began to laugh, caught himself, sputtered to a stop. "We had to pack your mother into an ambulance then, too."

"She said she'd taken too many antihistamines. For an allergy I'd never heard of until that moment," Charles said. "I never asked her how many antihistamines you had to take before you passed out in the gravy."

Ken reached over to pull the boy close, but Charles remained stiff in his arms. Frances caught the edge of a whisper: "—you will try to come?" Augusta's son remained impassive, and Kenneth sighed. He took out his wallet, removed some cash, put it in Charles's hand. With a nod to Frances, he got in his car.

Frances looked over at Charles, who seemed to have aged ten years. She wished she had a jacket to lend him.

"This has been an exceptionally odd day," she said.

"Not really," Charles said. "It's my childhood all over again."

forty

The curtains rattled as they were drawn back around the cubicle where Augusta lay, prone and neck-braced, in the emergency ward. She struggled to raise her head, but a stabbing pain forced her to sink back onto the pillow. She tried to peer over the stiff brace. Perhaps Charles had come to see her.

It wasn't her son. She closed her eyes. Why hadn't he come? Frances was here, dispatched to the hospital's cafeteria to find coffee. Kenneth was here, sitting at the side of her bed, head hung low, hands clasped between his knees. But no sight of her boy.

Somewhere nearby a woman was gasping and crying to God. The air smelled of chicken soup and disinfectant. When Augusta opened her eyes, she saw a doctor leaning over her. He looked younger than Charles, but his eyes were cool and appraising. She didn't think she could outwit him.

"Miss Price?" he said, checking her chart. "I'm Dr. Khan. How are you feeling?"

"You should see the other bull," she murmured.

He didn't smile, but leaned over her to shine a small torch into her eyes. "Look to the right, please."

But when she looked to the right, she saw Kenneth and the livid purple bruise on the side of his head. The walking wounded.

Kenneth said, "Will you be able to discharge her soon, doctor?"

"I think so. It's fairly mild soft-tissue trauma," said Khan. "Although I'd like her to stay until the effects of the intoxicants wear off." He folded his arms across his chest. "How much have you had to drink this evening?"

Augusta's mouth opened, closed. She told him.

The doctor nodded. "I've already seen the toxicology results. I just wanted to know if you'd tell the truth." He touched her wrist lightly and left, drawing the curtain behind him.

Bloody doctor cares more about me than my own son does, she thought, and a phlegmy wave of self-pity washed over her. She heard Deller rise from his chair.

"You will be the death of me, Augusta."

"And you me."

He rubbed his eyes with the heel of his hand. "Must you always be on show?"

She slid her gaze away, for this did not merit the dignity of a response. On the other side of the curtain, the woman's sobbing had turned to a long, sustained groan. It was the ninth circle of hell; it was hell and she was alone.

"Ken," she whispered. "Why didn't Charles come?"

Under the harsh hospital lights, his face was exhausted and drained of colour. "He's not a dog, Augusta. He's not going to suddenly jump when you whistle."

"So it's all my fault."

She watched him pace to the curtain and back. After a minute he said, "You might at least have apologized to the lad."

Pain shot through her neck as she turned to glare at him. "For what, exactly?"

"For what?" He loomed over her. His voice, usually so low and measured, rose to a shout: "You made him choose between us!"

Augusta was wondering how best to damage his smug face when a nurse slid the curtains open and stared at each of them in turn. "Is there a problem?"

"No," said Ken. He sank back down on the chair.

"Only my taste in men," muttered Augusta.

The nurse shook her head, closing the curtains behind her as she left. Augusta folded her arms across her chest, ignoring the tears that had pooled near her ears. She wouldn't give the bastard the satisfaction of seeing her wipe them away.

She felt something placed at her fingertips, heard the crinkle of paper. With an effort, she raised her head enough so that she could see over the brace: a familiar shiny square lay on her chest, its blue-and-white wrapping unchanged since she was a girl.

"A peace offering," Ken said. "A Kendal Mint Cake. I remembered you liked them. There's a shop in Santa Monica…" His voice trailed off. He moved the hair off her neck, brushed the tears away with the back of his fingers. "Do you remember that time we went to the Lake District, like normal people?"

"And you left me in Windermere," Augusta said.

"Because you picked a fight with some old brigadier in the dining room. I can never go back to that B&B. I'm a wanted man in Windermere."

"Don't make me laugh, it hurts."

He unwrapped the sweet and put it on the table next to the bed, on top of a form that waited for her signature. Dear God, she'd have to pay for this somehow. She never imagined that she'd long for the NHS, with its filthy corners and day-long queues. How many arms and legs would she owe this expensive American hospital? Kenneth saw her gaze and flipped the form over.

Irritated, she reached for it and a hot pain seared from ear to shoulder. She cried out, and he took her hand awkwardly, as if afraid he'd make it worse. It occurred to her that she might be more badly hurt than she knew. A blood clot on the brain, perhaps. These could be their last moments together.

She said, "Ken, why am I not in your book?"

He looked at her as if she were mad. "Really, Augusta? Even now?"

"That's not an answer."

He shrugged. "I thought you wouldn't want to be."

"Perhaps a little, in a flattering light."

"Ah," he said. "So you wanted me to lie."

Her eyes flew open, and a little squeal escaped from her mouth.

"Oh, fuck," she whispered. "Your computer. I left it in my bag, in the bar." She closed her eyes. "It'll be gone by now."

"Is that all you're worried about?"

"Isn't that enough?"

He slumped back down on the chair. "Augusta, you are a savage. I have other copies of that bloody file."

For a moment neither of them spoke. Finally, she said, "All for nothing, then."

"I'm afraid so. Though I am upset at having lost all my porn."

Frances arrived with coffee to find them convulsed with silent laughter. She stood at the edge of the curtain, a cup in each hand, and wondered how you could want to kill someone in a single moment and laugh helplessly with them the next. It seemed an exhausting way to live.

forty-one

Augusta examined her neck in the gauzy reflection of her favourite mirror, which hung in the hallway of her flat. She had chosen the mirror because it was ancient and scratched and kind; Vaseline on the lens of her life. The soreness in her neck was slowly fading, as the doctor in Ventura had said it would.

The plane ride home had been agony, or would have been but for the bottle of Percocet in her carry-on. Augusta had reached in periodically to slip one under her tongue and wash it back on a tide of vodka. She christened this "The Velvet Hammer." Frances huffed every time Augusta bent down, wincing, to fill her plastic cup under her seat. Finally the girl snatched the bottle from her hand and stuffed it in the overhead bin.

Augusta stared into the mirror, stroking her throat. The sun had given her some colour; she looked reasonably healthy, all things considered. Ready for the camera.

"How is poor Kenneth?" asked Alma Partridge, seated at the dining room table. "Still suffering your abuse?"

With an effort, Augusta turned her head and smiled sweetly at her friend. "He lives, darling. My mission failed."

Alma chuckled. "I fully expect that the two of you shall come to my funeral, hand in hand, and retire to your bedsit in Croydon where you'll spend the evening watching *Midsomer Murders*."

"A love story for the ages," Augusta said, and sat down at the table to pick up her script. She did not tell Alma that Kenneth had paid her hospital bill, nor that he promised to show her his manuscript before it was published. Nor did she mention that Charles had not visited once during the two days she'd spent in hospital.

"Where were we?"

Alma adjusted her reading glasses. "I believe I was begging you not to reveal my nefarious sex-trafficking activities to the authorities."

"Ah, yes." Augusta flipped through the script and found her place. She sat up straighter, ignoring the pain in her neck, and spoke from her diaphragm: "It's no use, Jonathan," she said, in a voice high and strained. "What I've seen can't be unseen."

Alma responded gruffly: "Think of all we've been through, Tessa. I beg you. Doesn't our love count for anything?" Alma brought the script closer to her eyes and tossed it on the table. "What a load of yeasty balls! Good luck saying these lines, my dear."

Augusta sighed and reached for the teapot. Alma was right: *Circle of Lies* was melodramatic crap. But it would be award-winning, high-profile crap. Tessa was the role that would catapult her back into the public's good graces. First, however, she would have to read once again for the producers. The thought made her mouth go dry. It had been so long since she'd had to prove her mettle; what if her mettle had fled?

She shook her head, banishing the thought. "More tea?" She filled Alma's cup from a pot she'd found at the back of the cupboard, rinsing the dust away with hot water. Her flat was filled with tea. When she was a child, her mother had to choose between only two brands of tea, Typhoo and PG tips. It was all orange pekoe, builder's tea. Now the shops were filled with dozens of blends, a jungle of fruity and minty flavours.

She longed for a real drink but for the past three days she'd kept the longing in check. When she wanted to reach for a glass, she picked up the script instead. When she felt the storm of recriminations and guilt brewing inside her, she took a Percocet, and all was calm again. When Charles's pale face rose in front of her, aghast, she shut her eyes.

The doorbell rang. Augusta peered through the peephole even though she knew who it was.

"Darling," she said, as Frances came in. "You are punctuality itself." The girl looked exhilarated, as if she'd drawn energy from the air of California. The trip that had nearly killed Augusta had restored Frances's zing. Just as she'd promised.

"You look like a woman who could use some tea," Augusta said, and Frances raised an eyebrow at the pot. "Yes," said Augusta drily. "Actual tea."

Alma rose from her seat, balancing with one shaky hand on the table. Augusta took her other arm and drew her close. "Alma Partridge," she said, "please meet Frances Bleeker."

The young woman held out a hand: "It's lovely to meet you finally. Augusta has told me so much about you. Her old friend." Frances turned red as soon as the words left her mouth. "Not that I meant old—"

"And you are the new friend," Alma said, taking her hand. "Not an easy task. I congratulate you on surviving."

"I'm not actually Helen Keller," said Augusta. "I can hear you."

Her neck gave a twinge, and she put a hand up to it. She needed a Percocet. Before she could excuse herself, Frances placed an envelope on the table. "The outline for the next six chapters," she said. "Overcoming Despair, Dull Dinner Parties, Unwelcome Advances, Bad Haircuts, Fabric Stains, and Heartbreak."

"The totality of life," Alma marvelled. "I should have placed them in exactly that order."

"Thank you, darling," said Augusta. "I look forward to writing more of..." Her hand flapped in the air.

"*Deep-End Diva*," Frances finished.

"Precisely. I do appreciate that you're doing so much of the dreary shovelling, Frances. I'll be toiling with you as soon as I've finished work on *Circle of Lies*." Saying the title made it seem real, an apparition that wouldn't fade with dawn.

The girl picked up her tea. "I'm enjoying the writing, weirdly enough. I think perhaps I was meant to be a ghost."

Augusta slid a hand onto Frances's shoulder, patting awkwardly. A strand of dark hair had escaped from her ponytail, and Augusta had the sudden urge to tuck it in.

Her *Circle of Lies* script sat on the table, thick with notes. On each page Augusta had tried to mine some nugget that would illuminate Tessa's character. Its front cover was worn where she'd clenched it.

"You'll both remember the audition?" Augusta forced a note of confidence into her voice. "My two-person fan club?"

"Alma will pick you up in a minicab," said Frances. "And I'll meet you at the studio. I have it written down." She stood up, smoothing her denim skirt and wobbling ever so slightly on wedge-heeled sandals. For the first time, Augusta noticed, she'd made an effort to look smart. No, not smart—sexy. Gold hoops at her ears, a touch of lip gloss on her nervous smile.

"I'll see you both on Thursday," Frances said. "Lovely to meet you, Alma."

Suddenly Augusta didn't want to see her go. "You can stay for supper, if you'd like. Alma and I are going to Camden for a spot of rat kebab."

"I can't," said Frances. "I've got a date." She reached out impulsively and took Augusta's recoiling body in her arms. It was like a hug you give the dying, Augusta thought. "Don't worry," Frances whispered into Augusta's ear. "Everything will be fine."

forty-two

"This," said Stanley, "is pretty much *The Economist* of feline periodicals."

Frances brought the candle closer to the centre of the table to peer at the magazine. A tabby with green eyes stared at her with its species' singular blend of malevolence and self-belief.

"Look at the cover lines. They're doing some good work. There's a story about the crap hygiene in rescue centres. And here—" He flipped through the glossy pages, past adverts for flea drops and toy mice. "I've never read better reporting on feline herpes."

Frances stared at him, her lips twitching. He leaned back in his chair, flinging the magazine onto the table. "Fuck me," he said. "I'm actually considering becoming editor of *Caring Cat Monthly*." He slumped in his chair. "I'm a cat hack."

Frances smiled at him, an idiotic grin that reflected neither of their realities. Sitting here with him in a little tapas restaurant in Marylebone filled her with an unfamiliar joy.

He looked exhausted, but somehow lighter, as if losing his job had removed a heavy weight.

"It could be worse," Frances said. "You could be ghost-writing a self-help book for a pickled actress. For very little money."

"Is it as bad as that?"

Frances remembered the sharp stab of terror she'd felt when she saw Augusta crumpled on the floor of the bar. "No, not really. There's something quite endearing about pickled actresses." She poked at the *patatas bravas* on her plate. "It's not her I'm worried about. It's me. Where I go from here." She looked up at him, forcing a smile, and noticed that he'd missed his usual small patch of stubble while shaving. Before she could stop herself, she reached out and brushed his cheek, a fleeting touch. He caught her fingers and held them.

"You mustn't worry," he said. "I know it seems grim. I know it seems like the slough of despond, but—"

"At least it's not Slough."

"Yes." He let go of her hand to fill her wine glass. "You're going to be fine, Frances. You've still got plenty of good years ahead of you."

Count to ten, Frances thought and closed her eyes. *Count to ten thousand. You are neither going to hit him nor cry.*

"Stanley," she said after a minute.

"I've said the wrong thing again, haven't I?"

After dinner they began walking up Marylebone High Street, into a biting wind. Stanley's trench coat flapped behind him, and Frances tugged her jacket tightly around her.

"What I was trying to say before, quite badly, is that you have your whole future in front of you." Stanley stopped and looked down at her. He swung his hand toward her, palm up, and Frances realized he wanted her to take it. Without a word, she slipped her hand in his.

The moon came and went with the clouds. Stanley's palm was warm and dry against hers, a small point of contact that sent all of her dials spinning. Her shoulder bumped against his as he stopped by the wrought iron gates of St. Marylebone Parish Church. A collection of ancient headstones jutted from the grass in front of its walls.

"They all survived," Frances said, pointing at the graves.

"Until they didn't."

"The point is, they did survive. Cholera and tuberculosis and worse. Worse than anything we've had." She turned to him, but his face was lost in shadow. "Lift me up."

"What?"

"Lift me over this fence. We're going in. Let's see how long those poor bastards lasted. That should cheer us up."

"You're daft," he said, but she could hear something else in his voice. Admiration? Surprise? Frances lifted one leg toward him, her skirt falling back. He took a half-step toward her, his hand under her leg. One thumb traced the swell of her thigh, and she heard him say, "Frances…"

"Leg up," she whispered. "And I'll meet you in the graveyard."

Stanley braced himself and thrust her upward. She grasped the spikes at the top of the gate and moved to—

"Everything all right here, Miss?"

They froze. Stanley's hand was lost under her skirt, her leg halfway up the fence. Slowly, they both turned to find a policeman staring at them, unamused.

He said again, "You all right, miss?" Frances sank back down the fence till both feet were on the ground.

"Does it look like she's being assaulted?" Stanley had moved away from the fence and now stood glowering at the cop. She put a hand on his arm.

"I wasn't talking to you, sir. Miss?"

"I'm fine, officer, thank you. We just decided to go for a walk and…" She aimed for a girlish giggle. "Well, the church is so pretty. I was hoping to see it up close."

For a moment the cop peered at Stanley's face, which had begun to look like a kettle on the boil. Finally he turned to Frances: "That's fine, miss. I'll have to ask you to leave the churchyard, please. It's locked for a reason. You can come back in the morning."

"Have a good night, officer."

"And you as well, miss." He turned to Stanley with an expression of barely controlled distaste. "Sir."

They watched him head south down Marylebone High Street, occasionally peering into parked cars as he went.

She tried to tug Stanley away, but he resisted. "What the fuck was that about? He thought I was an old perv, didn't he?" He stared off at the policeman's retreating back and yelled: "It's my hair. It's PREMATURE!"

With that, Frances was lost. She bent double with laughter, wheezing. Every time she tried to catch her breath, the absurdity hit her again and she started shaking.

"It's not nice laughing at an old man," Stanley said gravely.

"You're right. I might have given you a coronary." Frances was still wheezing, and she turned to him, grabbing the lapels of his coat to steady herself. *Take the hint*, she thought. *For once, take the hint.* For once, he did.

He brushed the back of his hand across her face and bent toward her. It was as if her strings had been cut. She felt the buckle of his belt scrape against her belly, tasted salt and wine as he kissed her. She pulled his head down so she could press her lips to the small unshaven patch at the curve of his jaw.

forty-three

It was 10:19 a.m., or, less than a minute since she'd last checked the time. Frances forced herself to put her phone away. Staring at it wouldn't help. She tried to smile at Augusta's agent, sitting opposite her, but his expression was frozen in dismay. He looked as if his face had been caught in a bus door.

For the fourth time in ten minutes, David got out of his seat, went to the outer door of the waiting room, and peered down the hall. He came back to his seat, lips working, and pulled his phone from his inside pocket. Even in her own anxiety, Frances felt sorry for him: he had no extra hair to lose.

"Her phone's off," said Frances.

She wished there was a window to look out of, but they were in the basement of a brutalist building in the South Bank. A water cooler with no cups sat in one corner of the little waiting room. Illustrious actors projected seriousness from the four walls. Their intensity somehow made her anxiety worse.

"The traffic was terrible on Waterloo Bridge," Frances said into the silence. "I noticed it when I got out of the Tube." She had arrived at the rehearsal space a half-hour before Augusta's audition appointment; David was already there. He looked at her blankly.

A second door swung open and a woman with reading glasses and a clipboard in her arms looked through. "Any sign?" Her voice had been friendly twenty minutes before. David shook his head and the woman withdrew without a word.

"I will kill her with my own two hands," David whispered. He went to the door again.

Frances couldn't resist looking at her phone: 10:23. She felt sick. "I think," she said, "that you had better go get some coffee. Black coffee."

David turned from the doorway, stared at her for a minute, then nodded. "I swore I would not let this happen to me again," he said, and then he was gone.

Her head fell back against the wall. She tried to push the feeling of dread away.

A door banged at the end of the corridor, and Frances sat up. An erratic clattering, like footsteps at the end of a dance marathon. She heard a familiar voice: "Coming, darlings!" She caught her breath. Maybe everything would be all right.

Or not. Alma Patridge lurched into the room, an ancient Sherpa with familiar baggage. She balanced precariously on her stick, staggering under a load of Augusta.

"Oh, shit," Frances muttered and leapt to her feet.

She took Augusta's other arm and led her, wobbling, to a chair. Frances stepped back to survey the damage:

Augusta's dark eyes were half-shuttered and strands of red hair escaped her careful chignon, but at least she was wearing a blouse that buttoned somewhere near the top. The problem was her head: it lolled like a peony on a broken stem.

David appeared in the doorway with a cup in either hand. Without a word, he handed one to Alma. Like a practiced pit crew, they worked together: David held Augusta's head, and Alma put the coffee to her lips.

"Goddamn Velvet Hammer," whispered Augusta.

David looked at her, confused, and Frances said, "Painkillers and vodka, I think."

The agent closed his eyes and whispered a prayer.

"I've seen her worse," Alma said. "She did an entire run of *Lady Windermere's Fan* and couldn't recall a single performance."

"Alma, you are singularly failing to cheer me," David said.

Frances, kneeling at their feet, wanted to shake Augusta. How could she have thrown away such a perfect last chance? Why did she have such a gift for self-sabotage?

The door to the studio opened again and the woman with the clipboard came out. Seeing Augusta splayed in the chair, she gave a little snort of derision. And that was all it took: somewhere in Augusta's brain the snort registered. A challenge!

Majestically, she unfurled herself. Her eyes opened, her pupils bloomed. With one graceful hand she pushed Alma's proffered coffee cup away.

"Darling," she said. "Are we ready to begin?"

"We were ready a half-hour ago," the clipboard lady sniffed.

Augusta played the penitent. "I am truly sorry. We witnessed a terrible motorcycle accident on Southampton Row and we had to stop so my companion here"—she placed a gentle hand on scowling Alma—"could collect her wits."

"All right, then," said the clipboard lady, softening. "Come through when you're ready."

Augusta rose to her feet, inhaled, and marched to the door. The three of them followed her into a small auditorium. Two men sat in the second row of seats, scripts in their laps, and she paused to greet them, laughing and smiling.

"Producers," David whispered.

Augusta climbed the stairs onto the stage without a wobble; there was no indication that she'd been nearly comatose ten minutes before.

"How does she do that?" Frances whispered.

Alma shrugged. "Actors like to be looked at."

There was already another actor on stage, a slim, grey-haired man with a resigned expression. He rose for a greeting and Frances noted, with a start, that Augusta's hands were shaking. *Nerves*, Frances thought. *It's just nerves. She can do this.*

Augusta sat on the other folding chair. The stage lights were turned on full, glinting off the grey-haired actor's glasses, reflecting the sudden sheen on Augusta's forehead. She had dressed carefully for this audition, a grey skirt suit and raspberry suede pumps. Nervously, she unbuttoned her jacket and picked up the script.

Frances could see the backs of the producers' heads from her vantage point. They sat still, expectant. A hush filled the auditorium. Frances could hear a technician whispering backstage.

"Augusta?" said one of the producers. "When you're ready. The line is yours."

Clearing her throat, Augusta bent to open the script. Frances could see the pages tremble in her hands. The bravado of a minute before had dissipated. Alma's knuckles were white on the head of her walking stick.

David whispered, "Come on. You can do this."

Augusta licked her lips, looked out into the darkness of the seats. Frances knew, suddenly and with a lurch, what was wrong. *She needs a drink.*

"Augusta?" said the producer, and there was less patience in his voice now. His partner was checking his phone. Augusta stared at them, frozen. Frances felt tears rise, except this time it wasn't self-pity bringing them on.

With as much dignity as she could pull around herself, Augusta stood and placed the script on the seat.

"You'll have to excuse me," she said. "I'm afraid I'm not well."

forty-four

Across the top of the bulletin board, the word MINDFUL-NESS was spelled out in pushpins. At least Augusta thought it was MINDFULNESS. So many pins had been plundered to hold up other notices—offers of babysitting services, complaints about the staff fridge going uncleaned—that it was hard to tell.

This clinic wasn't so bad, so far as clinics went. She had a room to herself, and from its window she could see the river, which gave her comfort. There were chores morning and afternoon, and meetings when there weren't chores, so she had little time to think. After supper each evening, she used one of the communal computers to work on an email to Charles. It hadn't been sent yet.

Augusta wandered into the central meeting room, pulling her scarf tight around her. It was family recrimination day, a torture familiar from Wreckford Hall. At this clinic, it was called Full Circle, and when the facilitator asked Augusta if she would like to join, it was a rhetorical question. She would have much preferred to stay upstairs and scrub the loo. You knew when a toilet was clean, but it was never apparent how long a hostile family member would speak. Always she underestimated the capacity for misery.

The chairs were arranged in a rough circle, and nearly half of them were already taken, patients and their families seated in clumps. There was little friendly chatter at the coffee urn or at the table holding a plate of gluten-free biscuits. Instead the air thrummed with the tension of unvoiced grievance.

In one corner of the room French doors opened onto the river path. Augusta walked over to look out at the muddy Thames. To think that she had ended up here, in dreary Chiswick, once again admitting defeat. She felt ancient. There were teenagers at the meetings who'd taken drugs she'd never even heard of.

"Augusta?" Petra, one of the therapists, beckoned her from across the hall. "Come see who's here. You've got a visitor." The therapist cupped a hand to her mouth, stage-whispered: "From America!"

Augusta froze by the door and put a hand up to smooth her hair. So Charles did want to see her, even if she hadn't properly apologized. Making the first peace offering. He had come here, to be heard, in front of these strangers. She wasn't sure she was ready.

Slowly she walked across the room, with Petra beckoning her forward. The therapist had waist-length dark hair done in a braid, and in one hand she carried a little doll from the Andes, which was meant to encourage the airing of complaints.

"Look, Augusta," said Petra, as she might to a five-year-old. "It's your first visitor at Full Circle."

When she saw Kenneth at the door, she wasn't sure whether it was disappointment she felt or something else. All of her emotions were close to the surface these days, roiling and uncontrolled. It was deeply unpleasant.

Unfortunately, he looked well. She'd grown used to a visual landscape of grey fleece and pilled wool, and here was Ken sleek in a dark suit with California colour in his face. He'd probably come to London to buy shirts, the vain bastard. Visiting her would have been an afterthought.

"Actually," he said to Petra. "I've been to these family therapy sessions before."

"You have never," said Augusta, outraged.

"Yes, I came twice when you were in that other place, in Hertfordshire."

Augusta opened her mouth to protest, but Petra held up the doll between them. "Julia says save it for the meeting." She walked to the centre of the room, calling the group together.

Ken took a step toward Augusta, and she didn't back away. He took another, then pulled her into his arms and held her for longer than was necessary. Her nose was buried in his shoulder. He'd smelled the same for thirty years.

"I did come to visit you twice," he scolded. "And I brought Charles, too. But you loathed those sessions. You said never to come again."

"Liar," she said.

He murmured against the top of her head, "You know you hate to be the audience, Augusta."

She was shoving him away just as Petra clapped for the meeting to begin. Everyone took a seat, the patients with their eyes downcast and arms crossed, their put-upon families looking nervously around. Who would speak first?

"What about you, Kenneth? Is there anything you'd like to tell Augusta about how her behaviour has affected you?"

Ken crisply shot the cuffs on his shirt, and sat down. "I think I'll wait a bit. See how it's done."

"Don't be embarrassed." Petra shook the doll under his nose. "If you feel uncomfortable talking to Augusta, talk to Julia instead."

Grimacing, he pushed the doll away. "Thanks. I'll wait for wiser minds to speak."

Augusta slumped in her seat with relief. Now she could tune out the various tales of woe, dinner dates and concerts missed, babies left crying in pushchairs, bottles hidden in the laundry basket. It was old hat. If she closed her eyes now, she could catch fifteen minutes' sleep.

She felt a sharp finger poke her shoulder and sat up with a start. "On the other hand," Ken was saying, "maybe I will add something."

Augusta slumped again. She couldn't meet his eyes, but she felt the weight of his gaze, heavy with thirty years of disappointment.

He drew in a breath, started to say something, stopped. Around the circle, tired, sympathetic faces waited.

"I can't speak for our son," he began, "because it's not for me to say. Augusta knows what happened. She knows what's true and...what is less true. And that is something they will need to work out themselves. I'm not sure that will ever happen, because they've both cocked it up so badly."

A few rueful laughs. Augusta balled the ends of her

sleeves in her fists, clenching them tightly. She wasn't going to cry in front of all these strangers.

He swung around to face her, and she felt her eyes rise to his, against her will. He took her hand, and she didn't resist.

"What I will say is this. I am angry with you, Augusta, and with myself. I'm angry that I still give a shit. I'm angry that you probably go months without thinking about me and yet you're in my head all the time." He paused, shook his head. "I know what happens. I know one person is always the horse and one is the rider…" His voice trailed off, and for some reason she couldn't fathom, she squeezed his hand.

The group waited, but when Kenneth spoke again, he was talking to Augusta alone. "I took a cabin in Big Bear last summer and when I was driving back to the city I saw a woman on a bridge who had shoulders exactly like yours. I nearly drove off the road. The woman startled me, because I hadn't been thinking about you. I thought, *My God, that's the first time Augusta's crossed my mind in three whole days.* And I was elated. *Elated.*"

They sat facing each other, the rest of the group forgotten. "That's all I came to say." He touched the back of his hand to her cheek, as he had in the hospital. "I don't want to be the horse anymore."

forty-five

A wind off the river ruffled the piece of paper in Augusta's hand, and Frances stole a glance at her friend. She was barely recognizable in a saggy blue Marks & Spencer cardigan, her bosom hidden from view, face makeup-free. Frances thought she looked magnificent.

Without glancing over, Augusta handed her the slip of paper. Frances unfolded it. Across the top, in blue pen, it said, "A True Story." Underneath, she had written, "I like to drink."

Frances folded the paper and sat looking across the river. There was a rowing eight in the centre, pulling against the wind and the tide. She could hear the cox berating them, his voice carrying on the cold air. An elderly couple came toward them along the river path, buttressing each other against the wind.

"I already know that," Frances said. She watched the couple approach, the old man leaning on his cane, his wife holding his other arm and propelling him along. Would she and Stanley be walking this same path one day, infirm but intact? She turned to Augusta. "I know you like to drink. But you've got to remind yourself that it's been ten days now, and you haven't had a drink, or anything else."

"That's true," Augusta admitted. "It feels like someone's arse-fucked my head."

The old lady spun around, horrified, and Frances put a hand up to cover her face. The couple scuttled off, the wife tugging her husband's arm.

The rowers slid under a bridge. Frances said, "I imagine you'll feel better soon. And when you get out, David said he's willing to—"

Augusta held up a hand; the nails were bitten short. "Don't. I can't bear to think about it at the moment."

They watched two seagulls fight over a chip at the edge of the path. Frances sat up suddenly. "I can't believe I forgot to tell you. Your editor really liked the outline of the book."

"You mean *Bitch in a Ditch*?"

"Sadly, she's rejected your new title." Frances fished for her phone in her purse, and scrolled through the messages. "I mean, now we actually have to write the thing, but she liked the direction we proposed. Apparently she's quite thrilled that you're in rehab —"

"Wellness retreat."

"Fine, she's happy you're in a 'wellness retreat,' because it gives the whole story a redemptive arc."

"The only problem is, for a redemption story I would need to be redeemed." Augusta pulled a cigarette from her pocket. She'd cadged it from the sad-eyed therapist who worked with the self-harming teens. Menthol. It was like smoking toothpaste. "You know, my counsellor asked me the other day what I saw when I looked back. And I said, 'I see all my failures behind me, like a trail of breadcrumbs.'" She lit the cigarette and took a long drag. "He told me I needed to work on my visualization technique."

Frances started to say something, closed her mouth. Tentatively, she reached over to put a hand on Augusta's shoulder. She was worried it would be shrugged off, but Augusta didn't move. They watched the gull snatch the fleshy chip from its rival and back away. The river hypnotized with its slow swell.

Augusta said, "Don't give the best of yourself to the world, Frances."

"What?" She was awake again.

"You'll be tempted to, but don't. Save the best part of yourself, the kindest and most resourceful part, for yourself." Augusta crushed the cigarette butt under her heel. "And for whatever annoying children you might have."

The wind had picked up, and Frances pushed the hair out of her eyes. She said, "Because you didn't."

"Darling," said Augusta, exasperated. "Clearly not."

Together they watched the triumphant gull lift toward the sky. Burdened by its trophy chip, hampered by the wind, it beat its wings against the heavy air until it finally broke free, soaring on an updraft. It disappeared from sight.

"Come on," said Augusta, "let's get inside. We have work to do."